MURDER IN SILVERPLATE

FIVE STAR

Other Five Star Titles by Don D'Ammassa:

Scarab

MURDER IN SILVERPLATE

Don D'Ammassa

Five Star • Waterville, Maine

This novel is a work of fiction. Names, characters, places and incidents are either the product of the author's imagination, or, if real, used fictitiously.

First Edition
First Printing: November 2004

Published in 2004 in conjunction with
Tekno Books and Ed Gorman.

Set in 11 pt. Plantin.

Printed in the United States on permanent paper.

Library of Congress Cataloging-in-Publication Data

D'Ammassa, Don, 1946–
Murder in silverplate / by Don D'Ammassa.—1st ed.
p. cm.
ISBN 1-59414-260-2 (hc : alk. paper)
1. Women detectives—Fiction. 2. Silver industry—Fiction.
3. Silver-plating—Fiction. I. Title.
PS3604.A46M87 2004
813′.6—dc22 2004051225

For all the survivors of
Sheridan Silver

One

It was one of those late August mornings that turns so surprisingly and unseasonably cool that you find yourself unaccountably shivering despite the actual temperature. Vicki Sanders patted the pocket of her slacks after locking the door of her Volkswagen, just to make certain that she had actually taken the keys out of the ignition. It was a habit she'd consciously acquired after once locking herself out of her previous car in the middle of nowhere at 11:00 in the evening. They jingled reassuringly against some loose change, and she turned with a half smile toward the walkway that led around the side of the building to the front door of Standard Silver Inc. Low hedges marked the path, poorly trimmed and looking more pathetic than welcoming.

"Doesn't look any better on Tuesday morning than it did on Monday afternoon, does it?"

Vicki looked around and waved to Mark Ross, who had parked half a dozen places beyond her spot in the office parking lot. A tall, dark-haired man in his mid thirties, Ross was theoretically an eligible bachelor and several young women in the office were flirting with him in a casual sort of manner, but Vicki had known him long enough to realize he wasn't really interested. He didn't appear to be gay, just neutral.

"Can't say that it does. On the other hand, not much of anything looks good to me this early in the morning. I'm definitely a night person. One of my eyes is still glued shut and the rest of my body is arguing that I really should be back in bed for another hour or three."

"Fortunately, we're all so devoted to our jobs that we rise above these little vicissitudes of life, right?" Ross had a particularly attractive smile and Vicki felt a twinge of regret. She enjoyed his company, but sooner or later she'd remember that his interest in her was only feigned. "Each day a challenge, a new horizon to reach, problems to be solved, a mission to be accomplished."

"Don't get me started on our mission statement again." She sighed dramatically. "The truth is, I'd rather spend the morning in bed."

He raised his eyebrows sardonically.

"Alone," she continued. "With production shut down for the week, you'd think I could have gotten caught up with the paperwork and taken at least a half day off." She turned to walk alongside Ross. "First the shipment from India arrived a week earlier than expected, and since the manufacturer failed as usual to mark the contents on each of the containers, I had to open twice as many as were really necessary to get representative samples of each product. Then Frank questioned the reject ratios on last month's summary report, and I had to dig up all the source data to prove that I was right. Joslin thinks it would be a good idea to establish a routine spot check of all finished stock over six months old, Ken Carlisle wants approved samples of the new line to take with him to Dallas, and Linda tells me at the very last minute that the reject codes haven't been posting properly to the cumulative files and may have to be rechecked manually before we can finish the month-end report. And naturally, the clerk most familiar with the data is on maternity leave."

They rounded the corner of the building and approached the large glass doors that led into the new office area, erected when the need for additional manufacturing space had crowded the administrative functions out of their comparatively crude lodgings in one corner of what was now the finished goods warehouse.

"Think of it as job security," Ross advised. "Where else would they find someone willing to put up with so much crap and put in so many hours for so little money?"

"There's more truth than jest in that, Mark," she replied wearily. "What are you doing in so early, now that I think about it? I think this is the first time I've ever seen you here before 8:00."

Ross shook his head ruefully. "Your friend and mine, Frank Antonelli, requested my presence at 7:00 sharp," he glanced at his watch, "just ten minutes from now as a matter of fact. It seems that he has uncovered some major flaw in the way the schedule for the Press Room was put together and wants it straightened out before work resumes next week."

"What's the hurry? Production doesn't start for days yet. He's even let his supervisors come in at 8:00 during the shutdown, a major concession in itself. Frank must be mellowing in his dotage."

Ross shrugged, then reached out to open the door. "Who knows what thought processes take place within that enigmatic skull of his? I've spent four years trying to figure out how his mind works, and I'm still completely in the dark. Sometimes I think he deliberately changes his behavior patterns just so no one will think he's too predictable."

"Or maybe he's just a crazy person." She slipped inside, moved forward quickly to open the inner door and hold it before Ross could pre-empt her. "After you," she said with exaggerated politeness, knowing that Ross would be annoyed. She felt petty teasing him this way, but sometimes she just had to poke to see at least a glimpse of the creature that lived behind his mask. Ross hesitated a moment, then stepped through into the hall, clearly discomfited but trying not to let it show. "Frank hasn't been a particularly early bird himself lately. Are you sure he's in?"

"I can't imagine him being late for a meeting that he called. He doesn't like having to deal with me in the first place, and he would absolutely never allow himself to be put in a position where he might have to apologize for wasting my time."

Vicki smiled. "Well, I wish you the best of luck. You'll probably need it. Keep your guard up and watch your back. Catch you later."

She walked briskly to her own office, taking the lefthand corridor, closing the door behind her. Two days after her twenty-fifth birthday, Vicki had unexpectedly been promoted to Chief Inspector at Standard Silver, one of the world's largest manufacturers of silverplated giftware. Two years later, the Quality Control Supervisor, an elderly man named Shepherd, had died in his sleep, victim of an unsuspected fault in one of the valves in his heart. If his death had come six months earlier, Vicki would probably still be Chief Inspector, but everything had changed following a shakeup in the top management level of the company; an interim appointment had quietly become permanent, and she realized one afternoon that, at least theoretically, she was the highest placed woman in the company's history, thanks to its long and enduring tradition as a bastion of male prerogative.

She called the office manager's number, let it ring twice, then hung up, realizing that Jennifer Grissom was unlikely to be in for at least an hour. Most of the office, as well as manufacturing supervision, had moved to a more relaxed work schedule during the annual shutdown. Vicki methodically emptied her in-box, sorting the reports and memos carefully into three piles. Pile number one had to be dealt with today, no matter what else happened. Pile number two would be cleared up as time allowed. The third and largest consisted of routine reports that were filed unread as part of some arcane ritual she'd never fully understood. Someone from the office pool could deal with it.

The intercom crackled to life. "Frank Antonelli, line one, please." It was Mark Ross. There was a thirty-second pause, then the call was repeated, at a slightly higher volume. She could hear the irritation in Mark's voice. Ross was imperturbable and almost immune to stress, at least outwardly, but Frank Antonelli enjoyed a unique ability to get under his skin.

Vicki smiled to herself. Apparently Mark had been stood up, another round of the game men played as they jockeyed for position in the pecking order. There was little love lost between the two men under even the best of circumstances. The nature of their respective jobs necessarily resulted in conflict. Frank was responsible for maintaining a steady, high level of productivity as determined by equipment utilization versus downtime and other statistical measures; Mark's job was to ensure that the correct items were given priority through the manufacturing process in order to satisfy the Sales Department, even if that prioritization sometimes reduced the overall efficiency of the plant.

And mine is to make sure that when those pieces are shipped, they meet the quality level that our Sales Department has guaranteed to our customers, she reminded herself, a mandate which sometimes put her at odds with both men. Vicki finished sorting paperwork only after agonizing a bit about whether or not to assign a high priority to reviewing the customer returns reports, one of her least favorite tasks. As she was doing so, the office door swung open and Ross walked in.

"What happened? That seems like a pretty short meeting."

"Frank never showed up." There was an edge in his voice. "Doesn't answer his page either." Ross glanced around the room impatiently. "The bastard never did display much consideration for others."

"Maybe he's in autopolish and can't hear you." The oversized rotary polishing machines were so loud that their operators were required to wear earplugs to avoid degenerative hearing impairment.

"The factory's down, remember? The place is a graveyard out there; not a soul in sight."

"Are you sure he's in the building? Maybe he had a flat tire, or called in sick."

"No," he shook his head. "I noticed his car on the way in. He's here all right."

"Maybe he went outside. Did you ask the guard?"

"The shift changes at 7:00. He hasn't passed the factory gate since then, and there's no one on duty at Post Number 2. I suppose it's possible, but I'm not about to go out and look for him."

"Well, I'm sure he'll turn up."

"Bad apples always do."

"That's not fair, Mark. Why are you so down on him today, anyway? Admittedly, Frank's a little obstinate at times, but he's very loyal to the company."

"He's pigheaded is what you mean."

"Okay, I admit he doesn't always see any point of view except his own." She started to say more, but Ross was agitated and overrode her.

"He's narrow-minded and too defensive. He makes no effort to understand how important it is to keep our customers happy."

"But he does do a pretty good job of keeping the factory going," she continued, ignoring his interruption. "They didn't make him Vice President of Manufacturing because of his good looks."

"You never can tell. No, I take that back. Not even our leaders could possibly think that Frank is an attractive person."

Vicki fought, unsuccessfully, to suppress a smile. "Oh, he's not bad looking, in an overbearing, macho sort of way. He has his talents, Mark; he wouldn't win any popularity contests, but his people work hard and smart. And you know he didn't get his job by playing politics and stroking egos."

"No, I would never accuse him of that." Ross sat down on the corner of her desk and ran one hand slowly through his wavy black hair. Not for the first time, Vicki noticed how strikingly handsome he was. At thirty-four, Mark was six years her senior, but the gap seemed narrower every month. "Frank never was very adept at winning the hearts and minds of his associates." He turned serious suddenly. "The problem is that he has also managed to alienate most of the people who work for him, as well as those who work with him. The union is in an uproar about his casual attitude toward contract language, and his supervisors plot behind his back. I don't know how long the management of this company is going to be able to accept the risk of a major work stoppage."

Vicki sat back in her chair, watching him closely as he paced back and forth in front of her desk. "That's overstating the case, isn't it? He's a bit inflexible, I admit, but there are situations in which his style is very effective. And didn't I hear you complaining about the overtime provisions just two weeks ago?"

Ross raised one eyebrow. "Is that Vicki Sanders I hear defending the man she described recently as a bigoted, chauvinistic son of a bitch? When did you change your mind and join his fan club?"

Vicki flushed. "I was a little upset when I said that. It had been one bitch of a day."

"If that was how you react when you're a little upset, I don't ever want to see you when you're really pissed off." He smiled, but it only took some of the edge off the words.

She nodded, realizing that he was trying to change the subject. "Okay, point taken. And he really is a chauvinistic bigot. He's not an easy person to work with, not for any of us, but he's not going anywhere and we have to make the best of what we have." Vicki was suddenly weary of the subject. "Don't you have any work to do?"

Ross ignored her, resumed his pacing. Her small office really wasn't suited for his restless movement, and he could take only a few steps before he was forced to reverse himself. "What do you suppose is going to happen if Catterall actually does make you a manager?"

The abrupt change of subject caught her completely by surprise. "I don't understand."

When Edward Catterall had been named President of Standard Silver, it had provided an enormous and unexpected boost to her career. Catterall had bucked tradition and some indirect pressure from the Board of Directors when he picked Vicki to become the first female supervisor within the manufacturing division in the company's history. The Sales Department continued to blame its declining performance on quality issues, and he had begun to make public noises about the advantages of making Quality Control a managerial rather than supervisory function. His strong support had been welcome even though it had led to some sour remarks about favoritism and teacher's pets. So far there had been no rumors that they were sleeping together, but she supposed that it was inevitable even if they were baseless.

Ross reached the side of her desk and stopped, leaned to one side, and perched his rear end on one corner. Vicki resented the gesture and made a mental note to reciprocate at some point and see how he reacted. "If you end up as a department manager, you'll have to come to the weekly production review meetings on Monday mornings. You'll be the first woman ever to attend."

"Yeah. They'll probably make me take the minutes."

He ignored her. "The first time Frank wants to make some heavy point, he'll stop in mid-sentence, turn to look at you, realize he can't swear because there's a woman present, and collapse into his chair totally incapable of proceeding."

Vicki's eyes widened. "Are we talking about the same Frank Antonelli? I can't picture him swearing under any circumstances."

Ross nodded. "Fastidious Frank isn't as perfect a gentleman as his public image might suggest. He's quite fluent in gutter talk while it's just us boys. Having a woman there is going to seriously cramp his style."

"Well," she shook her head in an exaggerated motion. "I guess we learn something new about people every day. And," she twisted her face into an exaggeratedly innocent smile, "if I do become manager, I guess Frank will just have to get his shit in order."

Ross was still laughing as he walked back down the corridor toward his own office.

Vicki turned back to the workload sitting on her desk. Once she had mapped out the day's schedule, she would feel justified in getting herself a cup of coffee.

She had barely started when Paula Danforth slipped in through the door, without knocking. Vicki, who had been about to put the weekly rejection reports into chronological order, set them aside resignedly.

"Hi, Paula. What's up?" She hoped she sounded more cordial than she felt.

The older woman slipped into the chair beside her desk. "The prodigy is in early this morning. Is he still trying to find first base?"

Vicki sighed. Two years previously, Paula had fallen for Mark in a big way and she had assumed that every other woman at Standard was a competitor. She made a pretty blatant, drunken pass at him during a company party, had been publicly rebuffed, and had alternated between infatuation and cold fury ever since. "Paula, you have a suspicious mind. Mark came in to see Frank, not me, but the meeting never came off for some reason. You haven't seen our resident redneck, have you?"

"Nope, not a glimpse. And I suppose Ross just happened to stop by to tell you about it, even though your door was closed. Or did he go into the wrong office by accident?" Paula, who was in her mid forties, had been divorced under rather messy circumstances just a few years earlier. Her ex-husband had beaten her badly enough that she had been hospitalized on at least two occasions before she had finally summoned the courage to end their marriage. Surprisingly, Paula seemed to have put that all behind her and she got along fine with the men she worked with, even Frank Antonelli. Mark Ross, on the other hand, seemed to irritate her even at his most innocuous.

"Mark and I are friends, Paula, and that's all. He's never even asked me to go out with him other than an occasional lunch, and I always pay my own tab. Just because we get along doesn't mean he's trying to get my clothes off. For that matter, I don't think he has ever dated anyone he works with."

"I've seen the way he looks at you, girl, and that's not friendship gleaming in his eye. The man is definitely smitten."

"Maybe so. But he probably gets the same gleam when Wendy LaRocque walks by." Wendy was a recently hired nineteen-year-old whose good looks had caused a noticeable increase in the amount of male traffic through the Customer Service area. "It's all in the hormones. Anyway, I'm not ready for any kind of new romantic involvement just yet. I don't want to get stuck with another Danny Sanders." She was happy to realize she could say his name now without wincing. "And when I am ready, I plan to keep my social and professional lives separate." Vicki realized that her voice had risen and she clamped her lips.

Paula nodded. "Right, sorry. I didn't mean to stick my nose where it doesn't belong." She rose and started for the door.

"Paula," Vicki called, then waited until the other woman turned toward her. "I didn't mean to jump down your throat. I'm a little tired this morning. But you do dump on Mark an awful lot. I don't expect you to pretend to like him in my presence, but it's pretty uncomfortable having you criticize him all the time. I'm not the only person who knows you have it in for him and you're going to cause yourself some unnecessary trouble if you're not a little more careful about what you say."

Paula stopped, one hand on the doorknob, turned her

head so that she was looking past Vicki's shoulder, not meeting her eyes. Vicki half expected an angry outburst, but if anything Paula's expression was bleak and unhappy. "I know. I don't know why I feel that way about him. It's probably just because I know it's only a matter of time until my department is integrated with his, and you know as well as I do what that means."

Vicki nodded. "He's already Production Control Manager. You'll probably end up as Assistant Manager. Isn't that a step up from Materials Control Supervisor?"

"It's a better title. Might even pay a little more. But it's not the same, you know? It'll still be his department. He'll set the policies, make the decisions, decide what shape things will take in the future. I'll slip into a kind of limbo, fade away a little bit each week, until finally you'll pass me in the hall and wonder who I am."

"It won't be that bad. You've been with the company almost ten years; he's only been here four. Mark's not stupid enough to ignore your experience. And he's not even bad about deferring to a woman, compared to most anyway."

"I suppose you're right." She didn't sound convinced. "I'd better get going. You have work to do and I should look busy even if I'm not. Catch you later." And without waiting for an answer, Paula turned and left, closing the door softly behind her.

Paula hadn't sounded as though she'd been convinced by Vicki's assessment, and when Vicki thought about it, she felt less confident herself. No matter how much open management Mark practiced, it was still ultimately his decision how Production Control would operate. The decision to dissolve the separate Materials Control function, formerly called Centralized Trucking, had not yet been made, at least insofar as she was aware, but it was only a matter of time. The shape of recent changes in the entire production process made such a consolidation inevitable. Remembering her own feelings of satisfaction when she assumed the Quality Control position, she could understand Paula's reluctance to lose the autonomy she had enjoyed. But it couldn't be helped. She would just have to adapt.

Vicki returned to her paperwork, trying to fight off the growing feeling that this wasn't going to be one of her better days. When everything was arranged to her satisfaction, she slipped down the corridor to the vending machines and bought a coffee, carrying it carefully back to her office. The plastic cup was hot to the touch, and she kept switching it from one hand to the other as she walked. The level of traffic outside her door was increasing steadily as more of the staff arrived. It seemed quieter than usual, however, and it was a while longer before she realized that the big difference was the absence of the muted rumble of the exhaust system from the Polishing Department, aptly named the "hurricanes." With the factory shut down for the week, there was no reason to operate the blower system that kept the particles of polishing compound from flushing out into the factory. No production would be performed except possibly the preparation of a few samples for an upcoming sales meeting in Dallas with one of the larger buying groups.

Shortly after 8:00, she decided to take a break from the paperwork. Setting aside a spreadsheet which steadfastly refused to crossfoot, Vicki left her office and stepped out into the corridor. There was no sign of life from Jennifer Grissom's office, but she could hear Jason Capwell's voice from around the far corridor. His nasal tones and perpetually whining disposition annoyed her at the best of times, and she turned and moved off decisively in the other direction, headed for the cross corridor that led to the production area. Although nothing much would be going on, it would at least give her an opportunity to stretch her legs.

The corridor was deserted but she caught up to Manny Soares, supervisor of Autopolishing, at the factory entrance. He was carrying his familiar lunch box and his expression was one of equally familiar dourness.

"Hi, Manny. Are you keeping banker's hours this week like everyone else? How's it feel to sleep late in the morning?"

"Don't know. Woke up same as always." Manny's accent remained strong despite nearly thirty years in the United States. He gave her a thin smile, which was about as much animation as he ever expressed. His black eye, which he had refused to explain, had faded to an unhealthy yellow.

"The body knows even if the mind doesn't," she replied. Manny stared back at her blankly, not saying anything. "After you," she said at last, breaking an uncomfortable pause, and followed him through the archway that led to the manufacturing area.

They walked along together down the narrow walkway that ran between the office and the main warehouse, the latter filled nearly to capacity at this time of year, the beginning of their busiest shipping season. Over forty percent of the year's sales would be completed between August 1 and November 15. Standard Silver produced a line of approximately four hundred silverplated gift items, ranging from coffee sets and water pitchers to dresser sets, pill boxes, picture frames, serving trays, chafing dishes, coffee urns, sconces, mirrors, casseroles, candy dishes, and compotes. Although the volume had been increasing slowly and steadily over the course of the last decade, margins had shrunk so dramatically that the Board of Directors had been clamoring for more efficient operations and even higher sales volumes.

The corridor had been painted a cheerful yellow some years past, but the passage of time had dulled it to a dingy shade, streaked with the intervening years' accumulation of dirt.

"It must be pretty boring for you this week," she said to her silent companion. "Even the maintenance crews are off on vacation."

"There's plenty to do. Have to make sure maintenance didn't screw up the rotaries when they cleaned 'em. Catch up on paperwork. Things like that."

He must be bored, Vicki thought. That was the longest string of words she'd ever heard from Manny.

They passed through the Packing Department, where each item was sealed into the appropriate gift box, the final inspection area, and into plating, an enormous area laid out symmetrically with two elaborate and now-silent plating lines, one located at each end. Vicki had always been fascinated by the electroplating process. Most of the items manufactured at Standard were constructed from brass, copper, zinc, or other base metals, sometimes with applied lead borders. It was only when they had reached their final form that they were attached to racks and immersed in enormous tanks of a fluid which contained silver particles in solution. She had never understood exactly how electrolysis worked, but she knew that the racks and their contents had the opposite electrical charge from that of the solution in which they were immersed, and since opposites attract, silver adhered to whatever appropriately charged surface was carried through its tanks.

Originally, the racks had been moved from position to

position by a team of nearly twenty men, back when there had been a single line, but an automated system had been installed a few years back despite strenuous objections from the union, and the second plating line, just recently installed, had doubled their capacity.

At the moment, the system was silent and motionless, the tanks having been drained during shutdown so that they could be patched and resurfaced.

Tony Capra, the Plating Department supervisor, waved a greeting from the opposite side of the room, then turned away when Vicki returned the gesture. Manny ostentatiously ignored the interchange; there was a coolness between the two men that Vicki had never understood.

When they reached the Automatic Polishing Department, Manny half raised one hand in her direction and started to turn away, intent upon his own duties, however inconsequential. Each of the large automatic polishing machines was enclosed in a plywood casing, except for a small opening through which the operator loaded and unloaded the items to be polished. Vicki paused, trying to decide whether to continue on into the pressroom or cut through soldering to the receiving dock, but before she could make the decision, external events intervened.

Luis Mello, newly appointed supervisor of the Press Department, ran out into the main aisle, appearing uncharacteristically disheveled. After a momentary hesitation, he started directly toward the door of one of the small, prefabricated offices that were scattered through the factory. Something about his face, though briefly glimpsed, and his headlong pace warned her that something was seriously amiss. Without thinking, she followed him, opened the door, and stepped inside.

Mello was standing, half crouched over the desk, the

telephone receiver pressed to his ear.

"Hello, Mr. Romero. This is Luis Mello down in the pressroom." Pause. "Yes, it is. Listen, Mr. Romero, I have an emergency out on the floor. There's been an accident. It's Mr. Antonelli, sir." Another pause, and Vicki turned to look down the narrow passage that led into the largest single open area in the building, where the massive single and double action presses were housed. What kind of accident, she wondered, could take place when everything had been shut down?

"No, I don't think that would do any good. Mr. Antonelli is dead, sir." Mello's voice shook with tension. Vicki turned toward him, blinking, not entirely convinced that she'd heard correctly. Frank Antonelli dead? It didn't seem possible; he'd been running the factory since long before she'd even come to work here. He was almost like a piece of the machinery.

Manny Soares appeared at her elbow. "What's up?"

"There's been an accident of some kind. I think he said Frank is dead." Her voice sounded strange, distant, as though someone else was talking.

Soares made an inarticulate sound and turned away, immediately striding off toward the press area. After a moment's pause, Vicki followed, marveling that her legs still worked properly.

It took a few seconds for them to locate Frank Antonelli. There were three dozen presses in the area, a full third of them the double-action giants that were used to stretch base metal from squares, circles, and rectangles into the basic shapes of water pitchers, coffee pots, wine coolers, and coffee urns. Often the degree of distortion required a series of operations, each stretching the metal slightly further, the reduced strain preventing the metal from tearing under the stress. The presses varied from six to fourteen feet in height, depending upon the length of their stroke. Their moving parts were covered with grease and the housings had been repainted so many times that the surface was bumpy and uneven.

Antonelli was in the row farthest from the entrance, where one of the Addison presses was set against the outside wall that abutted on the walkway leading from the factory to Guard Station Number 1 and the main parking lot. This entrance was used by the factory workers, and a few office workers who didn't have spaces in the smaller lot on the opposite side of the building. From a distance, it appeared that he was merely bent over, perhaps examining the fit of the bottom portion of a die set. It was only when they were within a few meters that they realized the upper die had descended until it had almost met the bottom, easily crushing whatever slight resistance the upper half of Frank Antonelli's body might have offered.

Vicki caught the odor as she approached, unmistakably that of blood, although it had already dried into a dark stain that was nearly indistinguishable from the coat of grease, oil, and dust that caked the press from head to foot.

"Shit." Soares came to a stop two meters away, and even his ruddy complexion had turned slightly pale.

Vicki told herself it would be embarrassing at the least and perhaps unprofessional if she fainted. It would merely reinforce the entrenched opinion that women didn't belong on the manufacturing floor. Nevertheless, she averted her eyes and went no closer. She felt better when she noticed that Soares had made no move to advance either.

Only a moment or two passed before Luis Mello joined them, stopping at the same distance, as though some invisible force field prevented them from approaching further.

He and Manny exchanged enigmatic looks, but neither spoke.

"Is the ambulance coming?" Vicki asked inanely, trying to find something to say that would release some of the tension.

"Yes," Mello replied. "I imagine so. And the police as well."

Soares flinched, crossed his arms, then uncrossed them immediately, obviously nervous. She remembered one of Antonelli's periodic tirades against OSHA and the detailed accident reports that they required; this was one case where he wouldn't have to worry about completing the paperwork. "How could such a thing have happened? I thought all of these presses were equipped with safety devices so that this kind of accident was impossible."

"They are." Luis Mello glanced in her direction. "This wasn't an accident. Frank was murdered."

Two

Detective Lieutenant Walter Henderson was an unhappy man. He'd been working long hours for the past three weeks, filling in wherever possible because of a sudden rash of absenteeism in the department. There had been a debilitating intestinal virus making the rounds which had already brought down three detectives and a handful of uniformed officers. At the same time, Zacharelli was still on vacation, Andreissen was on an extended leave of absence, and several others were involved in a cooperative regionwide federal operation directed against organized crime. The department had been strained to its limits, and the state authorities were disinclined to take up the slack.

Ben Dardenian had been teamed with the slightly older Henderson for fifteen years and knew his moods well enough to remain silent as they entered the front offices of Standard Silver. A balding, skeletally thin man tall enough to have played in the NBA met them at the door, his fingers intertwined at his belt buckle. A young, uniformed patrolman stood just beyond, looking uncomfortable.

"Come right in, officers." The man's voice was surprisingly high pitched, almost as thin as his body, the kind of voice that Henderson had always found instantly irritating.

"We are in, Mr. . . . ?"

"Romero. Carl Romero. I'm the personnel manager."

"I'm Henderson and this is Detective Dardenian." He pointed over his shoulder with one thumb, then turned to the patrolman. "Is Bidwell here yet?"

"The crime scene people have been in there for a while, sir." Marks was young, possibly a rookie, trying very hard to look both professional and calm. "Mr. Bidwell came in just a few minutes ago. Officer Lawrence took him out to the scene."

Romero was looking anxious and kept shifting his weight from one leg to the other. "Mr. Catterall has taken personal charge of the situation, Detective. He thought it wise to keep things quiet until the authorities were on the scene."

"Very sensible of him." Romero opened his mouth to speak again, but Henderson had already turned back to the patrolman. "Has the area been properly secured?"

"Yes, sir. The factory is closed today so there aren't many people about. Bill . . . that is, my partner, Officer Lawrence, remained with the body until the team arrived."

"All right, let's go. Ben," he turned to Dardenian, "why don't you see if Mr. Romero here can give you a list of everyone currently on the premises."

"Will do." Dardenian suppressed a smile when he caught the annoyed expression on Romero's face. Henderson was making his usual stunning first impression.

"Let's go," Henderson said impatiently, and Marks nodded and led him inside and along a corridor to a large arched doorway. Beyond was a larger open area which extended off to their right. They passed between rows of wooden benches, each covered with small lead castings, feet and handles for sugar bowls, then on through a succession of rooms of varying sizes, many filled with enigmatic machinery whose purpose was not always evident.

A gray-haired man in an expensively cut three-piece suit moved forward to greet Henderson as the two police officers came into view of a cordoned-off portion of the Press Department, his hand extended. Behind him, a half dozen men and women were busily pursuing their specialties.

"Hello, I'm Ed Catterall; I'm the Chief Executive Officer here. I appreciate your having come so promptly, Officer."

"Detective," he answered automatically, dismissing the man with a single glance and nod. The technicians were systematically cataloguing the crime scene, dusting for fingerprints, and taking samples of blood, dust, oil. They measured and photographed and recorded observations. A heavyset man stood near the body, his back turned toward them, one hand massaging his chin.

"If there's anything I can do to help . . ." Catterall started to speak again, but Henderson cut him off immediately, anxious to dispose of distractions as quickly as possible.

"Thank you, Mr. Catterall. We'll let you know what we need as soon as we've completed our preliminary examination. For the moment, if you would just remain outside the police line and let us do our jobs." Never noted for his tact, Henderson had little time to waste on public relations. That was more his partner's line. He turned away from the executive, stepped over the rope and stanchion barrier, ignoring Catterall entirely.

"Bidwell!"

The man near the body turned, dropping his hands to his sides. "Henderson! You're primary on this one too? Don't you ever sleep?"

"Don't remind me. What have you got for me?"

"What we have here is a dead Caucasian male, about age fifty to fifty-five." Bidwell half turned toward the body. "Cause of death is apparently, and I stress the word 'apparently,' extreme trauma resulting from having his head, collarbone, and most of his chest cavity crushed by a hydraulic press. Of course, he could have been dead before the fact. We won't know that until the autopsy."

"Time of death?"

Bidwell grimaced. "It didn't happen this morning. Judging by the temperature of the body, the congealing of the blood, I'd say at least twelve hours, most likely sometime between 4:00 and 6:00 yesterday."

Henderson turned to the patrolman. "What time was this called in?"

"Just after 8:00 this morning. We were dispatched at 8:05 and arrived at 8:11."

Henderson made a disgusted noise. "So the body spent the night here," he said aloud, but directed at no one in particular. After a moment's thought, he spun around and gestured for Catterall to approach.

Catterall responded promptly, but there was something about his posture that told Henderson he had already alienated the man, perhaps by refusing to play up to his vanity. "Yes, Detective. What can I do for you?"

"On the way in here, I thought I noticed a computer terminal at the guard station near the entranceway."

"Yes, we had it installed about six months ago."

"Do you log everyone in and out of the building?"

"Outside of normal business hours, yes we do. Not when the plant is in operation. There are almost four hundred employees when we're open; it wouldn't be practical." He smiled. "We don't deal in precious metals except for the silver, you realize, and that's not very attractive for thieves, at least not in the form we carry. There's not much market for silver cyanide, and the bars are locked in the tanks. We keep track of things for safety reasons as much as for security."

"I didn't see anyone on duty on our way in just now. If your plant is not currently operating," he glanced around, "and obviously it isn't, shouldn't someone be there?"

"No, under the circumstances, it seemed best to suspend our normal procedure. I sent the guard back to the office area to wait with the others."

"But anyone going in or out of the factory yesterday would have been logged through that guard location?"

"Either there or the other station, the one leading out into the employee lot. That one is manned twenty-four hours a day all of the time; the one you passed through from the office closes down at 7:00 in the evening, when the outer doors are locked for the night."

"But everyone would need to pass through one or the other?"

"That's correct." He paused, considering. "Unless they climbed out through one of the windows, I suppose. The safety doors are bugged all around; they can't be opened without a warning light going off at the guard post. There's been no record of that. But one of the windows could have been forced; there's no alarm on them."

"We'll check that out later. All right, Mr. Catterall. My partner, Detective Dardenian, is with your personnel manager. I would appreciate it if you would see that copies of both logs for yesterday reach him as soon as possible. We might require earlier records as well. If you make a practice of routinely dumping old data, please defer doing so unless you've cleared it with the department. I trust that we can rely upon your cooperation."

"Certainly." Catterall opened his mouth as though he wanted to say more, but Henderson had already turned away, cutting off further conversation. The executive's eyes narrowed momentarily, and this time his expression was clearly angry and offended. He regained control with a visible effort of will, then turned and strode off toward the office complex, deferring the contest of wills to another time.

Bidwell stepped forward when he saw that Henderson was ready for him. "We're about ready to move the body. Do you want to check it out first?"

Henderson's face twisted. "Not really, no, now that you ask. But I suppose I'd better." Despite the many years he'd spent as a police officer, even after examining more bodies than he cared to remember, Henderson still hadn't grown inured to the presence of death, particularly violent death. He walked in a slow circle around the press, forcing himself to examine everything clinically. There was rather less blood than he would have expected, and most of it had dried to a semi-solid, sticky mass, the largest stains running down the back side of the press housing and pooling on the floor. "Is there an ID on the victim?"

"Tentatively," answered Bidwell. "From the build and clothing, he's been identified as Francis Antonelli, a vice president here. Two of his co-workers have tentatively identified him as well."

"Next of kin?"

"We're working on it. No immediate family. He was a bachelor, living alone. There's a brother out in Utah according to his personnel record. No other family identified so far."

Henderson stepped closer. The dead man's legs were slightly splayed, his right arm extended through the breach of the press, although it had been thrust through the opening between the die set and the framework, and thus had not been caught by the descending ram. The left arm was extended backward and rested near the hip, a position that would have been awkward had the man been in any position to feel discomfort. Henderson half crouched, then slowly rotated the wrist.

The dead man's watch read 4:45. It had been shattered and was no longer running.

"Yes, I noticed that as well," said Bidwell. "There are traces of the crystal and some blood on the side of the press there." He pointed to a spot above and to the left of the bottom half of the die set. "My guess is that his arm jerked reflexively at the moment of death, smashing the watch. The time fits."

Henderson grunted. "Find any prints?"

"Many. They'll all be checked but they're not likely to tell us much; I don't think any of them are fresh enough to be relevant. Anyone who watches television knows enough not to leave prints at the scene of the crime. I don't even know why we bother any more, unless it's just to help keep these guys employed." The members of his team steadfastly refused to give any sign that they were listening.

"All right. You can take the body. I assume the photographer has done her bit with her usual thoroughness. Does someone know how to raise this thing?" He glanced up, following the lines of the hydraulic press. Its massive, blocky body extended ten feet into the air, the top lost in the shadows above.

"We have one of the employees standing by, the man who discovered the body as a matter of fact." Bidwell turned to the second uniformed policeman, presumably Lawrence, and beckoned him forward. "Would you retrieve Mr. Mello for us, please?"

The officer nodded and walked briskly off. Henderson watched him go, his face drawn and thoughtful.

He walked over to a set of metal utility shelves that stood to one side of the press, crouching so that he could examine the contents of the lower shelves. There were a number of unfamiliar tools, wrenches far larger than anything he had ever seen before, a couple of oil cans, a block of wood with lines and numbers written on its sides, an empty soda bottle, a clot of filthy rags, another clot of marginally cleaner ones, a roll of duct tape, a small notebook, two stubby pencils. "Done with this stuff?" Henderson asked a technician who was busily repacking the tools of his trade in a large black satchel.

"Sure thing, Detective. Knock yourself out."

Henderson poked at the items diffidently, picked up the notebook, and began thumbing through it. The patrolman returned, followed by a dark-haired man of about forty, wearing jeans and a plaid shirt.

"This is Luis Mello, Henderson," Bidwell explained. "He's the supervisor of this department." He turned to the newcomer. "Mr. Mello, we need to have the press raised. Is it possible for you to bring it up an inch or so and stop? We'd like to take pictures at intervals."

"Yes, I can do that." Mello looked like it was the absolute last thing in the world he wanted to do, but he didn't argue. Stepping over the barrier, he took up a position behind and slightly to one side of the dead man while carefully keeping his eyes averted. He spread his arms wide enough to reach each of two large red buttons. Each button was set within a recessed chamber about the size of a clenched fist, constructed in such a way that the buttons could not be depressed except by direct intent. "I'm ready."

The police photographer moved to a new vantage point and prepared to snap off a shot. Henderson decided that duty didn't require him to watch what was certain to be an unpleasant procedure, so he began flipping through the notebook. Page after page was filled with one series of numbers after another, some of which appeared to be measurements but others which were completely mysterious. There were occasional notations, such as "soluble oil only," "call for restudy," "have tool sharpened for next run," "check set-up," and other cryptic comments.

There was the sound of an electric motor starting, gradually changing pitch as it warmed up, then a brief mechanical clanking, terminating with a pop and a soft sucking sound. The press was at the periphery of his vision, and its movement caused Henderson to turn involuntarily as the ram rose a short distance, then froze in place. Flashbulbs crackled in the gloom.

"Up another inch or two please," instructed Bidwell. Mello had kept his hands in place, eyes fixed on some imaginary blemish on the upper die rather than stray to the grisly display below, and now the ram rose again, another small increment. More flashbulbs expended their lives.

This process was repeated several more times before Mello finally spoke. His voice crackled with tension. "That's it; she's all the way up."

"All right then. Thank you, Mr. Mello. If you'd move out of the way please."

Mello stepped away with alacrity, turned, and left the cordoned area, although he remained nearby, visibly shaken. Having no particular desire to discover just how Bidwell's crew planned to move the body to the stretcher they had prepared, Henderson joined Mello and showed him the notebook. "Excuse me, Mr. Mello. I understand that you work in this area?"

Mello nodded, his face pale.

"Could you tell me what this is?"

The other man seemed momentarily distracted, but he grew more animated and seemed to relax slightly now that he had to deal with something a bit more mundane than mutilated bodies.

"That's the set-up man's book. Here, I'll show you." He took the book from Henderson and opened it, apparently at random. "See, this up here is the part number; this one's the butter dish cover. These are settings for the stroke length, pressure, and these are the tool numbers, so he knows what storage bin to find it in. The tools are kept in a series of racks over near receiving. All of this information is supposed to be on the production order, but a lot of it's been put into the computer wrong and we can't go by what it says."

Henderson took the notebook back. "Is it normally kept there?" He pointed to the rack where he had found it.

"Sometimes. They're supposed to leave them in the office when they go home at night, so we know where to find them if someone's out sick or quits or something, but most of the time they don't."

"Is there anything else on the rack that is out of place, or wrong in any way?"

The two men moved to the rack and Mello took a few seconds to look over the shelves, his expression serious. "No, sir, everything belongs here."

"Is anything missing?"

Mello shrugged. "Not that I can think of. We're really not that careful about where things go around here."

"What's that block of wood?"

"It's a guide. See," he picked it up and held it extended in Henderson's direction. "These lines are measurements for the opening between the top and bottom dies. We line it up with this when we're running the first few pieces to make sure we've set it correctly."

"All of these tools belong here, then?"

"Yes." Mello raked the shelves with his eyes once more, just to be certain.

There was a prolonged wet sound from behind. Henderson resolutely refused to turn around. "I understand that you found the body, Mr. Mello."

"Yes. Yes, I did." Mello looked down at his shoes, his mouth suddenly dry. Mello appeared to be sincerely shaken, but Henderson had long since learned to discount and ignore his own first impressions. Some people were remarkably good actors.

"We'll be talking to you in detail later, of course, but just for the moment, I'd like to understand a few things. I'm told that you said right away that Mr. Antonelli had been murdered. How did you know it wasn't an accident of some sort? How do you know even now for that matter?"

Mello turned around. "It couldn't be, sir. These presses all have safeties built right into them. There's no way he could do that to himself. I can show you, if you want."

"That'll have to wait, I'm afraid. It'll be quite some time before we can allow anyone to touch this equipment."

"I can show you on another press. We have three more Addisons just like this one. They're all set up the same way." The man looked eager, although it wasn't clear whether that was to show off his expertise or just to quit the vicinity of the corpse.

Henderson considered the offer for a moment, then nodded. "All right, show me."

"Just over here." Mello hopped over the cordon and Henderson followed thoughtfully. Henderson glanced over toward Bidwell, who stood beside the stretcher. The body was already covered. "I'll be right back."

Bidwell shrugged. "Take your time. This guy isn't going anyplace until we take him."

The two men walked several meters down a dimly lit aisle to another press, one which Mello assured him was an exact twin of the one where Antonelli had died. Mello started up the motor, then stepped back, gesturing for Henderson to take his place. "You can try it for yourself."

Henderson held back, and Mello laughed, although his voice crackled with tension. "Place one hand on each of these buttons." He indicated the two recessed controls, both painted bright red, identical to those he had used earlier. "Don't actually press them yet, because that will move the press. Just make sure you're touching both of them."

Henderson cautiously did as suggested, stretching his arms wide apart. The righthand button felt sticky and he grimaced, assuming that oil or grease was splattered there. He was a fastidious man. He hated getting his hands dirty. He had never even learned to change the oil in his car or do other routine maintenance.

"All right, sir. Now lean forward and put your head between the two dies. Right here." He tapped a point directly inside the opening in the main body of the press. Henderson didn't move a muscle.

Mello laughed drily. "Don't worry. Nothing will happen unless you press both buttons simultaneously. Even then, you'd be safe. You'll see what I mean."

Taking great care not to apply any pressure to either control, Henderson bent forward at the waist. "I can't reach," he said after a few seconds. "I'd have to take my hands off the buttons."

"Exactly. That's the point of the dual control system. It's a safety feature. The press won't move unless both switches have been depressed, and no single person can do that and lean into the path of the ram. There's no way that this could have been an accident, or suicide for that matter." He licked his lips again, looking back the way they had come. "Someone else had to have operated at least one of the controls, maybe both. Frank was too careful a man to take chances even with the safety features on."

"I see." Henderson dropped his arms and backed away. "But there are mechanical failures. What if one of the switches was stuck in the closed position?"

Mello looked offended. "They're checked all the time, and even if one switch had locked up, why would Frank have touched the other?" He shook his head. "Even in a test situation, Frank would have gone through all the safety checks first. He was a real fanatic about safety, made us compete for the most days without a time-lost accident in our departments, the whole road show."

"Years of experience have taught me never to underestimate the capacity of human beings to perform unlikely acts under absurd circumstances. You're probably right, but we'll still want to check this equipment out, just to eliminate the possibility that it was in fact an accident."

"I can see that," Mello answered softly. "Do you want me to check it right now? I can strip down the control assembly in just a few minutes."

"No. The department will send someone down to work with you, if necessary. No reflection on you, Mr. Mello, but we need to have this confirmed by someone not associated with the company or the deceased."

"Of course." Mello sounded mildly offended despite the disclaimer. Henderson felt an increase in his own level of irritation. He was tired; there had been too many long days this month, nights when he arrived home too exhausted to do any more than heat something in the microwave and fall into bed exhausted, days when he walked around performing his duties mechanically, drinking more than his usual volume of coffee just to remain reasonably alert. On one occasion, he had dozed off sitting on his couch, attempting to read the evening paper, waking there in the small hours of the morning with a horrendous backache. This man's indignation was just another dollop of aggravation piled on a growing mountain of frustration. Not trusting himself to speak, Henderson returned to the murder scene with Mello trailing behind him.

Dardenian was waiting for him.

Henderson forced himself to speak calmly and in a neutral tone. "Did you arrange for an interview room?"

"All taken care of. One of the conference rooms has been set aside for us. Do you want to start now?"

Henderson considered his options. The crime scene people were still at work, but he could tell that they were starting to wrap things up. The body was already gone. "Let me know if anything turns up here, will you?"

Bidwell nodded. "Of course. How would you ever be able to solve a case if we didn't find all of the clues for you?"

"All right, let's go." Henderson gave Bidwell a parting sarcastic glare, which was cheerily ignored, then followed Dardenian back toward the office.

"We'll want to talk to anyone who was in the factory between 4:00 and 6:00 yesterday to start with, then we'll branch out if anything looks promising. There's a computer log that should give us a list of names."

"They're printing a copy for us now. I told them to have it delivered to the interview room. Catterall wants to talk to you again, by the way. At your convenience, he said."

"He can wait."

"Do you want them in any particular order?" They made their way down the narrow walkway that led to the office. As before, the guard station was unmanned.

"We might as well do Mello first; he's the guy who found

the body. But I want to get set up before we start."

Dardenian nodded. "There are four more uniforms up front. I put one of them on the front door and two more are going around with the security people, checking the building's integrity. The fourth I kept to run errands."

"All right. Tell Catterall or the personnel guy that no one is to leave the building without our permission." He glanced at his watch. "They can send out for lunch if they want to. The staff can go about their normal business, but no one leaves today without signing out, even after they're interviewed. Have the uniform posted at the front door check on that. And we'll want a list of all employees and their home addresses."

"I already have that." Dardenian held up the large, combination binder and notebook that he always carried when on duty. "The list is pretty long, around four hundred names."

"So I would imagine. Hopefully we can prune it a little before we start doing backgrounds." They passed back through the archway into the office area. "Which way?"

The conference room had been created by subdividing a larger area by means of a folding partition which ran along tracks in the floor and ceiling, locking into place on the far wall. There was a large oblong table surrounded by chairs, ashtrays scattered across its top, a screen for overhead projection at one end, a smaller table set against a side wall. There was additionally a portable wooden cabinet, its doors currently open, exposing a carousel projector and an extension cord. The lighting was relentlessly brilliant, a triple row of fluorescents which reflected off the plain white walls. A few photographs of giftware items manufactured by Standard were fastened to the wall, set in cheap plastic frames; otherwise the room was unadorned. Even the carpet was plain beige, disfigured by the pressure points where furniture had stood in the past, with clearly defined pedestrian traffic lines, and the occasional scorch mark of a discarded cigarette.

Henderson sat down at the midpoint of the longer side of the central table. Dardenian had remained outside, making arrangements with Romero and another uniformed officer, an experienced patrolman named Hescox with whom Henderson had worked previously. Catterall was nowhere to be seen, a fact for which Henderson was profoundly grateful. He'd dealt with enough executive types in the past to know that a bloated sense of their own importance was endemic among the species. He would have to deal with the man sooner or later, but right now he needed to develop a general understanding of what had happened and enough background to give it proper context.

When Dardenian entered a few moments later, he was carrying a fan-folded computer printout and a set of floor plans. "The list is here. Eleven people left the factory between 4:00 yesterday afternoon and 7:00 this morning when the new shift took over. Actually, all of the activity was last night."

"Is Mello one of them?"

Dardenian glanced through the list. "He sure is." He unrolled the floor plan and put it on the conference table. "This place is a rabbit warren."

Henderson glanced down at the diagram of the extensive factory and adjoining office and grimaced. "How many exits are there?" He counted them by pointing at each in turn. "Almost twenty outside doors?"

"That's right. But they're all supposed to be bugged."

"They're checking that out, right?"

His partner looked offended. "I don't overlook the obvious, Walt."

"Sorry."

Dardenian glanced back at the list of names. "There's someone else on this list who might interest you."

Henderson looked over to read the name his partner was pointing to. "I almost expected it," he said quietly.

"What are you going to do about it?"

"Nothing just now. We'll have to proceed as usual. When I have a chance, I'll talk to the captain. But right now, the man I want to talk to is Luis Mello."

THREE

Luis Mello appeared even more ill at ease when he was ushered in for the formal interview than he had been on the shop floor. Ben Dardenian was sitting at the side table, notebook open, pen poised over a small notepad.

Henderson pointed to the chair across from him. "Have a seat please, Mr. Mello." He removed his own notebook from a jacket pocket and began flipping through it randomly before setting it down on the table.

"This is a preliminary interview only, Mr. Mello, but you still retain certain rights which I will now explain to you . . ." Henderson went through the familiar ritual by rote; he had recited the words so many times they no longer held any meaning for him. He fantasized about a new law which would require that all citizens have their rights read to them on their eighteenth birthdays. "Your name is Luis Mello?"

"Yes."

"What's your home address, Mr. Mello?"

The interview proceeded, establishing that Mello was the Press Department supervisor for Standard Silver and had been with the company for two years.

"Where did you work before that?"

"Flynn Manufacturing. I was a set-up man there for two years. I came over here when Archer retired; he'd been running the department for twenty years or more."

"Could you please summarize your movements yesterday from 3:30 until you left the building for the day?"

"I think so." Mello looked thoughtful for a moment,

took a deep breath. "The production meeting broke up at 4:00, which was just like always, and right after that Manny Soares and I . . ." The words spilled out of him so quickly that Henderson raised a hand to stop him.

"Whoa! Slow down. First of all, tell me about this meeting. What was it about?"

"We get together every week." Mello looked back and forth between the two officers, took a deep breath, and visibly tried to relax and speak more slowly. "Frank Antonelli held a meeting with all of us supervisors every Monday from 3:30 until 4:00. We'd go over production schedules, changes in quality standards, new products and redesigns, layoffs and recalls, changes in procedure, things like that."

"I thought there was no production going on this week."

Mello gave a short laugh. "That wouldn't stop Mr. Antonelli. No matter what was happening, the meeting went on as scheduled. It snowed one Monday and everyone went home except us; we all had to stay until 4:00."

"All right. Who attended this meeting besides yourself and Mr. Antonelli? And please talk slowly so that Sergeant Dardenian over there can write down their names."

"All the supervisors who worked for him came every week, and sometimes representatives from the office area attended as well."

"Were any of them there yesterday?"

"No, there was just the seven of us."

"Then we needn't concern ourselves with the others just now. The names, please."

"Manny Soares, Art Richardson, Tony Capra, Donna D'Angelo, and Bill Elliot." Mello was mentally counting. "That's all of them."

Henderson glanced toward Dardenian. "They're all on the list," the other man said.

"And when did this meeting end?"

"Exactly at 4:00. It always ended the same time, no matter what. Antonelli said no meeting should ever last more than half an hour or less than ten minutes. He was a stickler for punctuality at both ends." Mello placed unusual emphasis on the word "punctuality."

"Would you describe Antonelli as a strong boss?"

"As strong and as old-fashioned as they come." Mello's face twisted in mild distaste. "He did a good job, don't get me wrong. I don't mean to speak poorly of the dead. It's just that he was strict about some things that didn't seem all that important to anyone but him. He was what they call an authoritarian."

"Tight assed, in other words."

Mello nodded. "He's been called that sometimes too. And worse."

"Where did this meeting take place?"

"Office number 2, out in the Press Department, same as always. It's the only one big enough for us all to sit. It was originally the plant manager's office, back before my time."

"And at 4:00 the meeting broke up?"

"That's right. Manny Soares and I went up to his department right afterwards to look at some dented trophy covers. Antonelli has been putting a lot of stress on quality lately. We make a line of standardized trophy sets with very plain surfaces so that they can be engraved. Manny was having problems polishing out some small superficial dents and we were trying to figure out how they were getting in there in the first place." Mello became more voluble now that he was on familiar ground. "We're pretty sure the cause is slivers of metal left on the tools during the trimming operation; they get caught between the die set and the stamped part when the edges are being crimped and we end up with tiny dents. They're so small they look like scratches or even imperfections in the metal. Wiping the pieces first doesn't help, because the slivers stick to the rags and just come off the next time you wipe."

"How long were you with this other fellow, Soares?"

"Maybe fifteen, twenty minutes at the most. It was a pretty obvious problem once we thought about it. I left Manny there and went back to the Press Department to find out what lubrication had been used on the job and who the operator was. And I made a note on the maintenance log to have the tool sharpened."

"Did you see anyone on your way there or coming back?"

Mello's eyes became distant as he tried to remember. "No, I don't think so. I know Antonelli was gone, because the records I needed were in the office and it was empty when I got there. I spent some time looking through them, then checked to see if there was another run of trophy covers coming up when we reopen next week, so I could flag the production order and have the job checked over while it was running. After that, I went down to receiving to look for Art Richardson, but the area was deserted and the lights were off, so I figured he'd already gone home. If there was anyone else around, I didn't notice and I know I didn't speak to anybody."

"What time was it when you left receiving?" Henderson was studying the floor plan, making small notations in his notebook while the other man talked.

"It must have been about 4:45. I went home myself right after that. Couldn't have been more than three or four minutes."

Henderson turned to one side. "What time was he logged out?"

"At 4:53."

Henderson turned back to Mello. "Did you see anyone

else on your way out? In the parking lot, say?"

"No, the place was deserted. There were still a few cars there, I think, but I don't even remember that too well. It's a big lot," he explained. "We don't have assigned parking on this side of the building and no one was anywhere near me. I think there were a couple parked over near the fence; one of them was probably the guard's."

"Could you show me on this floor plan the route you took?"

Mello leaned forward and pointed with his finger as he spoke. "I came back through here, casting and solder, then down through polishing to the exit near Storeroom B. Then out past the guard."

"And you didn't see anyone along the way? You didn't check back with Soares before you left?"

"Not that I remember, and no, I didn't speak to Manny again. The lights were on in autopolishing, as a matter of fact, so Manny was probably still in the building, but I didn't see him. It's a pretty big area, you know."

Henderson made another note. "Now, tell me what happened this morning, right from when you first arrived."

"Well, since we're shut down, we didn't have to come in until 8:00. Even Antonelli relaxes things a little during shutdowns. I was a couple of minutes late." He smiled nervously. "Get up an hour later than usual and your whole schedule is thrown off."

Henderson refrained from smiling and Mello looked away nervously. "I turned on the lights in the office and started the coffee. There really wasn't anything to do, so I took a walk around the department while it was brewing. I found Antonelli right away and ran over to office number three and called Mr. Romero in personnel."

"You didn't touch the body or anything around it?"

"No, sir, I did not. I stood there for a few seconds, I guess. I mean, at first I couldn't believe what I was seeing and I kind of froze. But after that, I left right away. I never even got close to him. I mean, there was nothing I could do for him or anything like that."

"And you say you were certain right from the start that it is impossible for this to have been an accident?"

"I wish it was possible, sir. I really do. But there's just no way that it could be. Even if the safety failed, he would never have pressed one of the buttons while standing in that position. It wouldn't have made any sense."

"Does the factory shut down like this often?"

"Twice a year usually. We take inventory right around Christmas, and everything comes to a stop while we count all of the product on the floor. Most years we shut down for two weeks during the summer, like now, because it gets pretty hot out on the floor sometimes. We spend the first week with the maintenance people cleaning everything up, getting the equipment in order. Then, during the second week, we let them go too, so they can use up some of their vacation time."

"If there's no production going on, why would the presses even be operational?"

"The power is on all the time; we just have most of the equipment turned off. Frank and I have been working on that particular press, number 27, for a couple of days. There's a new die set that was made specifically for it, but the tolerances weren't figured right and it doesn't work the way it's supposed to. It's for a new bread tray in the promotional line. Someone in the tool room really screwed it up, and they've already pre-sold a lot of them. We've been playing with the die set when we had time; with the power on there's not much involved in getting the equipment up and running for a test. You saw how quick I did it with the other Addison a while ago. It's not like the polishing equipment, where you have to worry about the exhaust system and the compressors and all that stuff."

"Did Antonelli have any enemies?"

"There were people who didn't like him much; you can't be a boss and not piss people off some of the time. And I don't think he had any real friends around here. He was fair most of the time, but he was a hard man to work for. I can't think of anyone with a good reason to kill him, which I suppose is what you mean, but a lot of people resented him and," he shrugged, "who knows? Sometimes people just get pushed too far. And people get jealous; he had a lot of power around here, and he wasn't afraid to use it."

"Did Antonelli have frequent arguments with people outside of his own department, with people on his own level?"

Looking extremely uncomfortable, Mello shifted in the chair and his gaze wandered away. Henderson recognized the significance of this immediately. Mello was going to lie, or at least edit what he was about to say for some reason.

"It's no secret that Mr. Catterall had been coming down on him a lot lately. He's determined to upgrade our quality levels and to reorganize our systems in general. Antonelli figured these changes were a kind of criticism of his own methods. The front office has been bringing in some new people with new ideas, and giving them a lot of authority to make changes. It's hard for an old dog to learn new tricks, particularly when he thinks people are trying to get ahead at his expense. Sometimes there have been real fights. He'd been feuding with Mark Ross, the production control guy, but it's all been pretty low key. Usually they did it behind closed doors, so I don't know how serious they were about it."

Henderson tapped his pen against his teeth. "All right, Mr. Mello, that's all for now. I'm going to have to ask you not to leave the premises for the time being. I'm sorry for the inconvenience, but we have a lot to sort out."

"That's all right." Mello, visibly relieved, rose and pushed the chair back. "I brought my lunch."

When he was gone, Dardenian rose and stretched. "One down, ten to go."

"At least ten." Henderson continued to tap at his teeth. "I don't think this is going to be an easy one."

"Any reason in particular?"

"No, just the way the eyes shift around here. Mello was trying to decide how to say what he wanted to say, and how much he could keep to himself without getting in trouble. He knows he's going to have to work here after we're gone and he's worried about saying something that will come back at him later. A lot of these old manufacturing places are like that. They're little closed societies."

"You think he's hiding something significant?"

"Not necessarily, but he's being careful about what he says. He might just be afraid that something damaging will get back to his employers and affect his job, but he might also know something relevant that he mistakenly thinks isn't important."

"Should we go on to the next name?"

"Sure, have Hescox bring in another."

"Any preference?"

"I'd like to talk to the other five people who attended that meeting, try to set up some kind of chart of their movements. And I suppose we ought to add Catterall to the list."

"I'm afraid so. If we don't, he'll make a stink about it."

"Leave him till last, though. He pisses me off."

★ ★ ★ ★ ★

Manny Soares was visibly upset. He was dressed in an olive drab work suit that stretched tautly over wide shoulders and a muscular frame. Soares had obviously been athletic in his youth, although he wasn't trim any longer, with a noticeable beer belly, and more than a sprinkling of gray hair. His eyes darted about the room nervously as Henderson informed him of his rights, and blinked with surprise when the detective finally asked a question.

"Your full name, please?" Henderson repeated.

"Manny Soares. Manuel Soares." He spoke with a strong Portuguese accent, kept shifting his weight from side to side in the chair, as though uncommonly uncomfortable.

"You're the supervisor of polishing, is that correct?"

"Yes."

"How long have you worked here at Standard?"

"Twenty-two years, first a grease buffer, a polisher, then setting up the machines."

"How long have you been a supervisor?"

"Since nineteen ninety-four; nine years."

"And how long have you worked for Frank Antonelli?"

"Right from the start. He hired me."

"Is he the one who made you a supervisor then?"

"Yes."

"What kind of a boss was he? Did you enjoy working for him?"

"He was okay." Soares' face worked, and Henderson waited for him to decide how to express what he wanted to say. "Mr. Antonelli was tough, but he was fair most of the time. He knew what he wanted and he made sure you knew it too. I had no problem with him."

"Did he have enemies?"

"Sure. The people up front, they don't understand how

the factory has to run. They gave him lots of trouble."

"What kind of trouble?"

"Arguments, paperwork." Soares shrugged. "All our time, we spend doing reports and stuff like that, and then they complain because our production figures are down. If they left us alone, they'd get everything they needed."

"Was there anyone in particular Antonelli argued with?"

"The new man, Ross. They went at each other a lot. The guy never once got his hands dirty, but he thinks he knows how to run a factory." The expression on Soares' face left no doubt what he thought of that possibility.

"Was there anyone else Antonelli fought with?"

Now Soares looked uneasy again. "I don't think he got along with the top brass too much. He used to come back from meetings up front in really bad moods."

"Catterall?"

Soares nodded. "And the personnel guy, Romero, and sometimes the salespeople too. They always want everything today, you know. You got an item, it's got five different parts, maybe thirty-five, forty operations altogether, and they want it in three days. You can't even set up all the equipment that fast, and there's other jobs running at the same time."

"Was there anything in particular that they fought about regularly? Particularly recently."

"Same kind of stuff, mostly. A couple of times they really went at each other right out in front of everybody."

"Let's talk about last night, Manny. You were at a meeting with Antonelli and the rest of the supervisors, I understand."

Soares nodded.

"What time did it end?"

"It's always over at 4:00. Mr. Antonelli was real strict about that."

"Tell us what happened when the meeting broke up."

"Well, me and Luis, that's the press guy, we went up to my department to check on some bad goods."

"How long did that take?"

"Half an hour maybe."

"Did Mello stay with you all that time?"

"No, he left to check something in his office. I finished sorting them after he was gone, then went over to hand polishing to find some goddamned work tickets that were missing. Didn't find 'em, either. Sometimes the operators throw 'em away."

"And then?"

"Decided it could wait until this morning, so I got ready to go home." He shifted uneasily. "I was tired," he added defensively. "Didn't sleep too good the other night."

"Did you see Frank Antonelli at any time after the meeting?"

Soares shook his head. "Saw Tony Capra heading toward the Press Department. He might've. I went the other way."

"And when was this?"

Forehead creased with concentration, Soares seemed uncertain. "I don't know for sure. It was just before I decided I'd quit for the day. Maybe 4:45 or a little before. Luis came through from the other direction right after."

"Did either of them say anything?"

"Nope, don't think they even saw me. I was way back behind the last row of polishing lathes. Sometimes they throw the tickets back there, see? Luis had his lunch box; he must've been going home."

"So this other man passed by on his way toward the press area, and then Mello walked past you on his way out, and right after that you left yourself?"

"Well, I started to. But I got to talking with some of the office people on the way."

"Where was this?"

"Plating. They were standing there and they stopped me to ask about the missing tickets. So I had to explain how I'd been looking for 'em and was going to check around again today."

"Their names?"

"It was Ross, the Production Control man, and the Sanders girl."

Henderson nodded. "You saw the two of them together?"

Soares nodded. "They say around the shop that he's got his eye on her."

"What time would this have been?"

"Just before 5:00, I think. After a couple of minutes, we walked back down to shipping. They went into the office and I left."

"Ben, what time was he logged out?"

"At 5:29."

Henderson glanced down at the floor plan and then back to Soares. "That's an awfully big gap, Manny. It should only have taken you a couple of minutes to get to the door. Are you sure about the time you left them? Could you have talked for almost half an hour?"

"No." Soares shook his head. "I couldn't tell them nothing."

"Then what took so long? Did you see anyone else after you left them?"

Soares shook his head. "There wasn't anyone. The lights were off in shipping."

Henderson glanced down at the floor plan again and frowned. "How could you tell that? If you left the others here," he pointed to the junction of two aisles, one leading back to the office, the other to the second factory exit near the Packing Department, "then you wouldn't be able to see the office in shipping at all, would you?"

"I used the men's room." Soares leaned over and pointed to a small square on the plan. "It's the closest."

"And how long would that have taken?"

Soares looked uncomfortable. "A few minutes." He licked his lips, and Henderson noticed that his forehead was beaded with sweat. Soares was quite obviously hiding something.

"We're talking about fifteen to twenty minutes at least, Manny. That seems like an awfully long time to take a crap."

The sweat intensified, glistening under the fluorescent lights. "My bowels haven't been working so good lately. It takes a while." Soares looked extremely uncomfortable now.

Out of the corner of his eye, Henderson noted Dardenian making a note. It was plausible, and Soares didn't seem the type to lie convincingly, but it would have to be checked.

"Is there anything else you can think of that happened out of the usual yesterday?"

Soares shook his head.

Henderson sighed. "We'll be talking to you again, Manny. If you remember anything that you haven't told us, even if you don't think it's particularly important, let us know right away."

When the man had left, Henderson pushed his chair back. "Why does everything have to be so complicated, Ben? We've had two people in here, both of whom are probably innocent, and both of whom act as though they're as guilty as hell about something, if not murder."

"Everyone feels guilty about something, Walt."

"I don't. My conscience is as unblemished as a baby's butt."

"That's because you don't give a damn, not because you aren't guilty."

"All right. Who's next? I want to get this over with as quickly as possible."

Arthur Richardson was the next to be ushered in by Hescox. He seated himself without being asked, a tall, heavy man with broad shoulders and a prodigiously drooping belly, probably in his late forties or early fifties. His mass should have been imposing, but there was a pervasive softness that ameliorated the effect of the man's sheer physical bulk. He stuttered slightly while providing his name and address and the fact that he had worked at Standard for almost fifteen years. It seemed to be a speech impediment rather than nervousness, and it disappeared quickly once the interview had started. In contrast to the previous two men, Richardson relaxed visibly once the interview started.

"How long have you been receiving supervisor?"

"It's been just over ten years now."

"You were at a meeting with the dead man yesterday."

"That's right; every Monday." Richardson went on to confirm that the meeting had ended at precisely 4:00, just as it always did.

"What did you do after that?"

"I went home."

"You went straight home? You didn't stop to talk to anyone or do anything before you left?"

"Well, I went back and shut off the lights. Then Frank

came by and asked me to check out a couple of things before I left, so I did that and then I got my stuff."

"Wait, slow down. You saw Frank Antonelli again after the meeting?"

"That's right. He came down to my office right afterwards. He wanted me to help him straighten out a problem with overages and reminded me about a lot of bad solder that I was supposed to ship back to the supplier."

"He didn't bring this up in your meeting? He came down especially to talk about it?"

"It didn't matter to the other guys. You see, we buy most of our base metals, copper and brass, in these big coils, sometimes as much as 2,500 pounds each. When we set up a job, they like to run the whole thing out so they don't have to unload the leftover and repackage it, but sometimes production control wants to save some for another job that takes the same specifications. So Frank wanted me to try to match coils to jobs a little better, so they wouldn't have to return so many bits of coils. It's an extra handling for them and my people too, so I didn't have any problem with it. I told him he'd have to talk to the dispatchers though, because they've been marking up the coils for us to take lately, instead of letting us pick them ourselves."

Although the explanation was plausible enough, Henderson once again had the distinct impression that he wasn't hearing the whole story. "Who do the dispatchers report to?"

"Danforth in materials. But she and Ross, the production control man, have been arguing about how to assign materials to jobs, so she's been changing things around, wanted to keep track of coils by purchase order and vendor. Stuff like that. She tries to use the oldest lots first, but he wants to pick and choose depending on what has to be made. Some of the mills make their brass harder than others, and they split a lot if they're drawn out too deeply."

"Tell me what happened when Antonelli came to see you last night."

Richardson hesitated for a few seconds. "We talked for a few minutes, you know, and after he left I went up to solder for a second to note down the lot number on the bad stuff. I wrote it on a piece of paper, put it on my desk so I'd remember it today, and then I went home."

"Do you know what time that was?"

"About 4:45, I think, or a little later."

"And you didn't see anyone else on your way?"

"No. There was someone in shipping, probably Elliot, but I didn't see him either."

"Then how do you know he was there?"

"Because I poked my head around the corner on the way out. The lights were still on in the office. Frank was always after us about turning off everything before we left. We'd get reamed out good if he found out we'd left the lights on overnight. Elliot had to be specially careful, because he and Frank never got on so good in the first place." Richardson glanced up sharply, to see if Henderson had taken note of the last sentence. The detective's eyes never flickered.

Henderson decided the indiscretion had been deliberate. "Why was that, do you suppose?"

"Well, Elliot's a colored, you know. Frank, he didn't much like the way Catterall stuck him with someone like that without even giving him any choice."

"I'm afraid I don't follow. Didn't Antonelli hire this man?"

"Nope. He wanted to take Cerrone out of packing and give him the job, but the new personnel man, Romero, said we had to hire some minorities. He and Frank went round and round on that one, and finally they had to go see Catterall. I've never seen Frank so mad as that time, when they told him he'd have to hire Elliot even if his qualifications weren't so good. It wasn't even that bad when Catterall made him promote the D'Angelo woman. Frank looked like he wanted to throw up. We were all pretty careful to stay out of sight that day."

"Has there been trouble between the two of them since? Antonelli and this Elliot fellow?"

"Well, they're not exactly the best of friends." Richardson leaned back and hooked both thumbs in his belt, expanding it as though to make space for his paunch. "Frank, he tried to get on Elliot's back about everything at the start, but Catterall talked to him about it a couple of times is my guess, because he backed off after a bit. And Elliot doesn't do a half bad job. I know a little about warehousing, and he makes good use of his space. Of course, he's got good people working for him too, not like these jackasses they keep sticking me with."

Henderson made a note or two, asked a few more questions about the apparent conflict between Antonelli and Catterall, but if Richardson knew anything further, he wasn't about to say it. In fact he seemed to grow increasingly cagey whenever Catterall's name was brought into the discussion, his answers shorter and less informative. Henderson finally dismissed him, but with yet another mental reservation. Despite his slovenly appearance, Richardson had been around long enough and was shrewd enough to know a lot more than he had said.

"He clocked out at 4:47," said Dardenian, after the door had closed behind the man's back. "So far nothing any of them has said hasn't rung true. Antonelli obviously wasn't a popular character with the brass."

"It doesn't sound like the people who worked for him were enrolled in his fan club either, and none of them seem to have an alibi so far. We'll have to timeline everyone, but even if we could get the precise moments they intersect, I suspect there are gaps long enough for each of them to have committed the deed. What I don't understand is how the murder was physically accomplished."

"How's that?"

"Antonelli was a big man and looked to be in good shape. It would take someone pretty powerful to have put him into that press, even if he'd been knocked unconscious first."

"At least we've narrowed the timeframe."

"How's that?"

"If Richardson talked with Antonelli until almost 4:30, that leaves only an hour and a half during which the murder could have taken place."

"True, unless Richardson is the murderer and just told us a lie." Henderson stood up and started walking slowly back and forth. "On the other hand, if we can believe the evidence of the broken wristwatch, Antonelli died at precisely 4:45."

"Unless his watch was set wrong," suggested Dardenian.

"Or unless the murderer noticed that it was broken and reset it to mislead us."

"So you think he was already unconscious when the press came down."

Henderson nodded. "I think it's probable."

"Why such overkill? The murderer must have known we wouldn't think it was an accident. Why not just beat his brains out with a wrench?"

"Maybe the killer didn't know how the safeties operated and thought we would interpret it as an accident."

Dardenian looked doubtful. "Wouldn't that eliminate everyone we've just talked to? They all knew better."

"Unless they're being really clever and wanted us to draw that very conclusion."

Dardenian shook his head. "This doesn't feel like a sophisticated killing to me."

"No," agreed Henderson. "I think the answer is rage. The killer hated Antonelli so much that he wanted to physically destroy him. Anyway, it's probably not going to be our problem much longer."

"You think they'll pull us off?"

"I don't think they have much choice. Do you?" Henderson sat down again. "Once word gets out, the captain will have to do something. Until that happens, we have to continue with the preliminaries. So who's next on the list?"

Dardenian looked down. "How about this Bill Elliot, the guy that Antonelli disliked so much? He's the supervisor of the shipping area."

"Sounds good to me."

Four

Although Ed Catterall had gone to considerable effort to reassure everyone in the office and convince them to return to business as normal, at least as far as was practical, Vicki Sanders knew she wasn't the only person simply going through the motions that morning. The death of Frank Antonelli under any circumstances would have been monumentally disruptive; he had cut such a broad swath through company procedures, union relations, office politics, and every other aspect of Standard Silver over the years, it was hard to anticipate what his absence would mean in the future. She supposed she should feel guilty because she felt little regret that the man was dead, but he had been cool toward her at the best of times, and openly hostile more than once. Indeed, he seemed to deliberately keep everyone at a distance, avoided forming even the transitory alliances that were common during the company's periodic internal warfare. Vicki doubted that Standard would provide any serious mourners at his funeral other than just possibly Manny Soares.

It had been clear for some time that Antonelli's style clashed with that of the more sophisticated Catterall. Antonelli worked from experience and instinct, judging backlogs and loading levels by walking through the factory rather than analyzing reports. He made snap judgments where necessary, avoided paperwork and detailed planning whenever possible, and preferred to allow past history to dictate present strategies. Although both he and Catterall were essentially authoritarian personalities, the latter tempered his personal style with tact and at least a veneer of respect for the ideas of others. Contrarily, Antonelli had been utterly convinced that his was the only correct path to follow, because that was how things had always been done. Manufacturing, he had said on more than one occasion, was a man's work, consisting primarily of producing the maximum number of units in the minimum amount of time. Cost reductions were a frill, and new ideas were invariably dismissed as unworkable or unnecessary. Participatory management was a waste of time, and his response to the recent effort to craft a mission statement for the company had been openly hostile. There was no room on his watch for theorists, computers, paperwork, detailed cost analysis, or delicate negotiations.

If Antonelli had died in an accident or from natural causes, it would have caused earthquakes; throw in a juicy murder and you had a disturbance of apocalyptic proportions. It would be the only important topic of conversation today from customer service to the janitors.

She was sitting in her office, pretending to herself that she was working on the semi-annual quality reports, when the door opened. It was Linda Marzocchi, the closest friend Vicki had here at Standard.

"You're not working, are you?"

Linda let the door shut behind her and moved the empty chair up close to Vicki's desk. Standard's data processing manager was nearly six feet tall, almost cadaverously thin, perennially pale because of a particularly violent allergic reaction to strong sunlight. Carl Romero had astonished everyone by flirting with her from time to time, but even if Romero had not been married, Linda considered him beneath contempt, a perennial "yes man" without the courage to speak up for himself.

"Well, I was trying to."

"Oh, sure. Well if you're trying to impress anyone, you should at least leave the door open. No one else is stupid enough to be passing up the year's most sensational gossip session."

Vicki sighed. "All right, all right. So what does the rumor mill say?"

"Oh, I suppose the best story right now is that the old bastard killed himself because he knew Catterall was going to fire him and he couldn't stand the thought of losing his position."

"Implausible."

"Why's that?"

"First of all, why should he care? If they canned him, Frank would have gotten six months' pay as severance, not counting accumulated vacation time and profit sharing. He had no family and, except for that antique car of his, no expensive hobbies that we know of. He lived in a bachelor apartment and probably banked most of his money. Payroll has to get after him every so often because he hasn't cashed his paychecks. Add unemployment to whatever he walked away with and whatever he had saved, and he could probably have lived better fired than he could working."

"Yeah, but he'd lose the prestige."

"Second," she ignored the interruption, "although he and Catterall didn't get along, I don't think it was nearly as serious as the scuttlebutt would lead you to believe. Frank thrived on conflict, thought it was the best way to get what he wanted out of the people who worked for him. If you'd ever seen him have a session with the union, you'd know he wouldn't think twice about telling Catterall where to put his fancy ideas. I expected things to get a lot hotter around here in the next several months, but Frank wasn't the kind to quit without a fight. He'd have dragged his feet for as long as he could before giving up a single inch of ground; he wouldn't abandon the field altogether unless the battle was over and he'd lost beyond any hope of recovery. If then."

"So maybe he killed himself for reasons that had nothing to do with this place. This isn't the whole world, you know. You should go out and look for it some time instead of being Miss Conscientious."

Vicki smiled with saccharine sweetness. "If this is the prelude to another attempt to get me to go to a singles bar with you, you can save your breath, dear. And the third reason I don't believe Frank committed suicide is because Luis Mello said there was no way that he could have done it even if he had wanted to; there are too many safeties on the press. It couldn't be an accident either."

Linda gave an exaggerated shudder. "So you think we've got a killer on the premises."

"I don't know. The blood looked pretty dry. Whoever did it could be long gone by now."

"You saw the body!" Linda leaned forward. "I didn't know that!"

Vicki shook her head. "Only from a distance. I don't have any juicy details for you, Linda. I didn't even want to be as close as I was. You shock me, lady; you are absolutely ravenous for blood and gore. Is this a side to your cool, clinical persona that you have been secretly hiding all these years? The man is dead, after all."

The other woman's eyes narrowed. "Don't be so critical, Vicki. I know he wasn't exactly one of your favorite people either. I never liked the man from the day I met him and I've worked here a lot longer than you have."

"Okay, I'm sorry. And you're right about how I felt

about the man. Calling him a Neanderthal insults an entire species. Still, I wouldn't have wished this on him."

"Nor would I. That doesn't mean I have to act as though I'm heartbroken by his death. It's going to make things a lot easier around here."

"Don't count your chickens. We don't know who's going to end up in his place." Vicki decided to let it drop. Her friend's insensitive attitude bothered her. Or maybe it was that her own emotional flatness made her feel guilty and this was a way of externalizing it? Lost in self-contemplation, she had to stop and think back a few seconds to realize what had just been said to her.

"The police? Oh, I imagine they're interviewing people right now."

"I know that." Linda rolled her eyes. "Stop daydreaming and pay attention. I wanted to know what usually happens. Do you think we'll all be interviewed? Will they close us down?"

Vicki thought for a few seconds. "It depends partly on whichever detective is assigned to the case; they all have different styles. They'll talk to a lot of people, but not necessarily everyone. It depends on a lot of things: the physical evidence, autopsy reports, things like that. They'll do background checks on at least some of us, search Frank's apartment, try to contact his family and friends, if he had any. Then they correlate all the information and see where that leads them."

"Any guesses about who did it?"

Vicki shook her head, openly distressed this time. "I don't even want to think about it. I don't see any way it could be an outsider, unless someone broke into the plant, which doesn't seem very likely. So it must be someone we know."

"Well, I just wish I could be a fly on the wall in there right now," Linda pointed with her thumb over one shoulder in the general direction of the conference room. "Bill Elliot was just going in when I came down the corridor."

Bill Elliot was in his mid thirties, a well muscled but compact man just under six feet tall. His short curly beard was thick and intensely black, but he already showed signs of hair loss on top and would probably be noticeably bald within another year or two. He took the offered seat silently, meeting Henderson's eyes squarely, challengingly, as the preliminaries were gotten out of the way.

"Mr. Elliot, how long have you been employed here?"

"Less than a year."

"And where were you working before that?"

"Immediately before that, I was unemployed, had been for about five months. I was assistant supervisor of traffic management at Percox Industries in Cranston. They went out of business a couple of years back. They got tied in with Van Dine Chemicals and couldn't stay afloat when Van Dine collapsed."

"Traffic management?"

"It's a fancy term for shipping supervisor. Some places hand out nice titles so they don't have to pay what the job is worth. Mostly I scheduled the right trucks for particular shipments, prepared manifests and other documentation when necessary, sometimes helped the material handlers with loading."

"This is your first full supervisory job then?"

"That's right, at least officially. My old boss at Percox had a drinking problem and I pretty much ran things for the last few months."

"You attended the production meeting last night, did you not?"

"I did. Attendance is mandatory. Can't get out of it even with a note from your mother."

"So I understand. And the meeting ended at what time?"

"Four o'clock, as I'm sure you know. Antonelli was as predictable as sunrise."

"You don't sound as though you liked him."

"Not particularly. Frank Antonelli was a petty tyrant with a big mouth and a bad temper. Our relationship was cool, as you either already know or will hear before the day is out. I was hired for this job over his very loud objection, and he made no effort to disguise the fact."

"And why did he object?"

Elliot smirked and took a pack of cigarettes from his shirt pocket. "Do you mind?" he asked.

"Go right ahead."

Elliot lit up and took a few puffs before answering. "He objected to having a key position filled by someone he hadn't chosen himself, and I'll even admit that I could see his point. I'm not qualified to psychoanalyze the man, but I think he had some difficulty dealing with people of unfamiliar backgrounds as equals."

"Are you attempting to say, in convoluted fashion, that Mr. Antonelli was a bigot?"

"I didn't use that word, but it's not inaccurate."

"Then why didn't you just say it and save us some time?" Henderson's voice reflected his irritation. "What is said in this room will be confidential except insofar as it is relevant to the prosecution of this case, Mr. Elliot, so don't feel as though you have to spare anyone's feelings, least of all those of a dead man."

"All right. Frank Antonelli hated my guts because I'm

black and because some years ago he'd said several times, publicly, that he'd never tolerate a situation where white men had to take orders from their inferiors. He was prepared to sacrifice one of his best production people, put him in a job for which he had no training, and live with the consequences rather than hire me. When his decision was reversed, he felt as though top management did it deliberately to embarrass him. Does that cover the ground sufficiently?"

"I think so. You could have saved a lot of time by saying that in the first place. You're obviously an educated man, Mr. Elliot. What are you doing in a job like this?"

"I'm an underachiever." Elliot stubbed out his cigarette and sat forward. "Sorry. Sarcasm comes easily in this place lately. I'm here because the job pays rather well and I flatter myself that my employment history is not indicative of my abilities. I had been out of work for a while when I applied to a blind ad, and I was hired after what appears to have been a significant battle between Antonelli and the front office. It also tickled me to death to watch Antonelli squirm."

"So it was actually Catterall who hired you?"

"That's correct, although Romero conducted the formalities."

"What is your opinion of Mr. Catterall?"

"He's a very able and pragmatic administrator. The profit margins here had been steadily declining until he came on board. Since then he's tightened things up and held things even, although he hasn't been able to reverse the trend. The cost system was revamped from the bottom up, he shook up the Sales Department, added an effective Customer Service area, and has brought in several outside consultants to advise him on changes to the physical plant. When he makes a decision, he sticks by it and doesn't attempt to shift the blame to others. He gets along well with people, and although I think it's at least partly an act, it's a good one and most people respond to him well."

"A good man to work for then?"

"As long as you produce. I said he was pragmatic and I meant it. He'd hire Adolf Hitler if he thought the return on his investment would justify it. I might not admire his motives, but he's done a great deal to eliminate some of the less enlightened employment practices of this company. It's all public relations and self-interest, of course; I don't think it really matters to him if a particular group of people get screwed, as long as it improves the bottom line. He's good at what he does."

Henderson decided it was time to get back to the matter at hand. "What happened after the meeting yesterday?"

"I couldn't tell you."

"Why is that?"

"Listen, some of the other supervisors in this place are probably good guys, but they all knew that Antonelli had it in for me. They avoid me like the plague, and I don't see any reason to make it difficult for them. I left the meeting alone and went back to my department. I was there working in my office until a few minutes before 5:00. That's when I decided to call it a day and go home."

"You didn't see anyone or talk to anyone?"

"Nope. Wait, that's not true. I stopped at the guard station and talked to the guard, the redhead, Pat something or another. He's a rabid Red Sox fan and we talk about the games sometimes." He smiled.

"Anyone else?"

Elliot looked thoughtful. "I saw Art Richardson poke his head into shipping for a minute, probably on his way out. I didn't say anything to him though and I don't think he saw me. I was up on the second tier checking an inventory count in the obsolete storage area when I saw him."

"What time was that?"

"Just before I left. I was out before 5:00; it must have been about five minutes earlier. I wasn't paying much attention. Antonelli was killed some time last night, I take it."

"The log says you left at 4:50," interrupted Dardenian. "Does that sound right to you?"

"Must be. I thought it might be a bit later, but I don't remember looking at the clock when I went out. If that's true, then Richardson must have been there about 4:45 or a bit earlier. I must have finished up quicker than I thought, because it takes a minute or two to climb up into the balcony storage."

"Is there anything else you can think of that might help us?"

Elliot shook his head. "Sorry. I didn't like the man, but smashing him in a press would have been an over-reaction, tempting as it might have been. I honestly can't think of anyone who hated him that much."

Henderson closed his notebook. "That's it for now, then. If we need anything further, we'll let you know."

Elliot rose to his feet, pushed the chair back into place, but he didn't leave immediately. His face worked, as though he was summoning the nerve to say something, or perhaps struggling to find the right words. "Look," he said at last, his voice less self-assured than it had been a moment before. "I don't like to squeal on people, particularly when it might not mean anything."

Henderson looked up at him. "I'll say it again, Mr. Elliot. Unless it is germane to our investigation, nothing you say here will go any further."

"Yeah, I know." He took a deep breath. "One day a

couple of weeks ago, Wednesday or Thursday, I think, I came in early, real early." He shifted his weight from one foot to the other, his eyes darting around the room, never quite meeting Henderson's. "Antonelli was out in the parking lot, standing beside Manny's car. That's Manny Soares, one of the supervisors."

Henderson nodded. "I know who you mean."

"Right, well," and he hesitated again. "They were shouting at each other. I was too far away to hear what they said, but they were both pretty excited. I was curious because Manny is—was—the closest thing to a friend Antonelli had around here, so I edged in their direction on my way in, but I couldn't hear anything. But I did see Manny take a swing at Antonelli. It didn't connect; Antonelli took it on his arm, and then they saw me and everything cooled down real fast. Manny went home for the day; I heard he was sick. I pretended not to have seen anything, but I don't know if they believed me."

"Did anything like this ever happen again?"

"No, not that I know of. But people here don't talk to me much. You might check around."

"We will, Mr. Elliot."

"Who's next?" Henderson's voice sounded so tired that Dardenian gave him a long, appraising look before answering.

"Anthony Capra, the Plating Department supervisor. Do you want to take a break first?"

"No. It's almost lunchtime. We'll sneak out for a few minutes then."

Dardenian was thoughtful as he walked slowly to the door and gave instructions to Patrolman Hescox. He'd worked with Henderson a long time; it was more than just fatigue bothering him.

Tony Capra was a thin, nervous man with a brush-stroke mustache, thick black hair, wearing clothes that seemed just slightly too good to be appropriate in a factory environment. His voice was nasal and whiny, and it grated on Henderson's nerves right from the outset.

"And how long have you been employed here, Mr. Capra?"

"Eleven years, no, make that twelve. Wait a minute . . ." He glanced to one side and bit his lip in concentration. "It's twelve years next month. Yes, that's right."

"Could you tell us what you did from 3:30 yesterday afternoon until you left the premises?"

"Why, yes, I'm sure I can. There was the meeting first, of course. You see, we get together every Monday to go over production plans and . . ."

Henderson raised one hand. "We know what the meeting was about. Just tell us what happened after it broke up."

Capra looked momentarily disconcerted. "Well, yes, naturally you wouldn't care what happened while Frank was still alive, would you? Now let's see, I left the office at 4:00; that's when the meeting ended. Frank always ended his meetings at 4:00, you know; he was very regular about that sort of thing. Frank was a real regular sort of guy, you know?"

"Yes, we know. Go on, please."

"Right. Well, there'd been some problems with the plating counts. There's this tray, we call it the 744 tray, which we produce in pretty good-sized lots. Anyway, my figures showed that we plated 11,000 pieces during July, and they only packed about 10,500, and Donna—she's the supervisor of finishing and packing—Donna said she didn't have any left, so there had to be a problem with the counts somewhere along the line. You see, either my department had overcounted, or she'd undercounted, or they were lost somewhere in finishing or maybe even boxed under the wrong number. So I was trying to figure out how many were plated each day so I could match the counts with the number polished. That way I could figure out where the problem was. That sort of thing happens a lot because quite a few of our items are just variations of each other and it's easy to confuse them. Some people don't seem to understand that, you know, and get all worked up when things don't match. I spend more of my time trying to trace down a handful of pieces than I do on the really important stuff."

Henderson was momentarily awestruck at the flow of words he had elicited, and only the sight of Ben Dardenian laughing silently out of Capra's line of sight prompted him to take a hand.

"All right, Mr. Capra. I think I grasp the basics of the situation. What did you do next?"

"Well, I locked up the chemical storage room. We have to be careful of that because of the cyanide."

"What time would that have been?"

"Oh, I'm not sure I know. It might have been 4:30, because after that I recorded the amperage from the plating machines. We use that to determine how much silver we've consumed each day, and I wanted to recheck them now that the inventory is over so that my records were adjusted to the right value. I closed up my office at 4:45 and that was about fifteen minutes later. I'm pretty certain of that because I glanced at my watch. I wanted to get home in time to watch the news."

"And then?"

"Then, well, I hadn't found anything wrong with my plating counts; they matched almost perfectly to what was polished. So I went over to tell Frank that we should recheck the packing figures, even though there didn't seem to be any way they could be wrong. I don't know where this stuff goes. Sometimes it's like, you know, gremlins come in at night and move the stuff around. Frank wasn't in the office, though, and I thought he might be busy so I didn't bother to page him. He gets really annoyed when you interrupt him for anything that's not really important, and I figured anything I had to tell him could wait until the next day."

"Did you see anyone else during any of this time?"

Capra looked thoughtful. "No, not really. I think there was someone in the Hand Polishing Department when I went to look for Frank, but I didn't actually see anyone. The lights were on. But I wasn't paying any attention, I was just kind of, you know, figuring out how to approach Frank with the problem."

"So what did you do when you couldn't find Frank Antonelli?"

"Well, I double-checked to make sure I had locked the plating office because we have some chemicals in there too and control is important, and then I went home."

"And what time was that?"

Capra was suddenly silent, and the next words came, if anything, even faster than those which had preceded them. "I sort of looked things over a bit to make sure there was nothing that needed doing and then I left. It must have been before 5:00 though, because the news wasn't on yet when I got home and I've got a good thirty-minute drive."

"And you still didn't see anyone?"

"No, no one except Stone, the guard. He was sitting in his shack when I drove out."

Henderson noticed a sudden stiffening of Dardenian's shoulders and the other detective turned slightly in his chair, nodding toward the printout before him.

"Excuse me a moment, Mr. Capra." Henderson arose, stretched his back theatrically, and walked over to the other table.

"He didn't check out until 5:30," Dardenian said softly, too softly to be heard at the other end of the room.

Henderson nodded and returned to his chair, his expression neutral. "What would you say is the latest you might have left, Mr. Capra?"

"Oh, I really don't know. I didn't look at my watch again after 4:45. I suppose it might have been 5:00 or a little after."

"Could it have been as late as 5:15?"

As an actor, Capra would have made a fine truck driver. Guilt and confusion battled for domination of his features. "I suppose it might have been that late. I wasn't, you know, paying much attention, like I said. I walked around and checked things out and maybe I lost track of time a little."

"Mr. Capra, you were logged out at 5:30. That's a full forty-five minutes after you said you decided to go home. Where were you for that period of time?"

For a moment, Henderson thought the man was going to stick to his story, but then he collapsed as if all of the air had escaped through a rip in his skin. "Is this, you know, what we say in here, is it confidential? It wouldn't get back to . . ." he paused. "I was going to say to my boss, but I don't even know who my boss is now. That's kind of funny." No one laughed.

Henderson relented. "Unless it is material to the investigation, nothing you say will be repeated to your superiors. But if you don't tell us what you know, you're going to be in some very serious trouble."

"Well, I sort of, you know, took a walk around the

Packing Department. Those 744s had to be somewhere and lots of times they get stuck in the back out of the way and people forget where they are and then say they don't have them and I end up spending time figuring out where the mistake was when it was in a different department all the time. I probably spent almost a half hour there, but I couldn't find anything wrong."

"Why didn't you just tell us that in the first place?"

"Well, Frank gets upset when we go spying on each other, as he calls it. Tells us we should work together. He'd have been really mad if he knew I'd gone in there and checked up without telling Donna, even if he doesn't—didn't—like her all that much."

Henderson sighed. "Mr. Capra, I don't think you have to worry about Frank Antonelli getting mad at you any longer, do you?"

Capra's face twisted slowly, as though he were wrestling with the concept. Finally his eyes opened wide in what was unmistakably a look not completely devoid of pleasure. "Why, I suppose you're right. It just hasn't penetrated yet, you know. You get used to working for someone for a long time and you think they're always going to be there and that things are going to go on the same forever, you know?"

Capra continued in that vein until Henderson interrupted. "That's all for now, Mr. Capra. Thank you for your time."

The last of the factory workers was Donna D'Angelo, a not unattractive blonde of medium build who wore her hair coiled up in a tight bun, large round eyeglasses with heavy black rims, and walked with a barely detectible limp. She had been with the company nine years, as a finisher for most of that time.

"What precisely is a 'finisher'?"

"It's a final polishing operation, a lot like what you'd do to silverplate in your home, bringing out the sheen, except that we use soft cloth wheels on a lathe to save time and give it a uniform appearance. It's kind of a fussy job. The amount of silver on the stuff we make, particularly the new low-priced line, is measured in millionths of an inch. It doesn't take much pressure to cut right through the silver and expose the brass or copper underneath. When that happens, we have to replate the whole piece."

"How long have you been in your current position?"

"I took over when Charlie Waters died three years ago. And just so you hear it from me, Frank Antonelli didn't want to give me the job."

Henderson frowned. "And why was that?"

She gave him a tight, humorless smile. "It's a long story."

"I'm not in any hurry."

"All right. When Charlie Waters died, Antonelli had a problem. The most senior finisher in the department, Jose Santiago, is a nice guy, but he's not the leader type. Even if they'd offered him the job of supervisor, he'd have turned it down, I think. Probably would have run away screaming, as a matter of fact. I was second in line. Frank wanted to give it to Carlos Soares instead."

"Why was that?"

D'Angelo shrugged. "He didn't think I could control the people in the department, or at least that's what I heard."

"And the unofficial reason?"

"I think he was afraid that some of the men would refuse to cooperate with a woman as boss. He was wrong about that, if that really was the case; I haven't had a problem with anyone. Or maybe he just didn't want to have to accept a woman onto his team."

"Could it also have been something personal?"

The smile went away. "No, not at the time. Afterwards maybe, if he was as mad about it as I think he was. We'd always gotten along pretty well before that. I was a good finisher, second best in the department, and Frank always liked people who could produce. But he was furious when he was overruled and had to give me the job."

"Who overruled him? Catterall?"

"Actually, it was Romero, in personnel, who did the dirty work, but I'm sure Catterall was behind it. Romero's kind of a wimp."

"Were relations between the two of you strained after that?"

This time she laughed outright. "Pureed rather than strained. Should I be telling you this? Am I making myself the chief suspect?"

"You should be telling me the truth, and if everyone who disliked his or her boss committed murder, the entire economy would grind to a halt."

"Right. Anyway, he got used to it, more or less, and to be honest, he treated me fairly. It just wasn't very friendly around here, if you know what I mean."

"Where did you go and what did you do after yesterday's production meeting?"

She sat back and sighed. "I've got a lousy memory for this sort of thing, but let's see. Tony and I, that's Tony Capra from plating, we walked back through his department and he headed toward his office. I went up to finishing and checked the line, found out we needed some buffs for a goblet job we're running as a special. I filled out a requisition and left it in the cubbyhole at Storeroom E. Then I went home. That must have been about ten or fifteen minutes before 5:00."

"You didn't see anyone else during that entire time?"

She pursed her lips and was silent for a moment. "No, I don't think so. Except the guard on the way out."

The interview went on for several minutes longer, but only one other item of interest came up, and that just as she was preparing to leave.

"There's one other thing, but I don't know if it means anything."

Henderson looked interested. "What was that?"

"Well, this morning when I came in, I was setting up a job in the packing room when I noticed that someone had been moving stuff around."

"What kind of stuff?"

"Nothing important really. But there was this skid of water pitchers I had set aside for re-inspection; it's been so humid these last few days, they have water spots. It's like mildew forming on the finishing compound probably. Anyway, I know I had pushed them to the front of aisle number two in dead storage, but they were in aisle number three this morning. And some bonbons were stacked differently."

"Anything else?"

"No, not that I noticed anyway."

"Well, thank you for telling us, and if you recall anything else out of the ordinary, even if it seems irrelevant, please let us know."

When she was gone, Henderson groaned loudly. "Five more of these to go? Is it lunchtime yet?"

"Almost. We can fit one more in if you want."

"Let's wait. There's a nice little Italian place down the street. I need a break."

Dardenian shook his head. "Getting soft in your old age?"

"Only in the head." He paused. "One more, you said?"

"I think so."

"All right; stop nagging. Let's get on with it."

The door opened a moment later to admit a woman in her late twenties with straight, cornhusk-colored hair bordering a plain face that might almost have been pretty if it hadn't been quite so long, the chin quite so pointed.

Henderson stiffened so abruptly that the legs of his seat scraped on the floor, although he tried to conceal his reaction.

The woman glanced at him and smiled. "Hi, Dad. How's it going?"

FIVE

"You might have warned me, Ben." Henderson's voice was calm but his partner flinched slightly, detecting the hidden anger.

"I tried, but you were too busy to listen." He turned away and a ghost of a grin played briefly across his face.

"I suppose I should have expected this." Henderson sighed. "As soon as I heard where we were being sent, I had a feeling she'd be right in the middle of things."

"Like father, like daughter," Dardenian replied with a twinkle.

"Dad's famous for not noticing the same little flaws he criticizes in others," Vicki added merrily, but although her tone was bantering, all three of them knew she meant it.

Henderson massaged his jaw. "I suppose I should be grateful," he said at last. "With my only daughter as a potential suspect, they'll have to assign someone else and maybe I can finally catch up on my sleep."

"Still working long hours?" Vicki's eyes took in the fatigue lines in her father's face and she resolved to be less flip.

"Longer than ever," he replied shortly. "And we still have to finish the preliminary interviews here before I can go downtown and disqualify myself. So let's get on with it."

Vicki promptly sat down. "Okay with me. I'm used to all your tricks, though." She turned toward Ben. "He used to give me the third degree all the time when I lived at home."

"I'll bet."

"Let's leave the teasing until later, shall we?"

Vicki turned serious, or mostly serious anyway. "Yes, sir. We can assume you've told me my legal rights. My name is Victoria Sanders, I've worked here five years, most of that time as a roving inspector. Promoted to Quality Control supervisor two years ago." A smile broke through. "Even though my father said I'd never get anywhere in a serious manufacturing job."

Henderson glared at her. "You were in the building late yesterday?"

"That's right. Mark Ross dropped by to tell me the production report from two weeks ago was finally ready. We had a problem with the computer and we've been waiting for it so we could reconcile the reject rates I've been getting to the actual pieces produced. The total numbers still didn't look right, so we went looking for the WAT associated with one of the worst jobs to see if we could figure out what had happened."

"The what?"

"The WAT. Work Authorization Ticket. That's what we call the traveler that accompanies each production run through the factory. Anyway, we decided to go out to the Packing Department and look for ourselves. Sometimes the WATs get mixed up and the wrong job is being reported."

"What time did all of this happen?"

"Oh, dear." Vicki scratched her head in what might have been an infuriating comic exaggeration if Henderson had not recognized this as a childhood habit Vicki had never outgrown, performed quite unconsciously. "Mark came by just after 4:00. The guard would know what time we went by. He has to log it in."

"The report says 4:29," Dardenian confirmed.

"We went up to final inspection and packing, but didn't

find the job in either place. It was a run of ice tongs and they don't take up much space. After a bit, we walked over to plating to see if maybe Tony Capra would remember if they had actually been silverplated at all, but the office was locked so we decided Tony had gone home already."

"How long did all of this take?"

"Maybe fifteen or twenty minutes. I could walk it again and clock it for you."

"Maybe later. Where did you go next?"

"We stayed in plating for about twenty minutes. Manny Soares was coming through on the way out. He runs polishing."

"We know."

"Right, of course you would. Mark asked him if he had sent the ice tongs into plating; we knew they'd been polished. He said he'd shipped them to storage like the ticket said. Storeroom C is right there in plating, and even though it's locked up, it's made of chicken wire so you can see what's inside. We walked over there and, sure enough, they were right inside the doorway."

"Did you see anyone else while you were there?"

"At 5:25, Jenny Grissom came by on her way to the parking lot."

Henderson held up one hand but Dardenian was already speaking. "She's on the list; it says here she's the office manager."

"That's right," Vicki confirmed. "And before you ask, I know it was exactly 5:25 because I was surprised when I saw her and looked at my watch. She's usually gone by 5:15, and it's not that often that we see her out in the factory either. We left right after that, walked Manny to the warehouse, said goodnight, and came back to the main office. That was probably at 5:30, right Ben?"

"One minute before."

"Were you and Ross together the whole time?"

"Every minute, within touching distance. But we didn't go anywhere near the press room. Is that when Frank was killed?"

"We don't have the exact time," Henderson hedged. "But it was sometime before 6:00 as best we can tell right now."

Vicki shook her head. "I don't suppose there's any way it could have been an accident?"

"We're checking it out, Vicki, but it doesn't look very likely. Is there anything else you can think of that we should know?"

"No, not really." She hesitated, glanced quickly toward Dardenian and back. "You look tired, Dad, seriously," she kept her voice low.

"Don't fuss, Vicki. You know how I hate it."

"Bullshit, Dad. You used to love it when Mom thought you'd been working too hard and made a big deal out of relaxing you."

"I only acted that way so she'd think she was helping."

"Oh, right," she laughed skeptically, but it sounded strained and she stopped quickly. "Seriously, Dad. Why don't I come over tonight? It's been a while. We should talk."

"If we can go four months without speaking, I imagine we can last a while longer." He cursed himself silently as a fool, but he was too stubborn to soften his stance once he'd taken it. "You're a busy woman; I'm a busy man. We both have our own lives to live."

Vicki opened her mouth once, closed it, opened it again, still searching for words. "Haven't you sulked about things long enough? It's not going to change anything. Danny and I are not going to get back together. He's not a bad guy, and I wish we could still be friends, but I don't love him any longer, if I ever really did before, and I'm not going to spend the rest of my life keeping house for him up in Managansett. I like working; I've made a place for myself here and I'm respected for what I do."

Henderson glanced toward Dardenian, who was pretending to be fascinated with the computer printouts. "This isn't the place to talk about this."

"No, but it's the place where I work, and where I plan to work for the foreseeable future. Whether or not you approve of it!" She took a deep breath and told herself to calm down. "We need to talk this out, but you're right, not here and not now." She licked her lips. "I'll stop by tonight, around 7:00. All right?"

Henderson's face was immobile as he struggled with conflicting emotions of his own. "All right?" she repeated, slightly louder. "Dad, I'm serious. I'm not going to drop this. We should have done this a lot sooner and that's half my fault, but I'm not going to let it slide any longer."

Henderson winced, but he knew his daughter's moods well enough to realize he wasn't going to be able to shrug her off. "Okay, okay. I don't know what purpose it will serve, but come on over."

"Fine. You get the beer and I'll bring the pizza. Now are we done? I'd like to get back to work."

"That's it for the time being. Whoever takes over for me will probably want to go over everything again."

She rose and started to leave, then paused. "Seven o'clock, remember!" And then she was gone before he could reply.

Despite his original plan to break for lunch, Henderson

decided to interview Mark Ross first. If Ross confirmed his daughter's story, it would eliminate one small distraction.

Ross was a moderately good-looking man in his late thirties, self-assured and well-spoken. After sitting, Ross leaned forward over the table in what Henderson interpreted as an unspoken and perhaps even unconscious challenge. After the preliminaries, during which Ross explained that he had been with Standard for just over four years, Henderson asked about the rivalry that reportedly existed between Ross and the dead man.

"There are constant disagreements between factory management and production control in any manufacturing concern, Detective. They don't mean anything, and they're forgotten almost immediately."

"What exactly does a Production Control Manager do, Mr. Ross?"

"I'm oversimplifying, but basically my office determines what items should be made, in what quantities, and when. We schedule, prioritize, and occasionally expedite."

"Didn't that overlap Mr. Antonelli's responsibilities?"

"Certainly it required a great deal of interaction, although the systems here are pretty primitive and the department supervisors have much more latitude than in most similar operations. In a more sophisticated organization, we would be scheduling individual machines, organizing the transportation of materials, coordinating each element of the production process, and interfacing between the people who do the work and the ones who sell the goods. Production control is the network of nerves, manufacturing the muscle, finance the brains." He laughed. "And I suppose that makes salespeople the mouth."

Henderson wasn't amused by what appeared to be a well-rehearsed speech. "Wouldn't anything that structured infringe on the authority of the production manager?"

Ross laughed. "No one here has unlimited authority, not even Catterall. Frank and I had a lot of fights, but I didn't kill him over a lagging production quota." His expression changed. "Sorry, I didn't mean to trivialize the man's death; it just doesn't seem real yet. You're right; a certain amount of tension existed between us, although for the most part it was a healthy one. When your priorities differ, there are bound to be diverging opinions. Frank's solution to most problems was to throw more muscle at it; he worked hard and drove his people to put out their best. We'd pay overtime to produce out-of-stock items that should have been finished weeks before without the premium pay. He had difficulty reconciling himself to a new situation where it was more important to work smart than work hard. And because I'm relatively new, there was probably some resentment there as well."

"Catterall hired you, I imagine."

"Yes, as a matter of fact he did. And that was part of the problem. To be perfectly honest, to some degree Ed used me as a foil in his struggle with Frank. Don't get me wrong; I have a great deal of respect for Ed. He gave me this opportunity four years ago and stuck by me while I was floundering around for the first few months. He's a very pragmatic type of manager; he looks for what works rather than what the common wisdom says will work. I don't have any idea what his personal prejudices might be, but he seems able to set them aside entirely in a business context and make decisions on a perfectly rational and objective basis. He's done a great deal of good in this company, and my own personal stake in his continued success is enormous." He sighed. "But he does tend to be manipulative at times, and on occasion I become the tool he uses to nudge people, particularly Frank Antonelli, into changing direction."

"Did Catterall and Antonelli fight often?"

Ross looked momentarily startled. "I didn't mean to imply that there was something openly hostile between the two. Ed couldn't possibly be responsible in any case; he was in Houston until late last night. I remember him saying that his wife was going to meet him in Boston. It wasn't openly hostile anyway; Ed was always in control of the situation. If he had been killed, I might have wondered about Frank, but certainly never the opposite."

Henderson pondered the situation for a few seconds, then changed the line of questioning. Ross recounted the events of the previous evening in a story almost identical to Vicki's version. He couldn't be as precise about the times as she, but nothing he said contradicted her testimony in any way. He confirmed that they had never been out of each other's sight during the entire period.

When Ross left the room some time later, Dardenian sighed. "Walt, we're going to have a problem here."

Henderson nodded. "I think I know what you're going to say, but go ahead."

"Except for Vicki and this Ross character, no one has an alibi. There's just not enough overlap. And none of the remaining three names on my list have been mentioned at all except the Grissom woman, and that was only in passing, so there's a good chance they don't have alibis either."

"Meaning that an awful lot of people had the opportunity to push Frank Antonelli into a press."

"That, and an awful lot of people seem to have had a motive to do him in."

"Few people get into a position as powerful as his without making a lot of enemies along the way."

"Maybe. But this Antonelli seemed to alienate everyone he dealt with. I never even met the man and I don't particularly like him."

"Can't say that I do either, but I don't go around knocking off people I find obnoxious. I wouldn't have time to do anything else." He pushed his chair back from the table. "Let's get something to eat."

Ordinarily, Walt Henderson delighted in his lunches. He'd been blessed with a racing metabolism that had allowed him to maintain the same weight for most of his life, although now that he was in his mid fifties, he was starting to notice that some of his clothing fit a bit more tightly than it once had. He loved to eat and he was a cuisinary internationalist—Chinese, Burmese, French, Mexican, and particularly Italian. Today, however, he picked at his lasagna, pushing the ricotta cheese around the plate with his fork, expression distracted.

"Is something wrong, Walt?" Dardenian was cleaning up his own plate with enthusiasm.

"I don't know, Ben." He placed the fork down beside his plate and crossed his arms. "Not enough sleep, long hours, too many complications."

Ben paused, a forkful of manicotti halfway to his mouth. "You think they'll pull us off this case?"

"Me at least. With Vicki involved, it wouldn't look right. They might leave you on with a new partner."

Ben grimaced. "Thanks a lot. Not only do you wish more work on me, you want me to have to adjust to another prima donna detective after all the years it's taken for me to get used to you."

"You're a remarkably adaptable man, Ben." Henderson smiled.

"Who do you think they'll give it to?"

"Beats me. That's the captain's problem. Everyone is working extra hours already, or home in bed sick. Maybe he'll take the case himself; he used to be a detective. Pretty good too, at least so he tells me at every opportunity."

Ben was silent a moment. "You and Vicki need to stop feuding."

Henderson gave him a sharp look. "Who said we were feuding?"

"Listen, Walt, I know you don't like to talk about your personal life. God knows, I've worked with you for over ten years now and I still only have a hazy idea of the Walter Henderson who goes home at night. But you're not entirely opaque; I've noticed the change in you since Vicki's marriage fell apart. You never talk about her any more. I didn't even know she worked here until I saw the name on the security log."

Henderson's mouth opened, but he didn't say anything. He looked off to one side for several seconds, then dropped his eyes. "Vicki is an adult and makes her own choices, for good or bad. Come on," his voice became more brusque and he pushed back the chair. "Let's get out of here."

Dardenian sat for several long seconds, watching his partner take the check to the cashier. "You're a good friend, Walter Henderson, but you're also a thick-headed bastard," he said softly, too softly for anyone else to hear.

When they returned to Standard Silver, Patrolman Hescox told them that Ed Catterall had stopped by and was still insisting upon talking to Henderson.

"How many people are left on the list, Ben? I've lost count."

"Three. Paula Danforth, the Materials Control Supervisor; Jennifer Grissom, she's the Office Manager; and

Kevin Mitchell, Purchasing Agent. And you told me to add Catterall at the end."

"That's right, and that's where he stays." Henderson turned back to Hescox. "If Mr. Catterall comes by again, tell him that I hope to be able to speak to him before I leave."

"Yes, sir." The younger man sounded slightly uncertain.

"And don't let him bully you, Hescox. He's a civilian, remember? We're in authority here, not him."

"Yes sir." His chin rose slightly and his voice was stronger this time.

Paula Danforth was ushered into the conference room a few moments later. She was in her late thirties but appeared even older, with dark rings under her eyes, hair just slightly disheveled, obviously ill at ease and anxious to be anywhere but where she was. She admitted to having worked at Standard for eight years.

"Just what exactly does a Materials Control Supervisor do?"

"It's a service function. We used to be called Centralized Trucking, but we got an upgrade in title rather than a raise one year ago." She attempted a laugh but it sounded brittle. "We make sure the work is moved to the right departments on time and keep inventories in the storerooms. Do a little recordkeeping. Run errands. Things like that."

"You must have worked with Frank Antonelli a great deal then."

"Actually I dealt mostly with his supervisors. Frank thought of my department as a sort of necessary evil. Most of my people are in his operating budget, and since they're all indirect labor—that's labor that doesn't actually physically change the piece being manufactured—it reflects unfavorably in his monthly reports."

"Do you attend the Monday meetings?"

"The production meetings? No, not usually. Every once in a while he'll call me in to find out why some job wasn't where it was supposed to be, but no, I didn't attend it normally."

"But you did go out into the factory yesterday afternoon."

"Sure, about 4:30. We've been having some trouble with labor being reported against the wrong work order and I was spot checking some that looked suspicious to me. You know how this sort of thing works; everyone double checks to make sure it isn't their own department that's responsible for a problem, then makes loud noises about how terrible the situation is."

"Where exactly did you go?"

"Automatic polishing, then down to the Solder Department. I checked tickets for a while, didn't find anything worth mentioning, then noticed how late it was and went home. That must have been about 5:30."

"Did you see anyone or talk to anyone during that period?"

She shook her head. "Oh, wait. I saw Tony Capra walking into the plating office when I came out, but I don't know if he saw me. His back was turned. Didn't see anyone else at all except the guard."

"How long were you in polishing before you went to solder?" Henderson was peering at his copy of the floor plan, reviewing earlier statements in his mind. He knew Dardenian would have taken detailed notes, which they would attempt to cross-reference in excruciating detail later, but he always tried to weave the unfolding stories into a tapestry of movement from which he could pick out patterns and contradictions.

"I don't know. Really. It might have been half an hour. I

wasn't paying that much attention. Sorry."

"You didn't see Frank Antonelli and you didn't go near the press area?"

"No, I'm afraid not. Or actually, I'm glad that I didn't. If I had stumbled in at the wrong time, I might have been killed too, I suppose." She was silent, considering. "You know, I hadn't stopped to think of that until just now. It's kind of scary."

Further questioning elicited nothing of interest. "All right. That's all for now. If you can think of anything you might have forgotten for the moment, please let one of the patrolmen know."

Once she had left the room, Dardenian spoke without prompting. "She checked in at 4:35 and out at 5:31. So far, everybody's story checks out. This isn't going to be open and shut, Walt. Someone has been very clever, or very lucky."

"Or both. For more than one reason, I'm glad someone else is going to have to worry about this one."

"I thought you enjoyed a challenge?"

"You must be talking about some other person. I like my murderers dumb and luckless. Who's next?"

Jennifer Grissom was a tall, strikingly attractive black woman whose hair was cut short and close to her skull. She moved purposefully and with self-assurance, taking the obvious seat without waiting for an invitation. She wore a scarlet pants suit that clung tightly to her body, and which managed to mix subdued sexuality with professionalism.

"My name is Jennifer Grissom and I'm the Office Manager here. How may I be of assistance?"

Henderson cleared his throat and sat forward, determined to recapture the initiative. "You could tell us how long you've been employed by Standard and then describe the nature of your duties."

"I was hired by Mr. Catterall three years ago. He wanted to reorganize the office so that the different functions interacted more smoothly and there was better utilization of the clerical staff. This was later expanded so that certain previously separate areas of responsibility were combined. He also wished to replace the established informal decision-making process with something more structured and felt that my particular skills would help to change the situation."

"Is it really necessary to be so cryptic, Ms. Grissom?"

She met his gaze levelly, then let her shoulders drop a bit and smiled slightly, though only for a moment. "In other words, drop the bullshit, right?"

"That would certainly be helpful."

"All right. Catterall walked into a beehive here. Every office and department was run like a separate empire; no one cooperated with anyone else, there was overstaffing because none of the big cheeses would allow their employees to take up the slack in other departments, and the department heads themselves resented Catterall's presence and style. His predecessor was an ineffective administrator, but apparently a dear man."

"And Catterall is not?"

"No, he's a realist and a pragmatist. You'll hear that term a lot around here; it's one of his favorites. When he realized he was in for a long campaign just to get the office revamped, he decided to provide an overwhelming demonstration of his power. Not only did he create the position of Office Manager, but he hired a young black woman to run it, and changed the organizational chart so that a couple of white men reported to her." Her jaw worked a bit, giving away just the slightest amount of suppressed tension. "The purchasing agent, a balding Irishman, quit the day I was hired. Wouldn't even shake hands with me when I was introduced. He was actually shaking with rage at the time."

"Don't you resent being used as a tool?"

"Not particularly. Every employee is a tool. And I'm paid quite well to put up with the aggravation."

"You don't mind the pressure? It must have been rather tense around here."

"I thrive on it." Her eyes flashed with anger. "The office here was filled with complacent, self-absorbed people who were more interested in shoring up their tiny little personal empires than in getting the work done. I took a great deal of pleasure in puncturing their bubbles. Most of them took steps of their own to improve the efficiency of their departments once they saw what would happen if they waited for me to step in. The company gains better personnel utilization, I hold onto a fairly high paying job, and if some of the people around here were more honest with themselves, they'd realize they've been maneuvered into becoming better managers."

Henderson decided to change the subject. "You visited the factory late yesterday?"

"That's correct. Kevin Mitchell—he's the new purchasing agent—and I took a walk down to receiving about 4:15. We've been having trouble with some receipts recently. One of our vendors mislabeled a shipment of solder, and we've been trying to figure out which lots were affected. Our Receiving Department is somewhat lax about providing sufficient detail to trace individual cartons back to the source documentation."

"That sounds like a purchasing problem to me. Why were you getting involved?"

For a split second, her calm professionalism started to slip, but she recovered quickly. Not quickly enough for Henderson not to have noticed. "It was a slow day and I was restless. When Kevin mentioned he was going down to check, I went along for the walk. I wanted to ask Art Richardson something anyway, but it turned out he'd already gone home when we got there."

"Could you show me which way you went?" He pointed to the floor plan.

She indicated a route that passed through solder and casting. "We searched high and low in the warehouse," she pointed with one finger, "but we couldn't find any of the suspect solder. Richardson must either have issued it to the factory or moved it to some separate location we didn't think of, so that he could check it later."

"Were the two of you separated at any time while you were in the warehouse?"

"Not really. Possibly out of line of sight, but we were calling back and forth the entire time."

"How long were you in receiving altogether?"

"Possibly half an hour."

"And you didn't see anyone at all while you were in the factory?"

"I didn't say that. On the way back, I noticed Mark Ross, Manny Soares, and Vicki Sanders standing in plating, but we didn't talk."

"That would have to have been just before 5:30. I thought you were only in the factory for about a half hour."

She shrugged, but her eyes betrayed her anxiety, controlled but visible. "It seemed shorter than that, but I suppose it could have been longer. I didn't look at my watch."

"That's all for now, Ms. Grissom. Thank you for your time."

As she was leaving, Dardenian turned toward Henderson. "The time checks out okay, Walt, but she was hiding something, you know."

"She sure was. Anyone who makes a point of always meeting your eyes when she's answering a question is trying to hide something. Let's see if this Mitchell guy's story checks out with hers."

Kevin Mitchell was also black, his hair neatly groomed, clean shaven except for a spiky mustache. His English was very precise, and Henderson detected what he suspected was a Jamaican accent.

"You're the purchasing agent here, Mr. Mitchell."

"Yes. I have been employed at this facility for almost exactly one year, Inspector."

"I'm not an inspector, Mr. Mitchell. Just a detective."

"Yes, sir. Sorry."

Henderson shook his head. "Are you an American citizen, Mr. Mitchell?"

"Yes." Mitchell seemed surprised at the question. "The accent, no doubt. My parents were from Pine Mountain, Georgia. My father's business required him to spend a great deal of time out of the country, and as a consequence, I spent most of my childhood in Nassau."

Henderson nodded. "Yesterday afternoon, you visited the factory?"

"Yes, Ms. Grissom and I went down to receiving to check on a consignment of ribbon solder which had been reported defective by the shop foreman. He had unwisely thrown away the packaging, so we could not immediately identify the particular purchase lot number. Since the quantity he reported was less than had been ordered, I assumed that the balance would still be in receiving and that I could determine the lot number by locating it there. I mentioned my intentions while Ms. Grissom was present and she offered to accompany me."

"What time was this?"

"We entered the factory around 4:15, I believe. The computer log will confirm this. A record is kept of all visitors, you see."

"We know about the log, Mr. Mitchell. Please continue."

"Well, there really isn't much to add. We searched for the solder in the warehouse. Richardson had gone home, so we couldn't ask him. But either it had all been issued to the floor or it had been moved to some unlikely location. We couldn't find it even though we searched pretty thoroughly."

"How long did all of this take?"

Mitchell leaned forward and scratched his forehead as though thinking. The fact that this concealed his eyes momentarily from Henderson's view did not go unnoticed. "Slightly longer than half an hour, I believe. Ms. Grissom lost interest and left shortly before I. It was almost 5:40 when I returned to my office; I noticed because some of the lights were already off."

"And you didn't see anyone else while you were in the factory?"

"No. No one at all."

Henderson asked him to trace his route out and back on the floor plan, but it didn't contradict Jennifer Grissom's story in any way.

After he had left the room, Henderson made a disgusted sound. "It's going to be one of those," he said. "When all the suspects have alibis, you can concentrate on each of them in turn, find out which one breaks down. But what do you do when nobody has an alibi and everyone had an opportunity to commit the crime?"

Dardenian shrugged. "I guess under those circumstances you ask the officer in the corridor to send in Mr. Catterall."

SIX

Walt Henderson instinctively disliked Ed Catterall. There was something in the way he carried himself, the angle of his jaw, the set of his eyes, that radiated disdain. Catterall expected to be in charge at all times, was uncomfortable when the players did not conform to his set of rules, and he was clearly planning to assert his authority in the presence of what he probably considered a couple of fumbling local policemen.

Standard Silver's chief executive strode directly to the table, was already reaching for the back of the chair, when Henderson raised his head from the notebook he was pretending to be studying, as though suddenly noticing the other man's presence. "Take a seat please, Mr. Catterall. I'll be with you in just a moment."

Catterall no longer seemed interested in sitting. "My staff and I are anxious to clear up this situation as quickly as possible, Detective Henderson. We reopen Monday and there's still a great deal of work to be done beforehand. Obviously, this distressful situation is causing distraction and uneasiness. I'd like to know how close you are to clearing matters up so that we can get on with our normal activities."

Henderson considered a number of replies, some less than tactful. It would be pointless to alienate the man further; it would just make things more difficult for whoever was assigned to the case in his place. "Mr. Catterall, I realize that a murder investigation is disruptive. We are moving as expeditiously as possible under the circumstances. Our first priority, however, is and must be the identification and apprehension of the person or persons responsible. There will be as little interference as possible, but I regret to say that some inconvenience is inevitable. I expect that you and your staff will understand that and cooperate with us as fully as possible."

Catterall was momentarily uncertain. He clearly recognized that he was being challenged, but Henderson's phrasing made it difficult to object. "All right. How can I help you?"

"If you'd take a seat please, I have a few questions I'd like to ask about your staff. We would also like complete access to personnel records of the individuals I have interviewed today, as well as the victim. There will probably be other requests as we think of them."

For a moment, it appeared that Catterall would continue to stand throughout the interview, but he seemed to think better of it and slid into the chair. Henderson noticed that he deliberately leaned as far forward across the table as possible, trying to silently impose his authority. Henderson had been in this business too long to be impressed by body language, although he was an acute observer of it.

"How long have you been with Standard Silver, Mr. Catterall?"

The man seemed surprised at the question, but he answered. "I was hired by the Board just over four years ago. My predecessor, Merrivale, had just taken early retirement."

"Was it voluntary or was he booted out?"

Catterall raised his eyebrows. "It was by mutual agreement. I was charged with revitalizing the company and preparing it to deal with the more competitive conditions of today's market. Merrivale's methods were outdated, and he lacked the energy to reorganize the company on the radical scale required to deal with the necessary changes."

"I gather that Frank Antonelli wasn't entirely supportive of your program of reform."

Catterall nodded. "It was no secret that Frank resented some of the programs I have implemented. A certain degree of conservatism in these matters is inevitable. But we weren't changing merely for the sake of doing things differently. Each new policy had to be defensible for its own sake. Frank wasn't entirely on board and sometimes made things more difficult than necessary. He fought any change which seemed to dilute his own authority."

"He wasn't overjoyed with some of your personnel changes either, was he?"

"Frank was cast from a mold now broken, or at least in disrepair. If we're going to move forward, we have to learn to make use of the best tools available to us, regardless of our personal feelings in the matter. Frank preferred to replace worn components with as close an approximation of the old as he could find; he was not open to the possibility of using a superior part that lay outside his experience."

"In other words, he was prejudiced."

"It could be phrased that way, yes."

"Then say it that way in the future, Mr. Catterall. Neither of us has time for the Chamber of Commerce version of events."

Catterall's back stiffened just perceptibly. "All right, then. Frank Antonelli was a bigoted bastard who ran the manufacturing area as his private preserve for years. Our relationship with the union is bad, production systems are archaic, information from the shop floor lacks integrity, and it is difficult to measure our inefficiencies, let alone correct them."

"So it's fair to say that you were less than happy with Frank Antonelli." Catterall nodded. "And it's also fair to say that some of your changes were designed specifically to provide the means by which you could control him in the future."

"I tried to limit the amount of damage he could do but I had no intention of controlling Frank Antonelli. Plans had already been laid to replace him by the end of the year. His death merely rearranges my schedule."

Although Henderson didn't react visually to this information, it struck him as potentially significant. "Was Antonelli aware of your intentions?"

"I doubt it. He was convinced that he was indispensable. The Board of Directors knew, of course. There are nine directors, three of whom opposed the ouster of Merrivale and distrust the direction things are taking. One of them may have seen fit to tip off Antonelli that his days with the firm were numbered."

"Was anyone else aware of your plan? Anyone here? Maybe Romero in personnel?"

"Only Mark Ross actually knew what I had in mind, although some might have suspected. Ross is a bright young man whom I recruited shortly after my appointment. I gave him two years to become acquainted with operations and the product line, promoted him to Production Control Manager, and have since laid the groundwork for incorporation of all material movement operations into his organization. That's scheduled to take place in another month or two. Ross has been carefully groomed for Antonelli's job, has proven himself capable and dedicated. I advised him earlier this year of my ultimate intentions; I had to be certain that he was prepared to take on a greater responsibility."

"Ross holds opinions closer to your own?"

"Absolutely. He's not without his failings, of course, but he gets the job done with a minimum of unnecessary friction."

"But some friction is always necessary, isn't that so?"

"An organization that requires consensus on all occasions lacks the will to survive."

"Which means it is sometimes advantageous to play your employees off against one another?"

Catterall's expression became guarded. "I'm not certain that I understand what you mean."

"Is it customary to deny a vice president the right to make his own supervisory appointments?"

"Oh, you mean Miss D'Angelo. Not necessarily customary, but certainly not unheard of. Donna D'Angelo was the best person qualified for the position; it would not have been equitable to bypass her for a less-talented individual. The fact that this reduced the perceived stature of Frank Antonelli was not without its downside, you know. I'm not averse to overruling my staff, but I try to prevent doing so publicly. Frank didn't leave me much of a choice in this particular case. It was his decision to oppose me publicly; I would have preferred to have dealt with it behind closed doors."

"How well did you know Antonelli? Outside of his professional life."

Catterall shrugged. "Frank was a very private sort of person. A confirmed bachelor, of course; he lived alone, a small condominium over in East Providence. He started here as a teenager, a floorboy at first, then worked his way up through several of the production departments. Proved himself quite resourceful early on; he was the youngest supervisor in the company's history, as a matter of fact. He had a reputation for tactlessness, but he knew the equipment and processes in this place better than anyone else."

"Did he associate with anyone here outside of work?"

"Not to my knowledge. There were occasional company functions which he attended, although he never seemed to enjoy himself and was always among the first to leave. Frank never spoke of family or friends, at least in my presence. Some of the others might know more."

Catterall had suddenly looked away and there had been an almost imperceptible flutter in his voice. Henderson was convinced that he had just been told a lie. Or if not a lie, a half-truth. "Why do you have two guard stations? Wouldn't it be more cost-effective to consolidate them into one?"

"Yes, it would, but practically speaking, it's a bit difficult. We have two separate parking areas; office and visitors' parking is on the south side, general employee parking and access to both shipping and receiving are on the north. The office has access through a separate door directly into the manufacturing area, the entrance you're familiar with, and the bulk of the finished goods warehouse sits squarely between the two entrances. There is just no place to locate one station to watch both without making major changes to the warehouse area. And since there is no travel through the office station after we've closed for the evening, we don't man it twenty-four hours anyway."

"Why didn't the guard report that Antonelli never left last night?"

"She probably wouldn't have known."

"She?"

"Our second shift guard is Jill Hawkins. She would have relieved Stone at 7:00 or a bit sooner. Our security people are primarily employed to report fires or other unusual events; they aren't even armed. The only precious metal we use here is silver, and that's dissolved in the plating solution. We're not a prime target for thieves."

"And it would not have occurred to the first guard to question why Antonelli had not left by 7:00. Isn't that a bit late even for a dedicated and old-fashioned man?"

"It might not have occurred to him under any circumstances. Stone is not the most observant of men. He's a retired police detective, as a matter of fact." The man's eyes positively twinkled. "Employed on the Managansett Police Force, if I remember correctly. If he did wonder, he probably assumed that Antonelli had parked in the office lot. He often did."

"Is that where Antonelli parked yesterday?"

"No, it is not. Frank's only obvious interest outside of work was antique cars, of which he owns two or three. I believe he's been driving an elderly Bentley all this week, and it most decidedly is not parked in the office lot."

Henderson tapped his fingers irritably on the tabletop. "I don't care how unobservant this guard of yours is, Mr. Catterall, how could he or his relief fail to notice such an unusual car sitting abandoned in the parking lot?"

The expression of self-satisfaction on Catterall's face grated on Henderson's nerves. "If you'd care to step out to the guard post, I could demonstrate for you why that would be quite impossible."

"Later, maybe. Why don't you just explain it to me for the time being?"

"Frank was apprehensive that someone might scratch a fender or put a dent in the hood. He never parked it with the other cars. Instead, he drove around the back of the building and left it in a small open space near the receiving docks. I suspect he told Art Richardson and his people to keep an eye on it as well. It would be quite invisible unless you were at least halfway into the lot, and even then it would be easy to overlook."

Henderson fought back a yawn. His sciatica had been acting up again and he hadn't slept well. He decided to bring the interview to a close, clean up his notes, and report back to Captain Nicholas. "I think that's all we'll need for now, Mr. Catterall. Thank you for your cooperation."

The other man didn't rise. "Aren't you even going to ask me where I was at the time of the murder? There is no question that it is in fact a murder, I assume?"

"The death is of a suspicious nature, yes. But we've already ascertained that you were not inside the factory during the relevant time period. I could ask you where you were between the hours of 4:00 and 6:00 yesterday, but it would be merely a matter of form."

"Well, then. As a matter of form, Detective Henderson, I was aboard a plane until almost exactly 6:00, at which point we landed in Boston. My wife met the plane and we returned home directly from there. During that flight, I was reviewing the personnel records of a number of employees, working out the details for a proposed change in the reporting structure of the entire management team."

Catterall was obviously not speaking without a purpose. Henderson had risen, but remained motionless, waiting for the punchline. "Is there a point to this, Mr. Catterall?"

"I just wanted to mention that one of those changes involved the promotion of one of our most promising staff members, a young lady named Vicki Sanders." He paused, tried unsuccessfully to keep his mouth from curling into a sardonic half smile. "You must be very proud of your daughter, Detective Henderson."

Henderson barely reacted, only his eyes moving suddenly. "My daughter is a very intelligent young woman and no doubt deserves the promotion. Is there any reason why you are bringing this up just now?"

Catterall was obviously disappointed by Henderson's imperturbability. "As a matter of routine I have thorough background checks conducted for all of my key personnel, which includes your daughter. I simply thought you should know right from the start that I was aware of the relationship. It's best if there are no misunderstandings in matters such as these."

Henderson observed Catterall's face and body closely as he spoke. This was the second discernible lie the man had told since the interview started; he was positioning Vicki for use as leverage, even though there was as yet no clear purpose to which this leverage could be put. If he wasn't challenged immediately, he would consider that he had played a powerful psychological card. "That's a load of crap," Henderson replied coolly. "You wanted to score a point by letting me know that you possessed information potentially embarrassing to me. Or that I might modify the way we conduct this investigation so that you wouldn't retaliate against my daughter." Henderson was walking slowly around the table as he spoke, and now he approached Catterall directly.

"Let me remind you once again, Mr. Catterall, that this is a police matter. It will be pursued according to the procedures laid down by the department." His voice began to deepen. "If you ever try to influence the conduct of this investigation again, I will personally cite you for interfering with a police officer in the pursuit of his duties. If you make any effort to retaliate in any way against my daughter, or any of your other employees because of their cooperation in clearing up this case, you will be exposed to various legal remedies available to them. Do I make myself clear?"

Catterall rose and retreated a step as Henderson moved even closer. "I had no such intention . . ."

"Bullshit! Any further attempt to impede this investigation, by you or anyone else, will be dealt with as harshly as I can arrange. For your information, Mr. Catterall, I have already disqualified myself from this case because of my daughter's involvement, and another detective will no doubt have been assigned before the end of the day. I suggest that you refrain from playing mind games with my replacement, since most of us aren't as even-tempered as I am. Detective Dardenian will give you detailed instructions before we leave as to the security arrangements which will be in force until such time as the proper authorities choose to lift them. Good day, Mr. Catterall."

Henderson turned away before Catterall could reply. The executive stood motionless for a few seconds, visibly shaken, before finally turning and storming out of the room without saying a word.

"I think you pissed him off, Walt." Dardenian was gathering up his own notes.

"Make sure you tell that asshole that no one is to go near the crime scene until further notice. In fact, we'll keep a uniform posted there all night. I want photocopies of those personnel files we requested, as well as the printouts. The usual stuff. And I'd like the autopsy results as soon as they're in."

"I thought you were going to have yourself taken off this case?"

"Oh. That's right. Skip the autopsy results then. No, let me know what they are anyway. Satisfy my curiosity."

"Will do."

When Ben Dardenian left the room, Henderson closed his notebook and replaced it and his pen in one pocket.

More than ever he wanted to be transferred off this case. Catterall's arrogant attitude and the way he had tried to exploit the fact that Vicki was his daughter just added another degree of unpleasantness to an already undesirable situation. Once he explained things to Captain Nicholas, another detective would be appointed and that would be the end of it. He rubbed his sore leg and yawned again.

While Ed Catterall was walking furiously back to his office, Mark Ross was slipping into the office where Vicki Sanders was once again attempting to concentrate long enough to wind up the month-end reports.

"Now what?" she said with some exasperation.

"Well excuse me," Ross answered brightly. "I didn't realize you were involved in a momentous project. I'll just leave quietly."

"No, wait. I'm sorry." She forced herself to relax and pushed the stack of weekly reports away. "I'm just staring at the same columns of numbers over and over without seeing them anyway. I don't suppose anyone's getting their work done today."

"No one but you even seems to be trying."

"How can they keep gossiping with so little to go on?"

"Oh, they watch to see who's in with the police and for how long, and what their faces seem to tell when they come out. I've already heard about ten rumors."

"I love rumors," she replied. "Who does the scuttlebutt say murdered Frank?"

"Ben tells me that Bill Elliot is considered the likeliest, although Donna D'Angelo and I are both runners up. Luis Mello, Tony Capra, and Paula are considered longshots. I don't know how Paula made the list; the others are pretty obvious."

"What about Ed Catterall? After all the fights those two have had, why isn't he suspect number one?"

"I suppose he'd have been the prime candidate, except most people are too afraid of him to say anything even behind his back. And realistically, if he wanted to get rid of Frank, all he had to do was fire him. Why risk a murder?"

"I don't understand why people are so afraid of Ed. He's forceful, but I've never seen him be anything other than polite, even when he is tactfully chewing someone out."

"Perhaps that's the secret. Everyone expects that one of these days he's going to explode colorfully and excessively and cut down anyone in his path. Actually, since the police only seem to be concerned about a short period of time yesterday, between 4:00 and 6:00, Catterall is probably in the clear. He was out of town, remember? Attended that seminar on Management by Objectives in Houston."

"How did your interview with Detective Henderson go?" Some of her co-workers knew that her father was a police officer, but she didn't think any of them knew his name. "I guess we're each other's alibi for the time in question."

"So it seems. I'm certainly glad I didn't walk out there alone yesterday. Under the circumstances, I would probably have been suspect number one."

"Why? You and Frank weren't at each other's throats that often. No more than anyone else at least."

"No, I suppose not. But it was pretty clear to most people, including Frank, that Ed wanted me to trim back the authority of the production people, instill some discipline on the entire process. That was almost certainly going to make Frank look bad at times and erode some of his authority. He was never one to retreat gracefully."

"That might give Frank a motive to murder you, but certainly not the opposite."

"Probably not. But I'm certainly going to benefit from his death."

"How? It'll make things simpler possibly, because you'll have a jump on whoever takes over, but it might actually slow things down in the long run."

"And who do you think is going to take over?"

Vicki shook her head. "I hadn't even thought about it. I don't know." She considered the department supervisors. "Someone from outside, I imagine."

"You couldn't think of anyone either, could you?" Ross smiled. "Luis is too young, Manny too hidebound, Tony is only marginally competent even at his own job, and the rest are too controversial or too weak. Not even Catterall is ready to appoint a black, a woman, or a gay as Vice President of Manufacturing."

"Is Art really gay or is that just an act?"

"Definitely, or so I'm told, but he's reasonably circumspect about it, even in these enlightened times." He was watching her with an amused expression. "Can't you think of someone else?"

Her brow wrinkled, until something in the twinkle of his eyes tipped her off. "You? You think Catterall will appoint you as Vice President?"

Ross looked behind his shoulder to make certain the door was closed, then spoke in a lower tone. "As a matter of fact, Vicki, Ed has already told me so. He'll have to wait a decent period before making it permanent, but I'll be acting in that capacity officially as of Monday morning. The move was coming anyway, sometime during the next year. Ed had already decided it was time for Frank to go." He sat back, looking smug. "This is just between you and me, understand. I was supposed to keep this all quiet for the time being, but I had to tell someone or burst, and you're the only one I can trust not to send a group e-mail as soon as my back is turned."

"Well, congratulations. Or commiserations, which might be more appropriate. You're going to have to deal with a lot of serious problems, you know." She held out her hand. "What's going to happen with your own department? You can't run production control as well as the factory, can you?"

"Don't you think Paula can handle it?"

Vicki's face struggled to remain expressionless. "I don't see any reason why not. She's not very forceful, but she knows the line and she's always been willing to try something new. It might take a little bit of stroking to get her over the first few weeks, but intellectually she can handle it."

"I don't see any reason why she couldn't be acting Production Control Manager within a few weeks, maybe full manager by Christmas."

"That'll sure relieve her mind."

He frowned. "Relieve it of what?"

Nonplused, Vicki considered a cover story, but discarded it immediately. Mark had trusted her; she felt compelled to reciprocate. "Paula was concerned that she was going to be phased out, or at least knocked down a notch. Because of the consolidation, you know. She's run that department almost without a boss for years, and it was beginning to look like she was going to lose most of her direct authority, end up second-string quarterback on a first-rate team."

Ross smiled. "I'd have let her run with the ball even if she was second-string; I know talent when I see it."

"I believe you, but then I'm not sitting in her position. And the quarterback doesn't run with the ball; he throws long passes."

"Right. I never did understand football." He grew more serious. "Who do you think murdered Frank?"

Vicki became solemn in turn. "I'd like to think someone managed to sneak into the factory somehow, maybe someone from the outside who had a grudge against Frank. I never heard much about his private life, but with a personality like his, I imagine he must have had enemies we've never heard of."

"I wish that was a possibility, Vicki, but there's just no possible way they could have gotten in. Except for the two main exits, every door is bugged and alarmed. The police have been checking them all, and the windows as well, but you and I both know they're unlikely to find anything."

"Then it has to be someone we know, I suppose. It's not very pleasant trying to decide which of the people you see every day might be capable of taking another's life."

"Well, one of them did. Any candidates?"

"You don't really want me to suggest anyone, do you? You're always thinking a mile a minute, way ahead of the rest of us. Do you already have things solved? Are you ready to present the completed case to the police?" She turned her chair sideways, placed her right elbow on the desk, and leaned forward, resting her chin in the palm of her right hand, staring at him. "Come on, Sherlock, spill the beans."

"I'm not quite that far ahead of you. Unfortunately, Frank was far from being the most popular man here at Standard. I could concoct a motive for almost anyone. Even Manny Soares, as much a partisan as Frank ever had, was under a lot of pressure because of lagging production efficiency and miscounts. There's also a drinking problem, so I'm told. He came to work pissed out of his mind a while back, and he's a belligerent drunk."

"The production rates aren't his fault, or at least not entirely. You told me yourself that imposing the lower run sizes would have that effect because his equipment would have to be changed over more frequently."

"Yes, and you told me that you'd increased the polishing cycle on a number of items to upgrade the quality, and that cut down his productivity as well. I didn't say Manny wasn't doing his job, only that he was under a lot of pressure from Frank to find a way to maintain the old ratio of up time to down."

"Is he your nominee then?"

"No, as a matter of fact, if I had to name a name, I'd nominate Tony Capra."

Seven

Walter Henderson had lived in the same small house on the west side of Providence since the year of his marriage. There were only two bedrooms, both small, one now theoretically his den although months passed between uses, and a single bath, all on the second floor. The den was formerly Vicki's room, abandoned six years previously when she impulsively and perhaps unwisely married Danny Sanders. Margaret Henderson had died when her daughter was fifteen, victim of an unsolved hit and run accident. Her widower husband had devoted as much of his free time as possible to his teenaged daughter, and had thought that marriage to a well mannered, responsible, and successful young business executive would safeguard her future. Danny was undeniably handsome, though not vain, and his personality resonated with his new father-in-law so closely that Vicki had joked that Danny had only married her for her father. Walter had been sure that his daughter had made a decision that would last a lifetime. He had been wrong.

When Vicki's car pulled into the driveway, its headlights played briefly across the wall of the front room where Henderson sat reading the paper, or at least pretending to read it. The intricacies of city politics were a fact of life he had to deal with every day on the job; he wasn't particularly interested in hearing more about it when at home. The fact that property taxes were going to rise, that two people had been shot to death in their car in nearby Cranston, and that the state legislature was up to its usual shenanigans were all things he would quite readily have deferred learning about almost indefinitely. The engine noises died, a car door opened and shut, and there were faint footsteps on the porch. Sighing, he set aside the paper and rose to let her in.

"Mushroom, pepperoni, and black olives," Vicki said brightly, waving a large red and white carton in his general direction. "Got the beer?"

"Come on in." He held the screen door open until she was inside, then let it slam shut behind her. The door had swelled slightly with the heat and humidity, and it bounced back before settling into place.

Vicki began clearing magazines off the coffee table to make room for the pizza. "Let's get cracking, shall we? Where are the plates and drinks? Move it, mister."

Henderson had been uneasy about this moment, fearing that his nervousness might be interpreted as coolness. With her customary air of disarming ingenuousness, Vicki had already stolen the initiative. Relaxing slightly, he went into the kitchen and found plates and utensils, added two cold bottles of beer from the refrigerator. No glasses. He had always preferred the fizzy taste of beer straight from the bottle, and Vicki had adopted the same prejudice.

"Thanks." She took the plates and attacked the pizza, two slices per plate, while he opened the bottles. No further word passed between the two of them until she was sitting in a chair, pizza in her lap, two long drafts of beer down her throat.

"You look tired."

Henderson bit into his pizza and settled back on the couch, his own bottle balanced precariously on the padded arm. "Things have been damned busy lately. The flu has half the detectives lying in bed and unfortunately all of the criminals seem to be immune. This business where you work just adds to the backlog."

"Any chance you'll wind that one up quickly? It's kind of spooky not knowing who to trust."

"You know the routine, Vicki. We're still gathering data and we don't even have the coroner's report yet. I'd like to know if the victim was already dead or unconscious before he was put into the press, for example. If he was alive and conscious, it would have taken someone pretty strong to overpower him. Antonelli was a big, muscular man; he wouldn't have been easy to handle, alive or dead."

"It was definitely murder then?"

"I don't see how it could be anything else. The technical people have confirmed that the press couldn't possibly have malfunctioned, so it wasn't an accident. And no man alive is enough of a contortionist to press both those buttons simultaneously while holding his head between the two halves of the die set."

Vicki shuddered. "I hope to God he wasn't conscious."

"Bidwell couldn't say either way at the scene. We won't have complete results for a while yet, and it's possible they'll be inconclusive. If he was hit over the head just beforehand, the subsequent massive damage may have destroyed any evidence of the earlier blow."

"If you're disqualified, who's going to get the case?"

Henderson bit off a large bite of pizza and chewed it sullenly before answering. "I'm still on it."

Vicki paused with her mouth half open. "How did that happen? I thought it was a violation of department policy or something like that."

"Technically it is. Rules get bent sometimes when there isn't enough manpower to go around. Captain Nicholas went over my notes, decided you were not a suspect, and then told me how shorthanded he was and how my experience with this kind of crime gave me a decided advantage in bringing things to a satisfactory resolution."

"Isn't it still going to look kind of funny? Doesn't the oversight board routinely review the assignment of investigating detectives?"

"Technically, I'm only assisting. The record will show that Ben Dardenian is the investigating officer." He laughed. "I suspect Ben has secretly wanted to be my boss for a long time. On paper at least, he is, for the time being. He looks alternately uncomfortable and delighted."

"I don't suppose there is any way this could have been done by an outside party? A break-in?"

"You know there isn't. The security at Standard is sloppy but adequate. There's a remote possibility that someone hid in the building overnight and escaped in the confusion this morning, and I suppose one of the guards might be an accomplice, but those scenarios seem pretty remote." He took a long drink of beer, emptied the bottle, and set it aside. "Vicki, is there any way you can take a leave of absence for a few days? Use up some vacation time or something? Call in sick?"

"Why?" At first she looked confused, then realized what he was hinting at. "Dad, this is my job we're talking about, remember? I have responsibilities there that I can't just walk out on."

"You also have a murderer working with you."

"So I'll be careful not to stroll around after-hours without company; I do have some common sense. But I'm not going to pick up my things and run off like an hysterical woman. I need this job."

Henderson felt his gut tighten a bit. "You don't need the job, Vicki, you want it. Danny offered you a handsome alimony and you turned it down. There was never anything forcing you to work. Your mother never worked a day in her life."

"I don't want Danny's money. He earned it and he deserves to enjoy it. I still value his friendship, you know, and that wouldn't have been possible if I'd accepted a handout. Look Dad, most women work nowadays; it's nothing unusual or anything to be ashamed of. Mother may have never held a formal job, but she certainly worked all her life." She smiled impishly. "You think cleaning up after the two of us was easy? I know I'm supposed to be an adult, and I think I know what I want to be when I grow up, but even now my room is generally a mess. I never got into the habit of picking up after myself because Mom always did it for me." She glanced around the room, noting the piles of discarded newspapers, magazines, dirty dishes, junk food packages. "Doesn't look like you did either."

Henderson refused to be sidetracked. "Most women work because they need the income to support their families. It's an unfortunate situation, but I accept the necessity of it and I give them a lot of credit. But that isn't true in your case. Danny Sanders will probably end up one of the wealthiest men in the state; if you had wanted a cleaning service to take care of the drudge work, I'm sure he would have agreed without a second thought."

It was Vicki's turn to sip at her beer while she considered her reply. When she did speak, her words were measured, but there was a discernible undertone of tension. "Danny is a nice guy. I still like him, but if I ever loved him, that feeling is gone. I don't know if he ever loved me, but he did like me and we're still on good terms. We had dinner together just a couple of weeks ago. The problem was that Danny wanted his wife to be a showpiece, someone to entertain customers when they visit, or more accurately to entertain their wives. I couldn't even get him to let me do the household budgeting. He's not interested in a particularly close personal commitment, because his job keeps him on the road for most of the year. If I ever marry again, it won't be to an absentee husband. And my husband will know that I have interests deeper than the daily soap operas and how best to prepare shrimp scampi." By the time she had finished, her voice had risen sharply.

There was an awkward silence, punctuated solely by the ticking of the grandfather clock standing in the front hall. "You're sure that this is the kind of future you want for yourself, working in a factory environment?" Henderson asked finally.

"Yes it is. I have a good eye for defects, strong organizational ability, and my analytical and math skills are pretty good, to misquote my resume. I need to work on my administrative skills, learn how to direct the work of other people, do long-term planning, a few other things, but my staff is small and generally competent and I'm concentrating on overcoming my weaknesses. They seem to recognize my potential at Standard, and Ed Catterall is willing to promote people based on their performance rather than their sex. I'm not likely to find the same advantages elsewhere and I think I have a good future with the company. Even more important, I enjoy the work and it pays pretty well. My salary is probably close to yours this year, if you include the profit-sharing and the 401K contribution."

Henderson realized that he was outgunned and decided to abandon the field of battle, at least for the moment. "All right, maybe you've found the right job. I gather you think highly of Catterall?"

She paused to consider the question. "I admire his managerial abilities. Whatever his personal feelings might be, he seems to be objective in his decision-making. There's no question that he's turned the company around financially; we've reversed a steady decline in profitability since he's been with us. Of course, I may be prejudiced by the fact that he promoted me, and the grapevine has it that I might make manager by the end of the year."

"He knows you're my daughter. He let it drop at what he thought was a strategic point in our conversation."

"Yes, that doesn't really surprise me. He always seems to know a lot of the background on people, and he has no compunctions about using that information to influence things in the direction he wants. Ed definitely has an amoral streak. I suspect it's less an honest interest than a tool to manipulate people, but he's unobtrusive about it."

"He seems to have an inflated opinion of his own importance."

"He's very full of himself. I don't know if anyone could reach that level without a powerful ego. Ed was running a small company while still in his twenties and he's clawed his way up from there. He's brilliant and ruthless, but basically fair, at least as far as I'm able to judge."

"Do you think you could be ruthless if you had to be?"

She regarded him squarely. "I would do whatever was necessary to get the job done, so long as it didn't conflict with what I think is ethical. If an apparent necessity required something I was unwilling to do, I'd challenge it or look for another job."

"That doesn't really answer the question. Could you be ruthless if you had to be? Are you prepared to make difficult decisions that will affect people's livelihoods, exploit weaknesses in your rivals in order to further your own programs?"

"Yes, within limits. Business is by its very nature a form

of conflict. I've had to fire people and lay others off. I didn't enjoy either, but I don't feel any regret. Both decisions were justified."

Henderson made a noncommittal sound. "How well did you know Frank Antonelli?"

"Too well. I don't like speaking badly of the dead, but Frank was impossible. His methods and attitudes had fossilized and he was too stubborn to admit that what worked twenty years ago, or even ten, won't always work now. He had an acid personality, tactless and insulting, and he made no effort to conceal his prejudices. He ran manufacturing as his personal fiefdom and defended it fiercely against any encroachment from outside."

"Would you say he had a lot of enemies?"

"Is this an official question or are we just passing the time of day? I'm not sure whether I'm talking to my father or Detective Walter Henderson."

"A little of both. If you're going to continue to work at Standard, as it appears you are, then as a father, I want the guilty party apprehended and out of there. As a police officer, I want this goddamned case off my workload so I can catch up on everything else I have backed up. Take your pick."

Vicki sat back in her chair, setting aside the remains of her pizza. "If you want a complete background, how about another beer?"

"Done." Henderson brought a second for himself as well.

Vicki sat quietly, nursing her second beer, and Henderson knew her well enough to keep his own counsel for the moment, occasionally picking at the discarded pizza crusts on his plate. Vicki had always liked the crusts best, he remembered.

"I don't know if anyone really liked Frank," she said at

last. "An awful lot of people detested him, both in the factory and in the office. Paul Joslin in sales blames him for losing at least a couple of big accounts, because production schedules were so screwed up that we had constant delivery problems last year. That wasn't entirely fair, but Frank certainly didn't do much to help remedy the situation." Her eyes were distant, as she recalled bits and pieces of the several heated arguments which had erupted during their last busy season.

"His supervisors considered him a tyrant, even Manny Soares, who was the closest thing to a supporter Frank had. Manny came up through the ranks and since Frank made him the first Portuguese supervisor in the company, I guess he felt a degree of loyalty. Certainly he never participated in any of the anti-Antonelli crusades. But even he was under a lot of pressure." She took a longer pull at the beer.

"There have been a lot of changes in reporting procedures, priority control, run sizes, quality standards, and even the very nature of our product mix. A lot of these have resulted in reductions in the efficiency of the production area, at least when measured in traditional ways, although there are offsetting benefits. Sometimes the front office has been slow in realizing that we're changing the rules and they still expect the old performance scores. To that extent, Frank was used unfairly. Unfortunately, he wasn't sophisticated enough to understand why his ratios were slipping, and he responded to any criticism by putting pressure on his line supervisors to reach the old figures. Sometimes this just wasn't possible. Maybe he even realized that and just felt it was his responsibility to put the screws on anyway; that's the way production management was viewed when Frank was younger."

"Did he work at Standard all his life?"

"I really don't know. His personnel files would say, wouldn't they? I know he's been here close to thirty years, and he's run the factory for most of that time. It's not going to seem like the same company without him."

"What doesn't change, dies."

Vicki nodded. "Anyway, I'm sure you already know about the tension between Frank and Bill Elliot."

Henderson nodded. "Catterall forced him to hire the man, isn't that right?"

"Actually, Carl Romero fronted for Catterall. He's the Personnel Director. Carl has been hinting pretty openly that we're ripe for a complaint to the EEO, so he was just waiting for a supervisory position to open up in the factory. I'm sure he wouldn't have proceeded without Ed's backing though; Carl is basically an invertebrate."

Henderson looked puzzled. "He's a what?"

"No backbone," she explained. "Catterall was more directly involved with Donna D'Angelo, because the union told him unofficially that they would file a complaint if she didn't get the position. That was pretty open and shut anyway; Frank didn't like it, but he didn't protest very much, at least not out in the open. She was obviously the best qualified person we had, and she's done a superb job. In Bill's case, there was some doubt about his qualifications; he lacked the formal background of some of the other applicants. But as it turned out, he's worked out fine. Frankly, I don't think we'll be able to hold onto him for long. I think Bill worked as hard as he did because he was determined to make Frank look like an ass, and because he wanted to beef up his resume before looking for something better."

"What about the rest of them?"

"I don't know much about Luis Mello; he keeps to himself most of the time. He caught hell one day because he mentioned something to Ed Catterall without telling Frank first. Ed takes a walk through the factory almost every day, always without warning, asks questions, makes mental notes for meetings later. He's extremely observant and a lot more knowledgeable about manufacturing procedures than most people realize. On one of his tours, he got Luis Mello to tell him that the maintenance schedule had been extended so that the double-action presses weren't down so much of the time, and Ed sprung that unexpectedly on Frank during a staff meeting. Definitely not the way to get on the man's good side. He liked to be in control all the time and he demanded an almost feudal loyalty from his people.

"Art Richardson is a strange bird. He and Frank were always distant with each other, although I don't remember ever seeing them actually fight. Frank used to make cracks about Art when he wasn't around, about how slow he was, things like that. There were probably sexual references, but he never made that kind of comment in front of me. Art is gay, you know."

"I know. He was arrested for soliciting once, when he was younger."

Vicki blinked, digesting this tidbit. "Rumor had it that Catterall wanted to fire Art, but that Frank saved his job. I don't know if that was true, but it might well be. Art's a lazy bastard; if he didn't have such good people working for him, we'd have a real mess down in receiving. His paperwork is usually topnotch though, so I guess he's not entirely without merit.

"Tony Capra is the last of the line supervisors. Tony's another odd one. Tony started with the company about the same time that Frank became Vice President; I'm not sure if he actually hired Tony or not. There has been a lot of tension between them just recently. Our silver consumption in plating hasn't checked out right for a long time. At first they both blamed the standards set by the Cost Department. Whenever we plate an item, we make a bookkeeping adjustment to the amount of silver that is presumed to be held in solution in the plating tanks. Since we control the thickness of silver we apply, we can tell what our consumption should be by keeping track of which items we plate and in what quantity."

Henderson nodded. "Sounds reasonable, but how do you know how much you're really using? Don't you have to weigh the item before and after?"

"Actually you can come up with a pretty accurate approximation just by calculating the surface area of the piece. But the silver thickness isn't uniform over the entire item; it's an electrolytic process and there are differing concentrations. Anyway, the standards were rechecked and that didn't seem to be the problem, so we installed more sophisticated monitoring equipment on the plating line as a cross-check. But we still ended up with a shortage whenever we sent the remaining solution out for analysis."

"Someone's stealing silver?"

She shook her head. "Not likely. This isn't gold, remember? A few thousand dollars per year isn't going to tempt anyone to take the risks and overcome the difficulties of disposing of raw silver in this form. No, it's more likely just sloppy recordkeeping on Tony's part. There have been a lot of discrepancies between the counts he reports and the number of pieces that show up in the Packing Department. He's probably picking up the wrong item numbers, or the wrong quantities, or both."

"That sounds like it would be easy enough to check."

"The simplicity is deceptive. We have problems keeping

track of replates; those are repaired items that have to be plated a second time. Customer returns and rejects often have to be refinished, and they get mixed up with new production and distort the counts. We could set up methods of accounting for all of the dirty data, but we'd need a small army of clerks to do it right, and what we would gain in accuracy wouldn't justify the expense."

"What about the others, the three from the office: Danforth, Mitchell, and what's her name, Grissom?"

"None of them had any particular reason to like Frank, but Paula Danforth was the only one who had to deal with him on anything like a regular basis. Jenny and Kevin knew about his problems dealing with Bill Elliot, which they certainly resented, but I can't imagine them committing murder without a better reason than that. Paula disliked the way he constantly downgraded her contribution to the company, but they never overtly fought about it, as far as I know. She was pretty well cowed by him and I don't know if Frank could have brought himself to quarrel with a woman publicly." She smirked. "A couple of times I went out of the way to provoke a fight myself. He always managed to dodge me. I probably had as much reason to murder Frank as anyone else."

Henderson reacted sharply, sitting up straight. "I don't recommend that you repeat that, no matter how iron-tight your alibi. What was your beef with him?"

"Frank wanted to block my promotion to manager; he was upset enough when I took over as supervisor, first because I was a woman, and he didn't like having his people take direction from one of us uppity bitches, and second because quality control was transferred from manufacturing to administration. I report directly to Ed Catterall now, even though I'm not a manager. That creates one more set of eyes watching what manufacturing is doing. It was only natural for him to resent the way things turned out."

"Sounds logical to me, checks and balances."

"What's your current opinion of the Civilian Review Board, by the way?"

"Those meddling jackasses! What have they got to do with anything?"

"Checks and balances, Dad. Remember? Sounds logical to me."

Henderson's eyes slitted, then he laughed, openly and with more genuine amusement than he'd felt in some time. "Okay, I see what you mean. And presumably if you are promoted to manager, that would have made things even more difficult for him."

"Correct. Not only does the title carry more clout, but I'd have to be included in staff meetings, I'd be on wider distribution for reports and memoranda, and so on. Potentially, I could have been quite a thorn in Frank's side. Temperamentally, I almost certainly would have been."

"And you still could be to whoever replaces him. Hopefully, that won't be the murderer. Who is the most likely candidate, I wonder?"

"Mark Ross thinks he's it." She laughed when she saw her father's expression. "Rein in those horses, Dad. I can absolutely guarantee that Mark didn't kill Frank Antonelli, at least not unless he found a way to get back into the factory unobserved after 5:30. He wasn't out of my sight before then. His motive is more apparent than real, anyway. According to him, Ed Catterall had already made the decision to get rid of Antonelli. There was no reason to rush matters along. Mark seems to be generally truthful; I don't think he made the story up to impress me."

"Yes, your Mr. Catterall told me essentially the same

thing earlier today. Vicki, forgetting about motive for the time being, which of these people strikes you as emotionally capable of committing murder? I know that really isn't a fair question, but you've always been a good judge of character. Do any of them strike you as the kind to strike out violently when emotion is high, or mentally unstable, or cold blooded enough to have planned this in advance?"

Vicki crossed her arms. "That's an interesting question. Art Richardson strikes me as too soft and Luis Mello too timid. Manny Soares might be capable of it; he's a bit of a cipher. So is Tony Capra. He's a frenetic type, never sits still, sometimes gives the impression he's on the edge of a nervous breakdown. But I don't think he'd be able to stand up to questioning; he'd fold up or go to pieces. Donna and Bill Elliot talk tough, but I don't think they have much capacity for violence, although Bill did grow up in a bad neighborhood. He's from Detroit originally, told me once he used to run with a tough crowd, collected a couple of minor police charges when he was a teenager. Paula's not the type; she's afraid of her shadow. Squeamish too; I can't see her committing murder under any circumstances, but certainly not in such an unpleasant fashion. She might poison someone but she could never crush her victim to death. I don't know Kevin well enough to judge, but he doesn't seem a likely candidate to me either. Jenny is a tough lady, but underneath she's very sweet and gentle. I find it hard to believe about any of them; they just don't act the part."

"Few murderers act like murderers, and some of them are otherwise very nice people."

"You know, I could keep my eyes and ears open for a while. I don't think Ed Catterall told anyone else about us; he likes to feel as though he's in sole possession of secret knowledge. Someone might let something slip. Didn't you say once that most murderers can't resist the temptation to tell someone how clever they were at some time or another?"

"The answer is no, you absolutely may not play amateur detective, not under any circumstances. Thanks for the thought, but I don't want you acting like a female Sherlock Holmes, no matter how careful you might be. You'd either scare the guilty party off or muddy the waters further or worse yet, get yourself nominated for secondary victim. This isn't a game, Vicki; this is the real thing."

Her expression turned stubborn. "But I wouldn't have to do anything out of the ordinary. It's just that I belong there and no one would think it out of place if I gossip a bit and maybe keep an eye on people."

Henderson shook his head furiously. "Absolutely not! I know you, Victoria Henderson . . . Sanders, whatever. You always overdo things and you're overly fond of playacting. I'd end up arresting you for picking someone's pocket or ransacking their car, or I'd be watching them carry you out in a body bag. This isn't a game."

For a moment she was tempted to argue further, but she let it go. "All right, message received. Look, I have to get going. All of this excitement has cost me a full day at work, and I was already lagging behind schedule." She got to her feet and started toward the door. Henderson rose and followed her.

"Thanks for the pizza," he said awkwardly.

"And thank you for the beer. I had a good time, Dad. We should do this again, soon and more often."

He nodded, unable to speak.

Just before she left, Vicki turned back, biting her lip. "Oh, there's one more thing I almost forgot. I was talking to

Mark Ross today, about the murder of course, and he told me something I didn't know."

"What was that?"

"Mark said that Frank let slip to him a few days ago that he was going to fire Tony Capra. Apparently Frank had decided that even if Tony wasn't actually stealing the missing silver, he was incapable of correcting the accounting. It sounds plausible to me. The shortages weren't getting worse, but a lot more attention was being focused on them. And there have been other problems with Tony, none as important taken alone, but it all adds up after a while."

"Could Antonelli have carried through on that without Catterall knowing about it?"

"In the long run, no, but he could have maneuvered things so that Ed would have been forced to back him up even if he disagreed with the decision. That was part of his style."

"All right, thanks. I'll add that to the file. Thanks for coming by."

"My pleasure. Just give me a call the next time you're hungry for black olives and pepperoni. Good night, Dad."

"Night, Vicki. Watch yourself, will you?"

"Always."

And then she was gone. He stood in the doorway, long after her car had disappeared around the corner of the street, staring out into the darkness, looking into the past.

Eight

By Monday morning, most of the initial shock at Standard Silver had been displaced by speculative excitement. Antonelli's death was mysterious enough in itself, but of more interest to his former co-workers was the shape of the immediate future now that he was no longer part of the mix. Vicki kept her own counsel, but she couldn't help but be aware of the conflicting and sometimes wildly improbable rumors that proliferated around her. One story had it that Mark Ross had already been offered the job, another that Catterall was bringing in some unnamed hotshot from the outside.

At 9:30, Vicki realized that she had just opened her last package of pre-printed item rejection slips. She'd been sitting at her desk for almost two hours, a mild form of torture under the best of conditions, so she decided to walk over to purchasing to check the status of her re-order in person rather than use the interoffice telephone.

When she arrived, Kevin Mitchell was sitting at his desk, smiling broadly. Paula Danforth lounged casually in the chair opposite, and Jason Capwell, the controller, stood leaning against a wall, arms folded in front of him.

"Ah, Vicki, you're just in time to hear my marvelous story."

"Not another dumb blonde joke?" Dumb blonde jokes had been Kevin's favorite for the past few weeks, their crudeness a remarkable contrast to his precise, mildly accented English.

"No, no. This is a true story, and it's even work related. You remember the trouble we've been having locating a new source for spigots for the coffee urns?"

"Sure, Lawrence Metal Turnings went out of business, didn't they? I know that's where we used to buy them."

"They're dead and gone, all right. The building is locked up and their bank isn't talking. I've been trying to find out what happened to their tools. At this point we'd buy them if the price was reasonable and make our own, but so far I've had no luck at all."

"There must be other people who make urn spigots."

"Plastic and ceramic ones, yes, but unless we're willing to do a major redesign, we need them to be brass or copper."

Paula made an impatient gesture. "What about our competition? Most of them make urns as well. Where do they get their spigots?"

"An excellent suggestion, one which occurred to me as well." Kevin's face was highly animated, a sure sign that he was enjoying himself. "Unfortunately, Lawrence supplied most if not all of the spigots used in the industry, including most of our competitors."

"So where does that leave us?" asked Vicki. "We can't discontinue the urn line just because we've lost our spigot manufacturer. What about paying someone to build a set of tools for us? One of the smaller machine shops that make our screw machine parts might be interested."

"That might be the ultimate solution," Mitchell agreed, "but I had one more lead. Jennifer told me she had heard that Travis Giftwares manufactured urns. I had never spoken to my counterpart there, so this seemed a perfect opportunity to make his acquaintance. I called and spoke to a Mr. Tibbett. Mr. Tibbett was quite pleased to make my acquaintance and said that he would be more than willing to exchange information with me. So I told him that I understood Travis manufactured a line of urns. He admitted that this was so, although their volume was low and they considered it more of a sideline than anything else. Wonderful, said I, and would you mind telling me where you purchase your spigots?"

Mitchell paused dramatically, his eyes roving around the room to size up the audience. "There was a very long pause, which I thought was because Mr. Tibbett was reluctant to give me the name of his supplier. I was about to repeat the question when Mr. Tibbett cleared his throat and advised me that the line of urns which they manufactured were 'burial' urns, and that therefore they did not require spigots."

Capwell's burst of laughter was explosive, staccato, and disproportionately loud, as though his nerves were on edge. Paula laughed with more restraint. Vicki thought about Frank Antonelli's body lying in a morgue somewhere and wasn't remotely amused.

Paula stood up, shaking her head. "Does anyone know where Jenny is this morning? I looked in her office three times already without any luck. Eddie is out sick today and I need someone from the pool to collate and file all the movement tickets I've recorded. I brought everything up to date during shutdown, and I don't want to start off by falling behind now that production is running again."

Capwell shrugged. "Haven't seen her. Is she in?"

Kevin shook his head. "I think she had an appointment with someone from the Chamber of Commerce. Catterall wants us to get involved with their job training program. She said something about not coming in until after lunch."

"Her lights were on," said Paula.

"Maybe she stopped by on her way," suggested Vicki. The office technically opened at 8:00, but Jennifer Grissom habitually showed up earlier, was often standing waiting for the doors to be unlocked when Vicki arrived shortly before 7:00.

"Did anyone hear anything about Bill Elliot? How's he doing?"

"He's out of intensive care," said Capwell. "Carl told me this morning that they've apparently saved his leg, although he's going to need a lot of therapy before he'll be able to walk unassisted. We won't be seeing him here for a good long time."

"What about the other driver?"

"Didn't make it, apparently. He was coming home from a party, had a few too many. The usual thing. Jumped the median strip and almost hit Bill's car head on."

Bill Elliot had been driving home from the mall on Saturday evening when the accident occurred, crushing his left leg. It had added yet another element of uncertainty to an already volatile mix. "The other guy probably wasn't insured either," said Paula bitterly. A few months past, Paula's parked car had been hit by an uninsured driver, and her own insurance rates had jumped dramatically.

Vicki asked for an update on her overdue reject forms and Kevin promised to light a fire under the printer. She took a side trip to the cafeteria on her way back, bought herself a coffee and a sinfully sweet honey-dipped donut, then returned to her office.

There was an e-mail waiting for her, announcing a 1:00 meeting in the conference room. The distribution included all of the staff from supervisors up and it had been sent by Ed Catterall's secretary. There was no hint of the agenda.

She wasn't ready to return to her paperwork; one of the downsides of her promotion had been the inability to spend as much time on the production floor as when she had been merely Chief Inspector. She was determined not to become a paperwork executive, out of touch with the real work of the company, but there were times when it was difficult to ignore the growing piles of paperwork awaiting her review. If she had a good assistant to screen them for her, she could have used her time much more productively, but this wasn't a good time to suggest adding personnel.

She went out to the factory, bypassing the finished goods warehouse where Bill Elliot's leadman was nervously filling in for his disabled boss. Beyond was the Packing Department and beyond that the final inspection area. A row of benches stretched from one side to the other, each occupied by a trained inspector, predominantly female but with a smattering of men as well. Roller skate conveyors elevated to waist height were used to supply a steady stream of silverplated trays, bowls, candy dishes, goblets, wine coolers, and similar items to each bench, distributed by a harried-looking material handler who stood at the termination points of two motorized belt conveyors which disappeared back into finishing. The inspectors moved with practiced ease, rotating each item under a concave light hood so that they could detect any defect, water stains, scratches, blisters in the plating, and various less common faults. Acceptable pieces were wrapped in soft white tissue, slipped into a translucent plastic bag, and placed on the next section of conveyor, for transport to packing.

Vicki walked down the line, greeting each inspector by name. Toward the end, she noticed that Maria Castro's position was encumbered by a large pile of unwrapped trays.

"What's the problem here, Maria?"

"It's that new guy, the new finisher. He's cutting through the silver."

Vicki picked up one of the circular, twelve-inch trays and peered at it closely. Sure enough, there were faint yellow cut-throughs showing in a random pattern on the ornate border, primarily in the high spots, indicating that the silver had been removed completely, exposing the base metal. "Have you told Donna?"

"She's out there with him now." Maria gestured with one shoulder. "He's screwed up a lot of pieces already."

Vicki estimated that close to a hundred trays had been set aside. "How did so many of them get done without anyone noticing?"

Maria shrugged again. "I told Donna after about a dozen of them showed up. But they kept right on coming in that way."

"All right, I'll check into it."

Vicki didn't like giving Donna D'Angelo a hard time. It wasn't just because they were friends. Donna had been burdened by the active opposition of her boss, Frank Antonelli, and Frank had been an expert at turning a small mistake into a disaster of momentous proportions when it suited his purposes to do so. It was much easier and more pleasant for all concerned if problems were addressed quietly, without harsh words or recriminations.

She spotted Donna just inside the archway that led to finishing. "Donna," she called, "got a minute?"

"Sure," the other woman crossed the aisle so that they wouldn't have to shout over the rumble of the conveyors. The shrill sound of the polishing lathes made her teeth ache. Cloth wheels called buffs mounted on high speed lathes were used to create the final patina on each piece, but although the buffs were relatively soft, they were still being used to cut metal, and the result was high pitched and nerve wracking. "The trays, right?"

Vicki nodded. "How did so many get done before the inspector caught it? They're all going to have to go back to be replated."

"We've been backed up all morning," she pointed to the two conveyors, each of which was covered with tightly packed work. "All the fast run items seem to have hit us at once. I've told Frank . . ." she paused awkwardly, then resumed. "We need a third conveyor here. That new promotional line might be cheap to produce and very profitable, but there's an awful lot of volume involved and we're not set up to handle it. Now that they've got the automatic finishing machine back in operation, there's not enough room to put all the work directly on the belt. We're having to pile some of it on the floor and then load it when we find a gap. The double handling alone is a pain in the ass. There were almost four hundred trays finished before the first ones got inspected."

Vicki nodded. "I understand that, but particularly with a trainee finisher, we need to inspect a few pieces right away. I'd rather stop the job right from the outset than have to send hundreds of pieces back for replating."

Donna nodded, saying nothing.

"What happened anyway? Was he applying too much pressure?"

"I don't think so. I checked the set-up and it's the same as always. It looks to me like there's not enough silver on them."

"Did you tell Tony?"

Donna grimaced. "Sure, and he got pissed off and told me to mind my own business. I was going to try a softer wheel and ease off a bit; the job is stopped now."

"Can I have a couple of the pieces? Ones you haven't touched yet."

"Sure can. Help yourself to them all if you want."

When Vicki walked into the Plating Department a few minutes later, she held two of the suspect trays in her hands, neither of which had as yet been finished. Plating occupied a lot of floor space, with two fully-automated plating lines flanking a complex that included the department office, two storage rooms, the safe where silver bars or anodes were kept, and the growing complex of pollution control equipment which had been installed at the mandate of several government agencies: federal, state, and city. The two lines were similar in general operation, but differed in result. Since the amount of silver affixed to a piece was a function of the length of time it spent in the plating tank and the strength of the electrical current, Standard could market two separate quality levels. Line number one did high volume, low price, lower quality work, while line number two aimed at high price, high quality, prestige items—executive gifts, incentive awards, limited editions.

It took only a few seconds for Vicki to locate Nick Shasta, the Plating Department inspector, prime candidate to take over as Chief Inspector once Vicki had completed her reorganization of Quality Control.

"Nick, take these please and check out the plating thickness."

He raised an eyebrow. "Again?"

"I think so. See if you can test it without stirring things up until we know for sure. There's no point in upsetting Tony unless we have to."

"Will do." He winked conspiratorially.

The chain drives that carried merchandise through the plating lines clanked and groaned as they advanced from tank to tank, rubberized racks laden with product rising from the solution, dripping steadily as they were shunted to the next position and dropped back into solution.

Vicki continued on through automatic polishing, the loudest area in the factory. With all twelve rotary polishing machines and some of the subsidiary equipment running, it was impossible to speak audibly even by shouting and an informal sign language had developed over the course of years. Everyone in the area was required to wear ear plugs, although the old timers complained about them regularly. Each work station consisted of a rotating table with five fixed stations to which unpolished work was attached. A sequence of polishing wheels were arranged so that the movement of the table held each piece at a different angle in each position, resulting in a completely polished piece by the time the cycle was complete. The operator's duties were limited to loading and unloading, and occasionally changing the wheels. They were also supposed to inspect every tenth piece, Vicki reminded herself, although she knew that the incentive system in place here necessarily influenced the operators to check as infrequently as they dared.

Polishing was separated from the Press Department by the spinning area, a small enclosure which had declined in importance as more and more sophisticated tools were created to avoid hand operations. Only two of the eight spinning lathes were working at the moment, and there were times when the department was completely silent.

Then she was in among the towering Addisons and McKinleys and Delameters. The rhythmic thudding of single- and double-action presses, the bang of the drop hammer, and the unusual prolonged scraping of the embossing mills was familiar and almost pleasant. During shutdowns, walking through this department always depressed her; the deserted machines seemed to glare down reproachfully as she passed, reminding her of a lonely graveyard full of decaying vaults.

She stopped directly in front of the press where Frank Antonelli had died. The police had cleared it for use at the last possible moment before they reopened. Everything that might conceivably have had a bearing on the case had been photographed, measured, weighed, examined, and marked for further reference. The mechanical safeguards and operational procedures had been thoroughly checked and Luis Mello's pronouncement confirmed. There had been no malfunction in the safety equipment, no possibility of a bizarre accident. Vicki wished that it had been otherwise.

There was no good reason not to use the press, but Mello had managed to do without it today. Vicki wondered if he was superstitious or if he simply feared that some of the press operators might object.

Vicki would have bet a lunch that she wasn't the first person to pause here recently, nor would she likely be the last. It wasn't just idle curiosity, she told herself. Vicki had always fancied herself a bit of a detective. One Halloween she had dressed as Sherlock Holmes, complete with pipe, hat, and cloak. She had toyed with the idea of following in her father's footsteps, joining the police force, becoming a detective, but her father had discouraged her by explaining just how undramatic the job really was.

She was familiar with the safeguard procedure, which seemed to her quite foolproof. Each of the two operating buttons was almost entirely enclosed; in order to depress them, the operator's hand had to be almost completely enclosed within the box that housed the switch. Vicki's arms were so short that she was barely able to reach both controls no matter what position she assumed; if she bent forward toward the open die set, there was no possible way she could reach either of them. Even if Frank had been a contortionist, he would not have been able to accidentally crush himself in this press.

"Trying it out for size?"

Vicki jumped backward, turning at the same time, nearly stumbled when she bumped into a stack of metal stampings.

"Careful," Luis Mello said, his expression serious but his eyes dancing. "We wouldn't want to have to replace the Quality Control Supervisor too."

Feeling embarrassed and slightly guilty, Vicki laughed, just a bit too sharply. "Sorry, Luis. I got carried away for a moment."

"Don't worry about it," and his smile became more genuine. "You're the fourth person today to stop at that press. Did you know the switchboard is paging you?"

"They are?" Vicki turned her head instinctively toward the speaker set against the far wall. "I didn't hear it."

"You can take it in the office."

The call was from her father.

"Good morning, Vicki. How are things going?"

"Just fine," she answered, puzzled. "Things are still topsy-turvy here, as you might imagine. What's up? I thought we weren't supposed to know each other until this investigation is over."

He ignored her question. "Listen, do you have any plans for lunch? I'd like to talk to you about something."

"No, not really. What's going on?"

"Could you meet me at Leo's? Some information came up that I want to run by you unofficially. I don't want to talk about it over the phone."

"Sure, I guess so." She glanced at her watch. "But I have a meeting at 1:00. Can we make it a little early, about a 11:45?"

"No problem. I'll order for us in advance if you want; that'll save time."

"Does Leo still serve linguini with that great white clam sauce?"

"Still the best in the city."

"Are you buying?"

"Sure, you bought the pizza."

"You're on."

The linguini was as good as she remembered, but whenever Vicki tried to find out what mysterious event had resulted in the invitation, Henderson told her to wait until they had finished eating. When the plates were finally cleared away and coffee had been poured, he put on his serious face.

"How well do you know Art Richardson?"

"Not very." She laughed. "Why?"

He ignored her question. "Was there anything odd about his relationship with Frank Antonelli? Anything that might lead you to believe Richardson was exempt from disciplinary action, received special favors, anything like that?"

"Not that I know of, or at least nothing that stood out. I never understood how Frank could be so patient with him when he was so gung-ho with the rest of his supervisors; Art's a ditherer, never gets things done on time, but he's not blatantly incompetent and I suppose Frank figured there was no better alternative. Frank was a real macho type too, and it's possible that he felt uneasy dealing with Art because of his sexual inclinations."

"We've discovered a couple of things of interest today. When we went through Antonelli's apartment, we found that he'd written a number of checks to one Arthur Richardson. Once each month, in fact, for two hundred and fifty dollars each, for a period of rather more than two years."

Her brow wrinkled. "Could he have bought something from Art? Have you asked him?"

"Not yet. We'll be getting to that eventually. The other interesting bit of news came from the coroner." He sat back and watched her face very closely. "Frank Antonelli had AIDS."

"You're kidding!"

Henderson shook his head. "It looks to me like blackmail."

Vicki shook her head. "I don't see it. Frank was a bachelor, so he wasn't cheating on anyone. And if he was sleeping around, it would only have enhanced the macho image he worked so hard to project." The words were barely out of her mouth before she thought of an alternative.

Her father saw the recognition in her face and nodded. "And if Antonelli was resorting to male prostitutes, Richardson would have been in a good position to know about it."

"Ten years ago, that might have worked, but I can't see it today, Dad. It might even have worked to Frank's benefit. Catterall would have a much harder time getting rid of him if he could claim some sort of discrimination."

"From what I've heard about Mr. Antonelli, I don't think that would have mattered. I think he would have paid plenty to protect his macho image."

She nodded reluctantly. "You're right, I guess. But I don't see how this helps. If it really was blackmail, that might have given Frank a motive to murder Art, but not the other way around. He'd be killing the goose that laid the golden eggs."

"Unless Antonelli decided it had gone on long enough

and was threatening to denounce Richardson regardless of the scandal. Faced with the prospect of a jail sentence, Richardson might have decided that the gravy train was already empty so nothing would be lost by derailing it completely."

She nodded. "I see what you're saying, but I can't imagine Art having either the intelligence to plan a murder in the first place, or the nerve to carry it out."

He sighed and pushed back from the table. "Unfortunately, I agree with you and we're going to hold off confronting Richardson for the time being. I shouldn't be telling you any of this, you realize, but you know the parties involved better than I ever could. I thought if you knew, you might think of some other connection or line of inquiry that we're overlooking."

"I can't think of anything offhand. This is such a complete surprise."

"There's no hurry. Think about it though, will you? We're not going to confront Richardson about this for at least a couple of days. There are a few more angles we want to cover first."

She glanced at the clock over the bar and jumped up. "I have to run, Dad. I need to get back. I'll let you know if I think of anything. Will you be home tonight?"

"After 8:00, maybe earlier. Goddamn, I sure hope it's earlier."

"Thanks for lunch. It was great."

"My pleasure."

The gathering for the 1:00 meeting was unusually quiet. The partitions had been drawn back so that the two conference rooms were joined together; this provided enough seating to accommodate everyone. When Ed Catterall arrived with Mark Ross at his side, several people nodded to themselves as though their suspicions had just been confirmed.

Catterall was waving them to silence when Jennifer Grissom entered the room, obviously flustered. She crossed to where Vicki stood.

"Made it," she whispered. "The switchboard tipped me off as I came in. What's this all about?"

Vicki shook her head. "I can guess, but I don't know."

"Ladies and gentlemen, if you'll just give me your attention, please." The room had already been unusually quiet. "As you all know, Frank Antonelli died under tragic circumstances last week. Frank was a talented, experienced manager who had seen this company through some hard times. Although he was sometimes difficult to deal with, he was an effective administrator, one who knew when and how hard to push in order to get the job done, and he always acted in what he believed were the best interests of the company. We are diminished by the loss of his abilities."

Several faces expressed skepticism after the last statement, but no one said a word.

"We are entering a critical period for this company. The new high-volume line is gaining exposure in segments of the market which were previously closed to us as well as absorbing some of our excess overhead. That helps reduce costs for the rest of the product line as well. Our continued progress in improving the return to our investors requires that we move forward in an organized, forceful manner. Although we are a sales-driven firm, the ability of the manufacturing facility to provide the required goods in a timely fashion is a prime factor in achieving our goals of profitability and growth. As Chief Executive Officer of this firm, I cannot countenance any deterioration of the effective operation of our manufacturing assets. I'm sure everyone in this room realizes the importance of establishing firm control and providing for continuity in a situation such as this."

Catterall paused, looking around the room speculatively. Vicki was mildly amused by his conscious dramatics, too studied not to have been well rehearsed.

"To this end, I have appointed Mark Ross as acting Vice President of Manufacturing. His full appointment to that position on a permanent basis will be deferred until a suitable trial period has passed, after which I will make the appropriate recommendation to the Board of Directors."

There was a distinct but quickly muted murmuring.

"I'm sure all of you will continue to give Mark your cooperation as you have in the past. Some of you . . ." his eyes searched the room, rested briefly on Paula Danforth, then moved surprisingly to Vicki, who returned his gaze evenly. "Some of you will be called upon to expand your own responsibilities to take up some of the slack. I will be meeting with each affected person individually during the next few days, in order to clarify your responsibilities, and to address any issues you might wish to raise."

"Like salary increases," Vicki said softly, not realizing she had spoken loudly enough to be overheard until she noticed Jenny Grissom's expression.

"Looks like you might get that promotion sooner than you expected," the other woman said, grinning, her voice barely a whisper.

There were no questions, and the meeting ended shortly thereafter. Vicki made a point of joining the cluster of people who were congratulating Ross and shaking his hand, then returned to her office, mildly disturbed by the realization that Antonelli's death might well benefit her personally. It's a good thing I have an alibi, she thought, because now I have a retroactive motive.

She was still sitting at her desk, trying to summon the energy to return to her dissection of the quarterly quality reports, when she heard raised voices and running feet outside. Rising, she crossed the office and opened the door. Linda Marzocchi was standing against the wall at the far end of the hall, hands clenched over her mouth. Ben Colin from Maintenance ran by, giving her a brief, unreadable look but saying nothing as he raced toward the front door.

"Linda, what's going on?"

The data processing manager dropped her hands, and Vicki saw that her face was ashen, eyes wide, mouth trembling. "It's Jenny, in her office." She pointed with one hand, then covered her mouth again. "My God, I think she's dead!"

Nine

Vicki was never quite certain how she managed to get through the rest of that day without breaking down. The impact of Jennifer Grissom's death hurt badly, and not just because they had been on the verge of developing a genuine friendship. The murder of Frank Antonelli had felt like an external event, a violent response to some unknown stimulus. This was different; it hinted at a more general, perhaps less rational chain of events. Frank had spent his life making enemies. Jenny was liked and respected by her coworkers, and she'd led a life in many ways similar to Vicki's. It was the difference between hearing of a burglary in another neighborhood and hearing of one next door.

The police arrived quickly, almost as if they'd been expecting the call. Although Ben and her father headed the team as before, there were so many people to question that they had each conducted separate interviews. She caught a brief glimpse of her father when he arrived, but she didn't think he had noticed her. He looked angry and tired, but she admitted to herself that she might be projecting her own feelings. She suspected that he was blaming himself for Jenny's death. He had always found it difficult not to feel responsible for the victims he was unable to protect, even when events were clearly beyond his control.

Everyone had been chased out of the immediate area shortly after the alarm had been raised, and Vicki knew little of what had happened except that Linda Marzocchi had found Jenny lying on the floor of her office, and that she had looked "absolutely horrible." That was as much as she could hear before the nearly hysterical woman was ushered off into a private office by Carl Romero, who had demonstrated an unusual degree of good sense for a change.

Vicki was finally interviewed about two hours after the body had been discovered, and it was Ben, rather than her father, who questioned her. He was using the small interview room in personnel.

As soon as the officer who had escorted her in closed the door, leaving them alone together, Ben's face relaxed. "Hi, Vicki. How's it going?"

She gave him a brief, strained smile. "As well as can be expected, I suppose."

"Can you give me a quick statement? The usual, what you did today, when you last saw the victim, anything out of the ordinary."

Vicki ran through everything she could remember, mentioned having lunch with her father although she refrained from telling him what they had talked about. She summarized the announcement in the conference room and Jenny's hasty arrival.

"That was the first time you saw Miss Grissom today?"

"Yes, she'd been out at a business meeting of some sort. Kevin Mitchell, the purchasing agent, mentioned it to me this morning, but I wasn't paying that much attention. Something to do with the Chamber of Commerce. She came in just as the meeting was getting started. She was still carrying her bag, so I don't think she even had time to stop by her office. I didn't see her again after we broke up; I'm so far behind that I went straight to my office and worked alone until the shouting started."

Dardenian tapped his pencil repeatedly on the table. "Vicki, is there anything you know or suspect that might help? Officially or unofficially? Some connection between Grissom and Antonelli that didn't come out earlier?"

She shook her head. "No, nothing. It doesn't make any sense at all. There was almost no overlap between their responsibilities; I don't remember them ever even speaking to one another. Frank didn't like to ask for help so he rarely even used the office pool, and Jenny never liked being out on the production floor."

Ben nodded wearily. "So I've been told. But unless our killer is a nutcase, there has to be some connection." He shrugged and sat back in his chair, relaxing slightly. "Did you and your father patch things up the other night?"

From anyone else, the question might have been impertinent, but Ben was a longstanding friend, closer than her two uncles, almost a second father. "Some first aid was rendered. Most of the serious bleeding seems to have stopped." Vicki had always liked Ben; he seemed almost too gentle to be in this line of work, considerate and soft-spoken. If her father hadn't pushed him to apply for his present position, he would still be wearing a uniform. "I'm going to stop by and see him again tonight, or I was, at least. I don't know how late he's going to be."

"Don't change your plans. We'll be wrapping things up here before too much longer. We had too many suspects the last time, and this one is even worse. Fifty or sixty people had the opportunity, and we can't hold onto that big a crowd. Our killer isn't going to bolt." His expression grew darker. "Be careful, Vicki. There's no reason to believe this guy is going to stop with two."

"How . . . how did she die?"

He glanced toward the door. "I shouldn't be telling you this, but it was probably poison of some sort. Bidwell's got his crew in there and he's pretty certain it was cyanide."

She jumped, and he noticed. "What's wrong?"

"Just that we have a lot of cyanide on site, mostly in the plating area. It's used to help dissolve the silver anodes into the solution. I'm sure it's stored in some solid form as well, probably in the safe."

Ben made a note. "We'll check into it. Vicki, you've lost some color and you're shaking. Why don't you go home? Catterall has agreed that most of the office people should leave as soon as we're done with them. The factory shut down," he glanced at his watch, "about ten minutes ago, and we're not holding any of them either." He sat back in his chair. "Although I suppose it's possible that someone slipped into the office during that big meeting of yours. How many does that add? A couple of hundred?"

"Closer to three hundred, but the guard would have seen them come through."

Ben shook his head. "He was attending your little get together as well. Someone left their copy of the announcement on his desk, and he thought it was meant for him. Or at least that's his story."

She nodded. "That doesn't surprise me. Stone was on duty today. He's a nice man, but not exactly a mental giant. I think I will go home early though. It's obvious no one is going to do anything productive today. I'm still stunned. Jenny seemed so full of life, I can't process the fact that she's gone."

Standing, she slid the chair back in place and smiled weakly. "If you get a chance to tell him, let Dad know I'll still be over, will you? I'm supposed to be bringing pizza again, and it won't taste right if he hasn't laid in a fresh supply of cold beer."

"Sounds tempting. If I didn't already have plans, I'd try to wangle an invitation for myself."

"You'd be welcome any time, Ben. You know that." She turned momentarily serious. "He looks tired. How bad has it been?"

"It's mostly overwork. He'll be fine once we get the backlog down a bit and the flu runs its course. He told you about the epidemic at the department?" She nodded. "Karelski came in one day, looking pale, insisting he was fine. By lunchtime his temperature was back up to a hundred and two, and we lost him again. It's been a real bitch."

"Watch out for him, will you? And let me know if there's anything I can do to help." Without waiting for an answer, she turned and left.

Vicki returned to her office only long enough to grab her purse and keys. With a quick glance around the office to make sure she wasn't forgetting anything, she turned off the lights and slipped out into the corridor. The building was already quiet and largely deserted, although a uniformed officer stood at the end of the hall, watching the entrance to what had been Jenny Grissom's office.

Carl Romero was standing near the front entrance talking to Paul Joslin and Laura Vickers, both from sales, as Vicki approached the exit. She waved but didn't feel up to casual conversation, pushed through the doors and out into the bright daylight. For a moment, she felt that it should be dark, that the day had been so long, surely it must be night by now, even though it was only a few minutes after 4:00.

Kevin Mitchell was sitting a few meters away astride the double cement wall that served as a decorative border along the front walk. Small perennials had been planted in a broad row, mostly marigolds. He was staring off into the distance with a vacant expression. Vicki wouldn't have given him a second glance under normal circumstances, but there was something about the way he held his body, his arms tucked close against his sides, that struck her as unusual. She hesitated while Mitchell remained unaware of her scrutiny, and she realized that he was soundlessly but quite definitely crying.

She crossed the space that separated them without realizing what she was doing, and touched his shoulder gently. He flinched away. "She was a good friend, Kevin. I was just starting to get to know her. I know the two of you were close."

"You don't know," he said softly. "You couldn't know." His voice trailed off. One hand rose, clenched into a fist, then slammed down against his thigh. Mitchell was built like a professional dancer; he was strong and agile and never clumsy, almost glided when he walked. When she was younger, she had known several men who possessed that catlike grace, knew them from the dance studios where she had practiced three days a week for more weeks than she cared to remember.

Vicki's dance career had come to a halt with her engagement, of course. Danny needed for her to be home when he called, or arrived unexpectedly, often with unannounced guests, clients he had invited on an impulse. She still made an effort to keep fit, attended her aerobics classes religiously, and fancied she could still do a creditable job with the minor role in *Swan Lake* which she had held with the Rhode Island Ballet Society a few years earlier. But her dreams of a career had vanished along with her dreams of a perfect marriage.

"No, I suppose I don't. I don't understand it all." Her voice was unsteady and she paused to recover her composure, feeling as though she was going to burst into tears herself. "I can't believe she's gone."

"We were going to be married, did you know that? No, of course you didn't. No one knew. It wouldn't have been proper." The words seemed to escape rather than having been spoken. "We were talking about setting a date, sometime in the next few months."

Vicki had to try twice before she could answer. "I had no idea." She couldn't think of anything else to say.

"We were keeping it secret. I don't think old Catterall would take too kindly to having his office manager dating the people who work for her, let alone marrying them. One of us was going to have to change jobs, obviously, probably me." He laughed. "I was already looking. Guess I can hold off on that now."

She tightened her hand, squeezing his shoulder. "I don't suppose there's anything I could say that would help."

"No, I don't suppose there is." The words and tone were bitter and, under different conditions, Vicki supposed she would have felt offended.

She realized that almost anything she might say at this point would only make things worse, so instead she turned and walked to her car. Mitchell was still sitting there when she drove off. He looked like a softly sculpted gargoyle, staring outward with blind eyes.

Vicki never did go to her father's house that night. Just as she was preparing to order the pizza, the phone rang. She had been lying on her bed when the phone buzzed insistently.

"Hello." Her voice sounded strange, almost muffled.

"Hi, Vicki. It's me." Her father always assumed that his voice was so distinctive, no one would ever have the slightest doubt who was on the other end of the line. It always seemed to surprise him when someone asked who was calling. "I was hoping to catch you."

"Yeah, I was just about to order supper." She yawned and shook her head. "Are you home yet?"

"Just leaving the station. Look, why don't I pick you up and we'll go out someplace and eat? Some place with lots of lights and lots of people. Someplace cheerful."

"Sure, I suppose so." She wasn't sure she wanted to face a room full of happy people just now.

"You don't mind being seen in public with an old crow like me?"

"Not in the least. You're still a better catch than most of the younger men I meet."

"All right, I'll be by in about twenty minutes. Can you be ready that soon?"

"Did I ever keep a date waiting?"

"I'm on my way then."

Vicki rushed to change clothes, knowing her father's obsession with punctuality. As it happened, she could have taken her time because he was more than ten minutes late.

"Heavy traffic tonight," he explained. "Feels like a weekend out on the highway. There must be something going on at the Civic Center. A rock concert maybe."

"It's a convention, Dad. Don't you read the newspapers?"

He grumbled. "Who has time to read the papers? It's probably some weird religious cult, and tomorrow we'll read that they used some illegal hallucinogen in their services, and the feds will want us to detach another contingent from the force to help them track down the people who supplied the drugs."

"Don't get paranoid, Dad. Are we ready to go?"

Although she had intended to stay away from the subject of the murders, her resolve melted as soon as they pulled away from the curb in front of her apartment building. "Was it cyanide that killed Jenny?"

"Who told you that?" He gave her a sharp look. "Ben? He's violating procedure almost as much as I am lately."

"So was it cyanide or wasn't it?"

"Yes it was. Bidwell says it was quite a heavy dose, as a matter of fact. He found a high concentration of it in what was left of her coffee. Apparently she liked things really sweet."

Vicki remembered the pot that was brewed daily in Jenny's office, from which she had accepted a cup herself on more than one occasion. "Someone put it in her coffee?"

"More precisely, in the sugar bowl. Sodium cyanide, apparently. There was almost a full tablespoon mixed with the sugar, indistinguishable, virtually tasteless and odorless. And deadly."

"Any idea how it got there?"

"Sure. Someone put it there. As best we can guess at this point, it was added some time after noon yesterday and before 1:00 this afternoon, or perhaps even slightly later, although that would be cutting things pretty close. The window of opportunity is open so wide that it includes almost anyone who works at Standard, as well as a healthy number of outsiders who were in the offices at the right time, some of them unattended for at least part of their stay. There was so much traffic that even people who would ordinarily be out of place in the office area could have slipped in and out for long enough to do the deed. There was your big announcement today, during which time the guard post was deserted and the office area was deserted, and Catterall, whose office is right next to Grissom's, had each of the supervisors come in for private briefings yesterday. Someone could have slipped in when no one was looking, dropped the cyanide in the sugar, and been out again before anyone had a chance to notice anything out of the usual."

"But why would anyone want to kill Jenny Grissom?"

"You tell me. What connection could she have had with Frank Antonelli that would result in their both being targeted by a murderer?"

"You think it's the same person then?"

He gave her a sidelong glance. "What? You think there are two murderers working at Standard Silver? Nice opinion you have of your co-workers. Are you sure you want to stay employed at a place like that?" At her expression, he waved one hand. "No, don't bother. I'm just kidding. Of course it's possible that the murders are unrelated, but extremely unlikely. We haven't ruled that out of our thinking, but we're applying Occam's Razor and assuming this is a one-demon problem."

"Doesn't that narrow the number of suspects somewhat? There were only nine people on your primary list before weren't there?"

"That's right. The six supervisors, Grissom, Mitchell, and Danforth. We didn't get to eliminate many this time. I told you, there's just too wide a period of time to cover. No one can remember who they saw at what time this morning, let alone yesterday. At least with any reliable degree of certainty. The only reason we've narrowed it as much as we have is that we found someone who drank coffee there at lunch time yesterday and used the sugar bowl. The Marzocchi woman, the one who found the body."

"They were good friends." Vicki's voice cracked. "I was getting to like Jenny a lot too." She remembered Kevin's pained expression and looked away, fighting back tears of her own. It was the first time she had felt the urge to cry, perhaps because it was only now that she was beginning to accept what had happened.

"Well, obviously Grissom is eliminated unless there are two murderers."

"Bill Elliot too. He's been in the hospital since Saturday night." She bit her lip. "I guess every cloud has its silver lining. At least he's cleared."

"Only of the second murder, but he's certainly off our list of prime suspects. Which still leaves us with seven."

"Where did the cyanide come from? Were you able to trace it?"

"Probably from your Plating Department. Bidwell says the formulation is identical and it seems the simplest explanation. The security there is incredibly sloppy. I'm surprised the OSHA safety people didn't slap Standard with a hefty fine when they inspected last year. The stuff is dangerous. Silver cyanide is held in two separate storage areas, neither of which is secured during the day. They lock the goddamned things at night after everyone has gone home, but even then they don't always put the containers back inside before they close it up. Makes a hell of a lot of sense."

Vicki nodded. "I've noticed that myself once or twice. Tony didn't seem to feel it was necessary to keep an eye on it. I guess he figured that everyone knew how dangerous it was, so no one would mess with it."

"He was wrong. Frankly, Vicki, a lot of the security procedures at Standard are half measures as well, or are performed sloppily. You have two guard stations, but only one of them is manned around the clock. The guard abandons his post to attend a meeting without notifying anyone or questioning the lack of coverage. A distinctive, antique car sits in the parking lot overnight and no one notices anything unusual until the owner turns up dead the next day."

"Be fair, Dad. This isn't Fort Knox we're talking about, you know. The guards aren't trained professionals; they're rent-a-cops to make the insurance people happy. Flem Stone would probably faint if he ran into a thief; he certainly wouldn't be able to detain them."

"I realize that. But if you have an overnight guard, he should at a minimum walk the grounds a couple of times during the evening. Even if that car was parked where he couldn't see it from his station, he should have noticed it during his rounds and reported it to whoever he answers to."

"That would have been Frank Antonelli. Anyway, would you be any closer to a solution if you'd been called the night before rather than the morning after?"

He remained silent for a few seconds. "Possibly not," he admitted at last, his voice lower. "My frustration is showing. The Captain wants to know why we haven't arrested anyone yet." He laughed humorlessly.

They pulled into the parking lot of Fontana's, her father's favorite restaurant. "Vicki, let's have a good dinner and talk about old times. Let's not discuss murders, motives, your job, your divorce, or my work for a while. I'm getting stale, I think. I need a break and a fresh perspective. Not to mention about sixty hours of overdue sleep and a shower."

"Works for me. My nerves are on edge and I feel capable of settling small issues like capitalism versus communism, who should be President, the meaning of life, and stuff like that, but none of the big issues. You might even have to decide what I'm eating tonight."

"That's why we're here. Pick something at random; you still know it's going to be a treat."

It was too. Henderson had chicken cooked in a spicy tomato sauce, while Vicki finally decided to indulge herself with stuffed manicotti. The antipasto that came as the appetizer was almost a meal unto itself, and the two of them emerged an hour or so later stuffed to the gills and just the slightest bit lightheaded from the wine.

Vicki decided the ban on talking about the murder had expired. "So what's going to happen next?"

Henderson backed out of the parking lot and turned toward the highway. "I'm still putting off confronting Richardson about those canceled checks. Once he knows that we know, he'll yell for a lawyer and won't talk any more. I may have to do it though, question him about the payoffs, find out if there's anything there. I can't see it as a motive for murder but it's the best we've got."

"If you're right and Richardson isn't the killer, what does it hurt to let the cat out of the bag?"

"Just because I don't think it's the answer to the main problem doesn't mean it doesn't answer a related question. When I interviewed Richardson this time, I asked a lot of questions about his relations with Antonelli, and he probably suspects I know something. I could tell he was getting nervous; his answers got shorter and shorter. It might not have any bearing on the murder, but then again it might."

"But what would Art have against Jenny?"

"How should I know? Maybe she found out about the payoffs. Maybe Richardson let something slip and decided to silence her. If he's not the killer, maybe the real one knocked her off at random, just to confuse things, and it didn't really matter who the victim was. It hasn't escaped your attention, I trust, that Grissom was the most likely person to dip into that poisoned sugar bowl, but it could quite easily have been someone else, almost anyone else. Half the people I talked to today have taken coffee from that pot at some point or another."

"I've had coffee there myself."

He made an unpleasant sound. "And if it is camouflage, or if this is a motiveless killing by a psychopath who knocks off targets of opportunity, then you're in danger as well as everyone else."

"Don't start, Dad. I'm not quitting, I'm not taking an early vacation, and I'm not going to call in sick until you solve the case."

"At least you didn't say, 'If you solve the case.' "

"I have faith in my dad, even if sometimes he doesn't have faith in me."

"Is that fair?"

"Maybe, maybe not." She punched his shoulder. "I apologize anyway. You've been nice lately and I shouldn't be bitchy. Frank Antonelli was a bastard and while he didn't deserve to die, I can't honestly say I'm going to miss him. But Jenny was smart, personable, and we were starting to be friends, and I really want you to catch this bastard."

"We will, Vicki, sooner or later. Whoever it is thinks he, or she, has gotten away with something twice. They'll get cocky."

"Did you know Kevin Mitchell and Jenny were planning to be married?"

"No, but we suspected something was going on. The only time she wouldn't meet my eyes the other day was when she was telling me about their little walk down to receiving."

"Do you have any real feel for who might be responsible? I'm too close; I can't imagine any of these people committing a murder. The nasty ones are too incompetent."

"I'm convinced there aren't two murderers involved, but I've been wrong before. Once or twice. Despite the number of potential suspects, the realistic pool is small. I have the feeling we're missing something subtle but essential, and that when we do realize what it is, we're going to feel like fools."

"Maybe I could help."

"No!" It burst out, but Henderson made an obvious effort to regain control. "No, Vicki. We've gone over this before. No amateur investigations. Quite aside from the fact that it's dangerous, Ben and I have both told you more than we ever should have. If you let something slip, it might impede the investigation. Don't make matters worse by playing Sherlock Holmes."

"Don't worry, I wasn't planning any heroics. It's just that whoever is responsible is more likely to let down his or her guard in front of me, because I'm a familiar face. Other than Catterall, they don't know we're related, and most of them—even most of the women—tend to assume that I'm really not all that competent. For all his faults, Ed Catterall will always deserve my gratitude for one thing; he rewards performance, and he doesn't care about skin color, gender, age, national origin, or any of the other excuses the rest of the world seems to find to justify advancing mediocrity over talent."

"You like him, don't you?"

"I admire him in some ways, but not in others. Ed has an overwhelming, sometimes smothering, ego. He's also quite ruthless; he'd sacrifice one of his most loyal followers in order to advance the overall goals of the company, or more precisely to enhance his position there. On the other hand, I don't think I could ever consider him a friend. I think he evaluates personal relationships and loyalties emotionlessly. He's a good businessman, but a mediocre human being."

"I told you that you'd have to learn to be ruthless if you wanted a serious career."

"I remember. But there are degrees. Sometimes he treads dangerously close to overdoing things. You can't completely disregard the intangibles; if you do, you lose the support of the people who work with you, no matter how well they might be paid."

They rode on in silence for a while, until they turned onto the street that led to Vicki's small apartment.

"Vicki," Henderson said, "I know damned well that nothing I say is going to dissuade you if you really decide to take matters into your own hands. Despite appearances, your mother was a strong-willed woman, and I'm pretty stubborn myself. I can hardly complain if our only child seems to have inherited the same tendencies. But Margaret and I generally knew how to keep our impulses under control. I hope you're wise enough to do the same."

"In other words, be careful."

"That's right. Because whoever is responsible, no matter what the motive, has killed two people in cold blood, and in this second instance put the lives of any number of others at risk. He or she won't hesitate to add you to the list if you seem to be posing a threat of any kind."

"I know. I'll be careful. One of the things you taught me that stuck was always to know my limits. I try to keep my head well above water at all times."

Henderson frowned. "Keep your eyes open then. I'm afraid that if our killer thinks he can get away with two murders, then he can probably get away with three just as easily."

Ten

Vicki tried not to dwell on the two murders, but no matter how many times she told herself to concentrate on the matters at hand, she could not control her thoughts. It was particularly worrisome because she could see no logical connection between the two victims. If these were acts of random violence, perpetrated by someone who had slipped over the edge and was striking out at whatever target presented itself, then she might well be in actual physical danger. She felt a thrill of excitement when she realized that, followed by a mild anxiety attack that convinced her excitement was definitely overrated.

The disruption at Standard was another source of frustration, coming as it did during a very critical period for both the company and her own department. The general demoralization and distraction among the staff made people inattentive and short-tempered, and absenteeism was at an all-time high. The silverplated giftware business was very seasonal; if they missed delivering during peak sales months, they would have to wait a full year for the next cycle, and risked alienating major customers who might consider the lack of timely delivery sufficient reason to look for a new source. Product loyalty existed only at the very top of the high end line, and that wasn't enough to keep them on the right side of the profit and loss interface.

As she was driving to work the following morning, Vicki realized that even though she had not consciously decided to disregard her father's admonition against sticking her nose where it didn't belong, she could no longer remain a passive observer. She was going to conduct a small investigation of her own, discreetly, carefully, and as quickly as possible. Nothing that would interfere with the police, of course; a childhood spent with her father had included a thorough grounding in the prerogatives of the authorities. Her father had complained from time to time of criminals who escaped punishment because someone outside the department had decided to "help" and she knew that he wasn't exaggerating. But the fact remained that she was familiar with the personalities involved, the conflicts that divided them, the subtle interplays which couldn't be properly articulated during the police interviews. The alternative was to do nothing and wait for the next shoe to drop, and she had no intention of losing more of her co-workers.

She checked her mail slot and her e-mail and found nothing pressing. So she walked over to the Production Control office. Mark Ross and Paula Danforth were talking quietly at the desk, a stack of computer printouts spread out in front of them, two empty coffee cups set to one side. Momentarily she wondered which of them had made the coffee, and whether or not they had used sugar. She was now carrying a small supply of sealed sugar packets in her purse, just in case.

"Haven't you moved yet?" she asked brightly.

Mark glanced up, momentarily annoyed at the interruption, although his face changed almost immediately, the irritation swept away by his inevitable cheerfulness. "Not quite. I did arrange to have the sign on the door changed though. There are still a few things here I want to finish up, and it's more convenient if I stay until they're done." He glanced toward Paula. "If you don't mind the temporary crowding, that is."

Paula Danforth, who was now acting Production Control Manager, shook her head vehemently. "Stay as long as you like. I still have a lot of questions to ask before I'll feel comfortable." She smiled at Vicki. "Good morning, incidentally. How are you feeling? You look tired."

"A little wrung out," she admitted, "but I'll bounce back. What's the general mood?"

"Luis Mello gave two weeks' notice this morning," Ross replied, pushing himself back from the desk. "He was nice about it, assured me it had nothing to do with my being his new boss. It's just a case of bad timing. Barton Metal Products made him an offer recently and, understandably, he's feeling a bit nervous about this place. I tried to talk him out of it, but frankly I think he's more frightened than he admits. He wouldn't even talk about the possibility of staying on. By the time we were done talking, he'd made me almost as nervous as he was."

Paula nodded vigorously. "And Wendy LaRocque called in her resignation, or actually it was her mother who called. She's quitting, effective immediately, didn't even come in for her personal things. One of her friends is going to bring them home tonight. A few of the others have been talking about leaving but they haven't done anything yet. No one feels safe right now."

"Whatever happened to Frank's stuff?" Vicki asked suddenly. "I just remembered that he has no family. What's happening with the things he had in his office?"

"There wasn't much personal stuff, actually," Ross replied. "Some photographs, a spare sweater, a few desk ornaments, things like that. The police boxed them up and took them away the day after he died. I don't know what happened to them after that."

"Is his office locked?"

"No, it's open. Why? Do you need something from in there?"

"I'd like to check his files. Your files, I suppose. If you don't mind, that is. I worked up a rough report on scrap rates per item for Frank a few weeks back and I can't find my copy. If he kept it and I can locate his, it'll save me a lot of rework."

"Well, you're welcome to try. Frank's filing system seems to have been to put everything current into whatever folder was the thinnest. Jenny . . ." His voice fell and he looked away. "She was always after him to let one of the girls do his filing for him, but he insisted that he couldn't find things again unless he put them away personally."

Vicki nodded. "I think he was just embarrassed about how bad his filing system was, and he was never one to accept an offer of help anyway. Look, I'll leave you guys alone; I know how busy you must be. I'm going to see if I have any luck finding my report."

Frank's office was at the end of a corridor. Despite having established a legitimate, although totally fictional, reason to be there, Vicki felt nervous and furtive as she stepped inside, glancing up and down the hall to see if she had been observed before closing the door quietly once she was inside.

Frank Antonelli's office had always been spartanly furnished, a desk and chair, small closet, two four-drawer filing cabinets, three deliberately uncomfortable wire frame chairs for visitors, a set of metal shelves designed for books but currently overwhelmed by piled-up computer printouts and a few trade magazines. Somehow, now that she was actually here, the thought of searching through those eight drawers seemed alternately daunting and sacrilegious. For a moment, she considered abandoning her plan and leaving, but her father's stubbornness had bred true and she forced herself to stay.

At first she merely sat at the desk, poking through the overflowing in-basket. They were routine reports, mostly from data processing, and a flyer announcing the autumn company picnic. Vicki opened the center drawer of the desk, found it uncharacteristically orderly: the paperclips, elastic bands, pens, pencils, staples, and so on arranged neatly in little plastic bins. The drawers to either side held other supplies, blank requisitions, legal-sized lined pads, a tablet of graph paper, a calculator with its powerpack, a shoeshine kit that should have been taken along with the other personal possessions, more blank forms some of which were now obsolete, and similar items, nothing of interest.

Still unwilling to tackle the file cabinets, Vicki rose and picked through the shelved reports, opened the closet door, looking for anything that might be out of place. Since she couldn't stay here indefinitely without arousing suspicion, she would have to limit herself to a cursory search. Impatient with herself, she opened the top drawer of the first file cabinet, grimacing at the disorderly, overpacked mass of paper inside. You asked for it, she told herself, so don't complain. She began to sort through it.

At that very moment, elsewhere in the city, Walter Henderson was sitting in a semi-private office, not particularly happy about what he was hearing from his partner.

"So you didn't find anything at all?"

"Not a thing." Dardenian sat back and crossed his arms. "But that only means that Antonelli wasn't known to the local gay community. That's not unusual, you know."

"I know, it's just frustrating. Is there anything new on Richardson?"

"Nothing there either. He was flamboyant before it was fashionable, got into trouble a few times, minor arrests, solicitation, public exhibitionism. Nothing more recent than ten years ago. He's gotten more cautious."

"We need to spring something loose. I think we're going to have to confront him with those checks, pin him down, see if we can get anything that way. God knows, I think it's a red herring, but the captain wants us to try it and what else have we got?"

"I'd hold off for a while yet. He's squirming as it is; if he's our man, I'd let him heat up to a near boil before taking the lid off."

"And if we get nothing? What do I tell Nicholas then? He's in no mood to admit that we were only doing what he wanted. One of the Board members at Standard has connections in the Attorney General's department and has called in a favor. The Captain would like us to solve this case, at our leisure of course, any time in the next day or two." Henderson crumpled up an empty soda can and tossed it across the office. It struck inside the waste basket, caromed around the rim, and shot off into a corner.

"Walt, aren't you taking this case a little too personally?"

"What's that supposed to mean?"

"Cut the crap, Walt. You and I have been together so long that you tell me more by what you don't say than what you do, and we both know you don't give a rat's ass what Captain Nicholas thinks. You're on edge because Vicki's involved."

"She's not involved. She has an alibi."

"She's in danger then, or potential danger, if you must split hairs. You know what I'm talking about."

"All right, all right." Henderson's voice had risen, but he forced himself to ease off. "I suppose that's part of it. But there's something else too, something that just doesn't feel right."

"The fact that the two victims have no connection? That the killer is choosing victims randomly?"

"No apparent connection," he corrected. "That might be part of it. There may well be a link that we just haven't uncovered yet, although the Grissom murder feels wrong. I'm not sure I can explain just what I mean. I know this is unlikely but I'm beginning to suspect the murders weren't committed by the same person. One brutal, one subtle; one carefully planned and executed, one almost scattershot. Antonelli was overpowered and brutally killed; the Grissom woman was assassinated by subterfuge, poisoned, the traditional woman's weapon, and in a way that could have resulted in other deaths as well."

"You don't suppose that she wasn't the target at all, do you? Could the poisoned sugar bowl have been set up for someone else, someone who routinely drank coffee there?"

"People did stop by and have a cup of coffee with her from time to time, but there was no set pattern. It's too wild a shot, too random; there were too many ways for it to go wrong and strike down the wrong person, or persons for that matter."

"There's more than one way to explain that. It's quite possible that our killer has no compunctions about wiping out a few bystanders to get what he wants."

"But it's not a smart move. If Grissom had survived and someone else had died, then she would have been alerted to the fact that she was probably the intended target."

"And if the murders were connected, she probably would have realized that when Antonelli's murder was committed."

"Assuming she knew what the connection was."

"The second murder could have been designed simply to

confuse things further. To draw our attention away from Antonelli."

"Or his murder might have been intended to mislead us when Grissom was killed."

"What would that tell us, if Antonelli was killed to confuse us about the second murder, I mean."

Henderson shook his head. "I don't know if it tells us anything."

Ben nodded sympathetically. "So what do we do next? Do you want to bring Richardson in? I could have him here in half an hour."

"No, let's hold off a while longer. I'll look inscrutable when the Captain comes by and tell him we have a few leads we want to look into before we spill the beans. Besides, if we solve this too quickly, he'll have us helping Flynn and Heramia with that double knifing last week. They're not making any progress either and Flynn's blood pressure is acting up again."

Ben groaned. "The man has no mercy. Can't he get some of the guys back from the Feds? This interagency cooperation bit is getting carried too far. We can't get our own jobs done any more."

"Big drug busts and crackdowns on highly-placed organized crime figures and unscrupulous businessmen get better press. There's an election coming up, remember? The AG's office is putting a lot of quiet pressure on the department to play along. But I'll be sure to let him know how you feel about his assessment of priorities. Anything else come out of the background checks?"

"Minor traffic violations. Elliot almost got sent to a reform school when he was a teenager, but he seemed to straighten out during high school. Or maybe he just got smart enough to avoid being caught. Ran numbers, shoplifting, vandalism, and so on. Soares has been in a couple of minor fights in bars, nothing recently though, and he was only booked once, for drunk and disorderly."

"Did I ask for a background on Catterall?"

"After the fact. You really don't like that guy, do you?"

"He's pompous and has an overblown opinion of himself. Despite Vicki's opinion of him, I think the man's a phony. He'd cut the throats of as many people as necessary to promote his own position. He's one of those people who measures the worth of others by the size of their paychecks or by how many people jump when he says 'frog.' He uses people as game pieces, rewarding those things which contribute to his own advancement rather than the actual value they bring to the job."

"Sometimes that amounts to the same thing."

He nodded. "Granted. But I think he's a whiner. He'll lament the fact that employees aren't as loyal to their employers as they once were, but he doesn't feel that loyalty should flow the other way. Catterall strikes me as the kind who would throw people over the side of the lifeboat as soon as water began sloshing in, rather than wait to see if it was really necessary. He'd be methodical, and those to go first would be those most expendable, but he'd do it without a moment's regret. Certainly it would never occur to him to sacrifice himself. How could the world survive without him?"

Ben approached the next subject carefully. "Do you think Vicki might be in a position to help us?"

"What do you mean?" Suspicion glinted in his eyes. "Has she been talking to you about conducting her own little inquiries? I warned her about that."

"No, we didn't talk about it. Walt, she knows these people better than we do, has their trust. They don't know she's your daughter and they have no reason to suspect her. She's bright and perceptive and she's an insider. I'm not suggesting she get involved in anything dangerous, just that she keep her eyes and ears open."

"Catterall knows of our relationship."

"Excepting Catterall then. I don't think he's likely to make it public knowledge. He's waiting to play that card when it will mean something. But until then, she can ask questions that we can't, and she's more likely to get an honest answer."

Henderson shook his head. "No, definitely not. She's not a member of the police force, and it would be a violation of department procedure to employ a civilian."

"You're reaching, Walt. We've used informants before."

Henderson ignored the interruption. "Secondly, I've already discussed things privately with her and told her to keep her nose out of it. Damn it, Ben, this is my only child we're talking about, and whoever we're after has already killed two people."

"You underestimate the girl. She's got a good head on her shoulders."

"And that's where it's going to stay. Sorry, Ben, I know you mean well, but Vicki has agreed to mind her own business and that's how it's going to stay."

Ben's mouth moved as though he were preparing to argue the point further, but the determination in his partner's eyes never wavered, and he finally nodded and dropped the subject. But the idea remained in his mind.

Back in her own office, Vicki read through the small selection of documents she had removed from Antonelli's files, less anxious now that she was on her own turf, although she still carefully kept them mixed with some of her own reports, so that they could be camouflaged quickly if someone walked into the office. For the most part, she had taken memos which referred, however obliquely, to the growing tension between Antonelli and his foremen, including two confidential ones that threatened formal disciplinary actions, one involving Tony Capra and the other, to her surprise, Manny Soares. Capra's transgression was well known; the memo cited the consistent silver shortage, but the tone was a lot harsher than Vicki would have expected, even from a man as outspoken as Frank Antonelli. The memo to Soares mentioned an unusually high scrap level, and referred somewhat cryptically to "under-reported losses," which probably meant that Soares had made an attempt to cover something up. There was also mention of unspecified "personal problems" which were not associated directly to job performance, but which "indicated lapses of judgment and the potential for more serious problems in the future." She made a mental note to ask Paula for the yield reports covering the period directly preceding this last memo; if the Press Department had been hiding scrap, the counts on subsequent operations should be noticeably at variance with the lot sizes.

She slipped the contraband papers into her briefcase. Eventually she might have to return them, but she doubted their absence would be noted in the ordinary course of events. No matter how energetically Mark Ross attempted to pursue his new duties, it would be months before he would be able to spare the time to sort through old records. If ever.

And as if the thought of Mark Ross had been a magical summons, the door opened and he stepped into her office.

"Hi," he said cheerily. "Find what you wanted?"

"No, not really," she dropped her gaze, caught herself

doing so, and immediately re-established eye contact. "Frank must have thrown it out or hidden it somewhere in that idiosyncratic filing system of his. It overwhelmed me before I'd made it halfway through. I'll just have to reconstruct everything."

He glanced at his watch. "Not before lunch, I hope, which is almost upon us."

She glanced at the clock on the wall, which showed only a few minutes left before noon. "I had no idea," she said with genuine surprise. "I must have spent more time looking than I realized."

"I hope you'll feel some sympathy for me then, when I have to sort through everything and figure out what's worth saving and what gets heaved."

She laughed. "Knowing you, the wastebaskets will be full for days. How's the new job going?"

"It has its ups and downs. Most of the downs are trivial ones, at least so far. I have a set-up man claiming that someone walked off with one of his tools, one of those big wrenches for the double actions. More likely he mislaid it and it'll turn up in a day or two. The union wants to know if we're going to replace Luis from among the Class A press operators. They're not sure what their own position is, whether they want a promotion from within their ranks to a non-union job or not, so whatever answer I give is going to be wrong. Catterall sent me an e-mail asking what I'm going to do to make up for lost time on the promotional line, Joslin is after me to find a way to reduce the cost of the galley trays, and my hay fever is acting up. So how's it with you?"

"They're going to test you during the next few months in any case, you know. The union, I mean. Find out where you'll give and where you'll hold the line Frank established.

It's like being a teacher facing class on the first day."

"Probably, but no one's brought me an apple yet. Hey, what are you doing for lunch today?"

Vicki felt her guard going up. Mark was an habitual flirt, but she thought she'd managed to discourage him. She hoped that his recent promotion wasn't going to set their common neutrality back a few months. "I was going to grab a sandwich off the truck. I'm always so far behind."

"Why don't we go over to Hong Meas? I haven't had Chinese in a while. My treat. We deserve to get out of here once in a while at least."

Vicki felt conflicted, and not for the first time. She genuinely liked Mark Ross, although only as a friend. He reminded her too much of Danny to evoke any romantic feelings. At the same time, and considering things coldbloodedly, it would do her career no harm to establish a more informal relationship with a powerful, rising star in the company. She felt mild guilt about making decisions on that basis, but she knew that most of the men in the company viewed every social event as a potential political opportunity, and if she wanted to succeed she knew she would have to play the game.

But would Ross interpret her acceptance as tacit approval for more intimate proposals? Did she want her career to be influenced by the degree to which she was willing to play the cooperative woman? If Ross were to become romantically interested, how would she react? How would she deal with the inevitable office chatter that would follow their going anywhere together, no matter how innocent?

"All right," she said cautiously, "so long as it doesn't take too long. I have a ton of work to do. And I pay for my own lunch or it's no deal."

"Done," he replied without argument, and she suddenly found herself liking him a bit better.

After wolfing down a plate of chicken with lemon grass, Vicki returned to work with mixed emotions. There had been clear indications that Mark was still flirting, although with more restraint than before. She was also wrestling with the problem of finding a reasonable excuse to go through Jenny Grissom's files. Without sufficient cause, she would either have to forego the search or take some very big chances, chances that could cost her the job for which she had worked so hard.

What finally resolved the matter was her quick review of her stored e-mails from Jenny, business-related but always enlivened by her quirky sense of humor. She missed Jenny and resented the loss. Regardless of the risk, she was going to do whatever she could to find out who was responsible. It was just a matter of finding a time and opportunity which minimized her risks.

It would have to be first thing in the morning, she realized, before most of the rest of the staff arrived. The door to her office would be locked; Catterall had announced his intention of looking outside the company for a replacement. But one of the more arcane skills she had picked up from her father was the ability to pick almost any conventional lock. She was quite confident she could deal with anything installed at Standard.

ELEVEN

Vicki decided to act quickly, fearing that hesitation would only provide her with any number of reasons to avoid taking the next step. There was also the possibility that someone would move into Jenny's office, temporarily or permanently, reducing her chances even further.

A certain amount of preparation was required. First, she practiced unlocking her own office door with a credit card, assuring herself that she hadn't lost the knack. Since all of the offices had been constructed at the same time, she felt reasonably confident about gaining access. She tried to think of a plausible excuse for searching openly, but everything she considered seemed transparent or unsatisfactory.

She arrived early and had to wait for the guard to walk over from the other station to unlock the front door. Hawkins, one of the rotating night shift guards, greeted her cheerfully as he worked the keys, and Vicki struggled to act relaxed and casual even as she silently cursed the man's early morning volubility. Then she was inside, flicking on the light switches as she moved through the office area. No one else was in the building yet, although she thought she had noticed Mark's car turning into the factory side lot just before she entered.

She reached Jenny's door and hesitated, telling herself it was time to act boldly. Her hands were shaking when she took out her credit card, but the door opened obligingly at her first attempt. With a final glance in both directions to make absolutely certain that she was unobserved, she slipped inside, closing and locking the door behind her before turning on the light.

Jenny Grissom's personal belongings had already been removed, as well as the coffee pot, sugar bowl and creamer, and the small rack of cups, all of which the police had seized as evidence. The little cubbyhole which housed a diminutive refrigerator, currently unplugged, was otherwise empty, its two shelves bare. The adjacent closet held nothing except for a handful of coat hangers pushed into the extreme far end and a scrap of paper on the floor. She knelt and looked at it closely, but it was an advertising flyer for office equipment.

The desk here was newer than in Antonelli's office, a modern metal and plastic one as opposed to the solid though scarred oak behind which the Vice President of Manufacturing had sat enthroned. Except for a stapler, Scotch tape dispenser, empty routing boxes, and desk pad, it was uncluttered, just as it had been even when the office was tenanted. Jenny used to insist that she never felt right going home if there was any unresolved business waiting on her desk for the morning. Vicki couldn't remember the last time she had left knowing that she was caught up with her paperwork.

There was a single, four-drawer filing cabinet, shelves that held several reference works separated by artificial plants. There was no dust at the moment, but it was only a matter of time; it was impossible to keep these offices clean. Soot backed up through the air conditioner during the summer, through the heating vents during the winter. There were a few empty spaces on the shelves that showed faint outlines, where personal items had stood decoratively until their owner's death. Vicki could not specifically remember everything that was missing, even though she considered herself unusually observant. She knew there had been a large beer stein where Jenny tossed spare change, and an ornate jade and crystal dragon with unfurled wings, but there were at least four other vacant spots about which she could remember nothing at all. There were no windows, so Jenny had been forced to do without live plants, although she had a small greenhouse at her house where she grew an amazing variety of flowers and herbs.

Jenny's networked computer and printer stood on a table in one corner, just past the filing cabinet. Vicki glanced through the software, the usual word processor and spreadsheet programs, and found a CD labeled "memos." There was a small closet at the opposite side of the room, the door to which currently stood open. Vicki glanced inside, recognized more of the ever-present forms—materials requisitions, requests for vacation time, expense account forms, memo routing slips, telephone message pads, and so on. They were all arranged neatly and, she realized, in alphabetical order.

She tried the desk first, opening each drawer in turn, thumbing through the contents. She felt vaguely guilty, as though Jenny were still alive and she was invading her friend's privacy. Telling herself not to be silly, she continued, and ten minutes later she had gone through everything in the desk without finding anything worth the effort.

She was standing at the filing cabinet, flipping through attendance reports, when two people walked by the office, talking so loudly that she feared they were planning to enter. The moment passed, as did they, and she continued her search with more speed. File after file passed through her fingers, none of them revealing or even hinting at anything out of the ordinary. At least Jenny's files were arranged logically; there were entire folders she dismissed with a glance.

She found a thick folder that seemed promising. Several months previously, Jenny had fired one of the clerical workers, Nancy Lattimore, because of her consistently poor performance and unacceptable attendance record. Nancy was a constant source of tension in the office, with a brittle, hard-edged voice, a collection of well-developed prejudices, and an aggressive attitude that actually frightened her co-workers. Nancy had been quite vocal about her belief that she was being treated unfairly, had used some abusive and occasionally obscene language loudly enough to make herself a two-hour sensation at Standard, but Romero had been more than happy to see the last of her and the dismissal had stood.

One drawer proved to be empty, a second filled primarily with cleaning supplies, and most of the contents of the remaining two were routine, trivial, or duplications of items Vicki could have found in her own files. Each file in turn was organized neatly, nothing misfiled, duplicate copies removed, and outdated material carefully pruned. She had not found anything to justify taking the risk of breaking in.

The correspondence file contained evidence of ordinary tensions, inevitable in a business environment. Joslin in sales had complained about the timeliness of some of the reports he had requested, Brian Shipley in engineering had expressed his dissatisfaction with the necessity to familiarize several clerks with his chaotic recordkeeping system rather than a single one. This last was stapled to Jenny's response, citing a high turnover rate and the greater flexibility that would be possible if several people knew how to pick a path through his bewildering notes, logs, and memos. There was even an uncharacteristically petulant note from Mark Ross, complaining about the accuracy of some reports he'd had compiled by the clerical pool.

Vicki was just closing the top drawer when she heard voices again. She froze, waiting for them to pass, but there was a scratching at the door as someone fitted a key to the lock.

There was no good reason for her to be there, so she ran quickly and lightly over to the closet, stepped inside, and eased the accordion door quietly shut just as the outer door to the hall opened inward.

The voices were instantly recognizable, Carl Romero and Paula Danforth.

"I'm sure I left it here, Carl. It was just a day or two before she, you know, died."

"Well, you're welcome to look for it, but I was here when her personal effects were boxed up, and I don't remember seeing a cigarette lighter. Jenny wasn't a smoker, you know."

"Maybe she picked it up and put it in a drawer or some place like that, intending to give it to me later."

"Could be, I suppose." Romero sounded doubtful. "Just make certain that you lock up when you're done. Some of the personnel files are confidential. And turn off the light when you leave. Whoever closed things down last time obviously didn't bother."

The door clicked shut, and Vicki remained silent, waiting to see what would happen next. She expected to hear Paula opening desk drawers, perhaps the filing cabinet. Vicki couldn't recall having noticed a lighter during her own search but she might have overlooked it. Would Paula decide to try the closet and discover her hiding there? What possible explanation could she offer? Could she take Paula into her confidence, tell her that she was conducting her own informal investigation? Probably not. Paula was, after all, a suspect herself, with alibis for neither case. If she was discovered, she would have to say something, but should she claim to be nosing around for something relatively innocuous or admit that she was looking for clues? She didn't have to mention her father, just the desire to do something to bring Jenny's killer to justice.

That's what I'll do, she told herself. It'll work. Paula would believe her and even if she thought it was a stupid idea, she wouldn't raise a fuss. She wasn't the gossipy type. It was unfortunate, but it wouldn't hurt anything. So long as Paula wasn't the murderer, that is.

She was still holding her breath when the lights went out and she heard the outer door shutting firmly again, the lock engaging. Paula had apparently left, without looking in the closet, had in fact not been in the office for more than a minute or two. That in itself seemed odd, unless she'd found her lighter right away.

Breathing deeply in relief, Vicki slid the door to one side, and emerged into the inky darkness. With no windows, the only source of illumination was a thin line of light from beneath the hall door. As her eyes adjusted, she was able to orient herself and make out the general shapes of the furniture, although not with any clarity. After waiting long enough to assure herself that Paula had time to clear the area, she crossed to the door and turned the lights back on.

Had she forgotten anything? Her eyes swept around the office. The risk had been substantial, and she had discovered nothing of value. If there was a clue here, it was too subtle or too well hidden for her. She had almost turned to go when she remembered the CD where Jenny kept copies of all of her memos. Perhaps it included something that might help. But when she returned to the computer table, she discovered that it was gone.

Either Paula Danforth or Carl Romero had taken it, probably the former. But why?

Vicki listened until she was confident that no one was nearby, then turned off the lights, cracked the door open, peered out, and stepped quickly into the corridor, closing the door softly behind her until the lock snapped into place. So far so good.

Paula Danforth's offices, both the new and the old, were right around the corner. Deciding that there was no time like the present, Vicki went directly to the first, Production Control. There was no one there although the lights were on. Next door, in Materials Control, it was a different matter entirely. Paula stood in front of her desk as Vicki entered, sorting through her shoulder bag. Vicki thought that Paula started guiltily when she entered, but that might well have been her imagination. Certainly when the woman turned, her face was open and cheerful and if anything she seemed to be in quite a good mood.

"Hi, Vic. What's up?"

"Nothing much. Getting ready for the move?"

"I suppose. It's going to be hard leaving this office; I have a lot of memories associated with this place, both good and bad." She glanced around. "Of course, since the two departments are going to be combined, this will still be my territory, sort of. Who knows? Maybe I'll have a door cut between the two offices."

"Who's going to take on your old job?"

"It'll be split between Carvalho and Lucy Gomes. I think Lucy is going to get the title, but they'll both get token raises. He's got the organizational know-how, but he doesn't like directing other people. She'll ride herd on the material handlers and make sure they stay on the ball."

"Has anyone said who you're going to be reporting to? It

looks like Mark is planning to stay involved in the scheduling. I hope you're not going to end up having to fight with him the same way you both fought with Frank all the time."

"We're feeling our way. It looks like ultimately I'll continue to report outside of manufacturing, but until I've demonstrated my ability," she coughed dramatically, "Mark will still have a lot of say in how the systems are set up. I can live with that. Coming from the background that he does, Mark understands the importance of schedules and due dates. We won't always agree, but neither of us is likely to draw blood. I think everything will work out."

"You don't sound nearly as critical of him as you did a few weeks ago."

"No, I don't, do I? I guess I should have listened when you told me I was getting paranoid. He has certainly gone out of his way to treat me fairly since, hasn't he? I never did have a lot of self-confidence and I was probably projecting my problems on him." She laughed briefly. "I sound like I've been reading one of Romero's books on business cultures, don't I?"

"At least you didn't throw everything away and look for another job."

Paula looked uncomfortable. "Well, I was seriously thinking about it at the time." She bit her lip, was obviously searching for a safer subject. "Hey, what're you doing for lunch?"

"Me? I don't know; I hadn't thought that far ahead. Any suggestions?"

"The Bean Pot?"

She thought about the workload on her desk and was inclined to say no. Then she remembered the missing CD. "The hell with the monthly reports. No one reads them anyway. You're on."

"Great. I feel like having a cheap celebration."

Vicki disengaged herself as gracefully as possible and returned to her own office, but remained standing just inside the door. She watched as Paula made several trips back and forth between the Materials and Production Control offices, sometimes carrying armloads of paper or personal effects. It was almost 9:00 when she heard Tony Capra paging Paula on the intercom. A moment later, she came out of her new office and started down the hall toward the factory entrance.

Vicki stepped out into her path. "Hi, Paula. Where are you headed?"

"Plating. Tony's complaining that the movements tickets aren't with the work again, and that the counts are getting fouled up because the lots are getting mixed together and no one knows which should be reported against which lot number. He's determined to prove that the count problem isn't his fault."

"That's what it sounds like. Look, could you do me a favor while you're out there?"

"Sure, name it." But her eyes narrowed almost imperceptibly.

"I'm expecting some new AQL Inspection forms and Art doesn't answer his page. If you're in the area, could you stop by and ask him if they've come in and if they have, bring me a handful?"

Paula looked visibly relieved. "I think I can handle that. See you."

Vicki waited until she was quite sure Paula was no longer in the office building before surreptitiously entering the Materials Control office. The shoulder bag was no longer on the desk, but Vicki knew Paula habitually kept it in the lower righthand drawer of her desk. It slid openly silently, revealing the brown leather bag, wrapped with its own strap.

It only took a second for her to find the CD, tucked into one of the side pockets. She flipped it back and forth for a few seconds. Paula's computer terminal was dark. Vicki considered substituting a blank CD, but she was afraid that the other woman would suspect something. She returned to her own office, slipped the CD into the drive, created a new folder on the network share, and quickly started copying all of the files from the CD. A succession of cryptic filenames laddered their way down the screen until the copy operation was complete. She closed the window on her screen, replaced the purloined CD in its case, then returned to Paula's office, determined to replace it before it was missed.

But she should have realized things had been going too well.

Paula was sitting at her desk, sorting through another stack of reports.

"Hello again. I asked Art about your forms but they haven't come in yet. He said he'd send a package up as soon as he could. Then he and Tony got into an argument about a chemical delivery and I decided I had better things to do than listen to them shouting at each other. I'll see Tony later, after he's had a chance to cool off."

"Oh, right, okay. I guess I'll have to talk to Kevin." Vicki concealed the CD behind her back, leaning against the door jamb in what she hoped was a casual pose. Fortunately, she had closed the desk drawer; it was unlikely Paula knew that anything was wrong. But somehow she had to have access to the shoulder bag again before Paula discovered that the CD was missing.

"How did your meeting go with Brian yesterday?" Brian Shipley was head of engineering. He was supposed to be choosing a location for an additional semi-finished parts storage area on the manufacturing floor, but as usual he was making a major production out of what should have been a routine project.

"It didn't. Mark has him tied up designing a way to check the silver usage more precisely. I think he's decided to call Tony's bluff. I heard him saying that he wanted to go over the silver usage reports for the past month, and Tony wasn't able to convince him that he'd need several days to gather all the information. That's his usual excuse, you know. Antonelli accused him once of cooking the books so that everything came out right in the end."

"I wouldn't put it past him."

"I'll try calling Tony again after lunch, if I'm in the mood." She glanced down at her desk. "As long as you're standing there, I've got a question. Is there any reason why we couldn't incorporate your reject reporting into the payroll system, so that we could use the same input to find out how much rework is being separated from the runs? I'm having the devil of a time figuring out how to explain some of the fluctuations we're getting in the counts. I know the right number of pieces end up being made, within acceptable limits, but I can't make the counts match the issues."

"I've wondered the same thing, for other reasons," Vicki nodded. "Let me get some of the reporting forms we use and some other stuff and we'll go over it."

It was a great excuse for staying, but as the minutes passed, her investigation seemed suddenly of less interest. Paula's offhand question was something she had hoped to implement for reasons of her own. She had raised the idea before, but had always been greeted either by disinterest or active opposition. Labor reporting had been handled through Antonelli's timekeepers on the floor, and he was unwilling to give them a more responsible role. Ross had already reassigned them to production control, answerable to Paula. She slipped the CD into her pocket and for a while forgot about it completely.

They worked together for a considerable time, their discussion frequently technical, and Vicki found herself drawn further and further from the murder investigation as the possibilities of an integrated production and quality reporting system began to develop. They were still at it just before 11:00, when Vicki remembered the CD and began to worry again. They were supposed to be going to lunch together at noon and Paula would certainly take her bag, although there was still a chance that she might not notice that the CD was missing.

Her thoughts began to wander and she was about to apologize and ask Paula to repeat her last remark when the sound of a man shouting from somewhere outside the office distracted them both. After a second, it was repeated, even more loudly, and someone else was joining in. A woman laughed.

"What the hell is going on out there?" Paula looked up from her desk.

Vicki shrugged. "Doesn't sound like an argument."

There was more shouting, still indistinct. "Let's check this out," Paula rose from her seat. "Maybe Joslin and Carlisle are finally going at it." The Vice President of Sales and the advertising manager were as temperamentally mismatched as was humanly possible, and a major battle had been brewing for months. Technically speaking, Carlisle reported to Joslin, although he had ten years more seniority and was known to have friends on the Board of Directors. Even Catterall had been circumspect in his dealings with Carlisle, who reminded Vicki of a ferret.

"You check it out," Vicki replied. "I'm getting close to having this licked," she indicated the proposed new reporting format they had been drawing up. "If I go away now, I'll lose my train of thought and never get it back. When you have the hot hand, you don't pass the ball."

The other woman rose and walked to the door. "Okay, but you might be missing the fight of the century out here."

"I'll catch it on instant replay."

Paula disappeared and Vicki pulled the CD from her pocket. This might well be the only chance she would get. She pulled the drawer open, dropped the jewel case in approximately the same place where she'd found it, then closed the drawer and returned to her seat.

Just in time, as it turned out. Paula swung the door open almost immediately, looking bored.

"What? No bloodstains? No gobs of gore?"

"Just someone's birthday in customer service. Edie's, I think. I didn't bother to go in. Too many balloons and some guy in a gorilla suit."

"Oh, one of those kinds of birthdays. Who sent them?"

"Who knows? Who cares? Want to get back to this or take a break?"

Vicki's head was spinning and her heart was racing. "I've got a load to think about already. Why don't we drop it for an hour or so, and we can start up again after lunch?"

"Sounds good to me. I really ought to get some more of this stuff moved." She glanced at her watch. "See you in thirty minutes."

Vicki intended to close her door and check the files she had copied, but before she had taken two steps, she heard Paul Joslin paging her. Although he had no specific authority over quality issues, Joslin possessed a great deal of company-wide influence because of his success in opening up new markets and expanding the customer base dramatically after only a very short period of time with the company. She was careful to be cooperative and prompt whenever he requested her assistance, particularly since he was known to have expressed some only semi-private doubts about her maturity and background.

Joslin had received a complaint from a major customer about tarnish spots on the 15416 Chafing Dish and wanted to know if the remaining stock could be checked.

"Isn't that on the discontinued list?"

"That's correct, Miss Sanders, but just because the item is no longer in our regular line is no reason to supply our customers with an inferior product."

Vicki flushed but contained her anger. "I wasn't suggesting any such thing. When you consider that the item in question was dropped from manufacturing three years ago and we still have stock remaining that sales has been unable to dispose of, it's probably doubly important that the quality be unimpeachable."

There was a short silence at the other end of the line. "The 15416 was a turkey from the start. The market test suggested it would be the least successful item in the baroque line. My predecessor was on record as accepting it on a trial basis only, and his reservations were obviously well founded."

"I never realized that," she said archly. "When the sales forecast came in at such a high level, I just automatically assumed that he considered it a prospective winner."

Joslin's voice wavered slightly. Technically, his old boss—Cosgrove—was responsible for the debacle with the baroque line. But Joslin had been his assistant at the time, and was already wielding more influence than his title suggested. "There were other factors involved that contributed to a forecast that was somewhat inflated. At the time it was considered necessary to market a wide breadth of product in each category. We needed to have an item at that price point to round out the selection."

"So in order to justify the high cost of re-tooling, sales forecasted an unrealistically high volume that promised to amortize the extra costs in a reasonable period."

Joslin paused, then laughed. "All right, I concede the point. But would you please do me a favor and find out if the remaining stock is in a saleable condition? My inventory listing shows almost six hundred of these suckers left, and if I'm going to have any chance at all of unloading them on some unsuspecting buyer with poor taste, they have to at least look as though we thought they might be a good item."

"I think I can manage that."

"Fine." Then, almost as an afterthought, "And listen, sometime next week, please stop by when you have a few minutes. I'd like to find out just where you think the quality level can and should be going, maybe set up some sort of periodic meeting between you and customer service."

"All right, how about if I take you to lunch?"

The pause was longer this time, but the laugh was more genuine. "You would too, wouldn't you? Sure, why not? How about next Wednesday?"

Twelve

Vicki walked purposefully through the Shipping Department, angling toward the rear staircase that led up onto what was known as the balcony. As the company had grown, Standard had added more and more items to its assortment, and had diversified into other product areas as well. Although the increase in stock-keeping units had raised their gross sales, there had been some growing pains, chief of which was the result of shortsighted planning when the stock room had originally been laid out. Complicating matters was the increasing volume of slow moving, obsolete, and discontinued items which took up a disproportionate amount of floor space that might better have been devoted to more volatile inventories. The only potential means of increasing the available space on the ground level involved expansion and a reduction in the size of the parking lot, but this wasn't a popular solution within the office, and was expensive as well. When the need for more finished goods stock storage had finally become overwhelming, the only alternative had been to expand upward.

It had taken a full year to make the alterations. The roof of the front quarter of the factory complex had been partially removed, new supports were added, the existing ones buttressed, and then the roof replaced. An elaborate series of platforms had been installed, not a full second floor, but a sturdy structure of catwalks and storage areas that hovered above the primary shipping level. Slow moving items were stored there, brought down by means of a small freight elevator only when they were needed to fill customer orders. Because of state licensing laws, passengers were not allowed on the elevator, although Vicki knew that the rule was frequently ignored. She had never even been tempted to save time by riding in that rough wooden box; she wasn't really claustrophobic, but the freight elevator looked too much like a cage, or a lobster trap.

She climbed the spiral staircase slowly, feeling the tension build in the backs of her thighs. It was time to start exercising again, she realized. Her aerobics sessions helped, but she had skipped two of the last three because of work, and it didn't take long to lose muscle tone. She sighed with relief when she mounted the last stair and oriented herself on the catwalk.

Although the merchandise on the ground floor was laid out in strict numerical order, the balcony was a different matter entirely. As items were discontinued, they were moved up piecemeal, stored in whatever space was available, sometimes in multiple locations. The inventory register told her there should be 577 pieces of the 15416 left in stock, and they weren't small items, so she was looking for a pretty substantial volume of merchandise. Bill Elliot kept a roughly drawn map on a whiteboard in his office, indicating where each item could be found, annotated with bin numbers, but she had forgotten to go look at it until she was already halfway up the stairway, and the idea of losing what progress she had made by that point was enough to persuade her to do a little treasure hunting.

She walked past several rows of boxes of various shapes, sizes, and printing strategies, four-color and two-color, some plain corrugated cartons, a few display boxes with transparent covers. It was almost like a brief journey through the recent history of the company. Familiar failures greeted her on every side—the desk barometer that was unreadable unless one stood directly above it, the wall sconces that were too ornate for current tastes, the Christmas line with imprinted dates, which became instantly obsolete once the 25th of December had passed, the pewter tankards that were priced thirty percent above comparable items from the competition because the Cost Department hadn't anticipated the amount of hand work that would be required, the incredibly ugly water pitcher with the hand-applied border, the serving dish shaped like a flounder, and the tennis racquet trivet that was so oversized that it wouldn't fit properly on a table.

Vicki was shaking her head in dismay when she turned the corner at the end of the row and found herself looking down a dimly-lit aisle. Less than a meter away, the sprawled body of a man lay prone, his feet extended back in her direction. Even in the poor lighting, she could see quite clearly that the rear of the man's skull was misshapen. There was a pool of dark blood on the metal plating under his head.

She froze for a few seconds, unable to process what she was seeing, then took one involuntary step backward and almost turned to run. But just before she surrendered to panic, she caught herself. Her father would never let her hear the end of it if he found out she'd run off in hysterics. She also remembered his habitual complaint that most people were poor observers and reacted inappropriately in a crisis; she wasn't about to be lumped into that category. She knew better and would do better.

First, she glanced quickly around to reassure herself that she was alone. Walking back rapidly along the main row, she glanced down each side aisle until she reached the far corner. It was still remotely possible that someone was hidden concealed in some obscure corner of the balcony level, perhaps having climbed in among the stock, but if so, they would not be able to approach her without making a quite considerable amount of noise.

Reasonably satisfied that she was alone, Vicki returned to the body and crouched down beside it, confirming her first impression. It was indeed Edward Catterall who lay there, quite clearly dead. The blood pooled around his face was almost dry. The concave wound on the back of his skull was about an inch or two wide, but very deep, apparently inflicted with a great deal of force. She suspected that Catterall had died instantly. Two meters further along the walkway, one of the oversized wrenches from the Press Department lay on the floor, the larger end stained, almost certainly the murder weapon. With its meter-long shaft, it reminded her of a medieval war axe.

She glanced at her watch. It was exactly 11:30. It could not have been more than three minutes since she had discovered the body. Briefly she considered searching the man's pockets, but good sense prevailed and she decided to leave that to the crime scene people. Working systematically, she scanned the floor and surrounding area, looking for anything out of the ordinary, the classic clues: buttons, matchbooks, an odd mark in the dust, anything that was out of place. There was a large rag lying across the top of a pile of boxes a few feet away, but that was the closest to an anomaly she could find.

It surprised her that she felt so little empathy for the dead man; she felt shock, of course, but no real sense of loss. Although she would never have called Catterall a friend, he had to a great degree been a champion of her career, and his death might well reduce her own prospects. He was an impersonal, sometimes ruthless man, and he could never have been accused of an excess of compassion, but at the same time he had never done anything extraordinarily nasty or hurtful. At least, not to her knowledge. She reminded herself that she was hardly privy to the maneuverings and conflicts which existed at the higher levels of Standard's management team.

For whatever reason, someone had decided to kill Ed Catterall, presumably the same someone who had previously murdered Frank Antonelli and Jenny Grissom. The same person who might strike again at any time. And perhaps at any person.

Breathing deeply for a few seconds, she used biofeedback to calm herself until she felt that she was firmly under control. It would not do to appear the hysterical female. It would certainly be remembered later as evidence of her weakness. Vicki returned to the staircase and began to descend to the ground level, where she would use the paging system to locate Mark Ross and have him notify the police.

If Walter Henderson had been in a bad mood following the deaths of Frank Antonelli and Jennifer Grissom, he was even more disturbed and upset by the third murder. The fact that Vicki had found the body only made things worse. He was determined to get her aside at the earliest opportunity and insist that she stay away from Standard until the killer was caught. While the crime scene crew conducted their enigmatic tests, he and Ben Dardenian sat in Catterall's office.

"This is getting to be a real bitch," observed Dardenian, who had ensconced himself in one of the less comfortable chairs designed for visitors after his partner had claimed the executive chair.

"I believe I said that myself not so long ago. Captain

Nicholas is going to be screaming for blood if we don't come up with something soon, and I can't say I entirely blame him. Three goddamned murders and we don't have any promising lines of inquiry."

"Maybe this one will break the chain. We haven't gotten statements yet. Somewhere along the line, the murderer has to have made a mistake. They all make mistakes."

"Is anyone clamoring to tell us anything?"

"You're kidding, right?"

"How do you want to do this? You're in charge of this case, Ben. Remember?"

Dardenian shook his head. "That's a convenient fiction and you know it, Walt."

"I don't know. I think I'd like to just sit back and watch you run things for a while. Maybe they'll demote me."

"Yeah, because we have so many other good detectives to put into your slot. Look, I have Hescox and Rollins taking statements from most of the extras. I told them just to get quick summaries of what everyone was doing this morning. Bidwell says Catterall probably died sometime between 9:30 and 10:30. One heavy blow to the back of the head, almost certainly delivered by that oversized wrench we saw, swung at an inclining angle. Bidwell is also reasonably certain the assailant was right-handed. I sequestered everyone we interviewed after the first murder, all seven of them. I thought you'd want to talk to them personally. They're all right-handed, incidentally."

Henderson nodded. "Why only seven?"

"Elliot is still at home with a bum leg. That pretty well lets him out. Vicki and this guy Ross vouched for each other last time, so I didn't count them."

"Add Ross to the list anyway. He and Catterall were pretty close. Maybe he can throw some light on things, if they were chummy enough. I understand he's effectively in charge now."

"Only for a couple of hours. Two members of the Board of Directors are flying in to take over."

"Dandy." He glanced around the office. "The key to this whole thing is sitting here someplace, Ben. It might be obscure, or it might be so damned obvious that we're going to kick ourselves when we find it."

"You don't think this is just a series of random killings then?"

"God, Ben, I don't know." His voice was strained with fatigue. "Sometimes I think it is, sometimes not." He was momentarily quiet. "Does anyone know what he was doing up there?"

"His secretary says he left the office at just after 9:00. He said he was going on one of his daily tours, and she didn't think anything of it when he didn't return promptly. Apparently this is pretty normal. He takes a walk around the building almost every day, not always at the same time, sometimes spending half an hour, sometimes most of the day. There was no guard on duty when he would have passed through into the factory, so we don't know exactly where he went, or if he was alone. So far, we haven't found anyone who even remembers having seen him outside of the office."

"Who have you been dealing with, Romero, the personnel guy?"

"No, Ross has been keeping him on the sidelines. Between you and me, I don't think he likes Romero very much. Ross is being very cooperative but he looks shaken."

"All right, we'll want this office sealed off until the gang has had a chance to go through it. We'll have all of his paperwork boxed and taken downtown. Take his computer too. I don't know if there's anything here that has any relevance, but I don't want to take the chance that there is and that someone else will dispose of it beforehand. Where are the interviews being done?"

"Both conference rooms and a small interview room in personnel. We could use one of the private offices if you want to start talking to people."

"Not just yet." Henderson leaned forward and reached down, slowly opening one of the desk drawers with just the tip of one finger. "This drawer has been opened by force. See if the secretary knows anything about it. If she doesn't, I want it dusted and the contents examined first thing."

Dardenian rose to his feet and disappeared into the outer office.

Henderson inched the drawer further open and examined the contents. A stack of manila folders lay neatly in a pile. Each had a name neatly handwritten on its tab, and the ones visible were Ross, Romero, Sanders, Shipley, Soares, Stone, and Vickers. Impulsively, he reached down and slipped Vicki's folder out of the stack, leaned back in the chair and opened it.

There was nothing of any substance in the file that Henderson didn't already know about his daughter, but the thoroughness of Catterall's research, his audacious invasion of privacy, was almost stunning. There was a summary of her work experience, with copies of performance ratings by her two supervisors at Standard, a list of pay increases, changes of title, and other personnel actions. There was also an absentee record, a summary of office gossip—apparently she had been suspected at one time or another of having slept with the maintenance supervisor, Ben Colin, someone named Gutierrez, and with Ross. There was a copy of her credit rating and a neatly typed report from Blake, Anderson, and Shorter, an upscale private detective agency. The report included a short account of her divorce from Daniel Sanders. There was also the summary of an interview with one of her ex-neighbors in Managansett who said that the Sanders had frequent parties and that Vicki had occasionally had male guests while her husband was traveling. Henderson grimaced at that, suspecting that he himself was one of those "guests." Included also were a high school yearbook picture, a transcript of her grades both in high school and for the two years she'd completed at Providence College before dropping out to marry Danny.

Thoughtfully, he slipped the folder back into place, assuming that the other folders contained similar information. Each would have to be examined in detail. It was entirely possible that the endeavors of Blake, Anderson, and Shorter would have turned up background information that normal police background searches would have overlooked. But even though it might help his own investigation, Henderson marked it down as just one more reason for his aversion to Ed Catterall, a dislike for which he felt not the slightest bit of guilt even after the man had been brutally murdered.

He was still sitting there, turning the situation over in his mind, when Ben returned. "She doesn't know anything about the desk being forced. On the other hand, she doesn't seem to spend much time in here, so she really couldn't say if it's been done recently or not. Apparently Catterall liked his privacy, even typed a lot of his own correspondence."

"We'll want to know everyone who came in here today, with or without Catterall."

"I asked that." He referred to his notebook. "Catterall spoke to Romero for ten minutes just before 9:00. No one else was in the office this morning." He paused. "That she knows of at least. There's a gap."

"How big a gap?"

"Well, it seems that after Catterall left for his little hike, she decided to visit someone named Norma in the Accounting Department. She thinks she left the office a little before 10:00, but didn't really notice the time, and she was gone thirty or forty minutes, counting a stop at personnel. She's not really certain what time she came back but it was shortly before the alarm was raised."

"And I assume Catterall's office wasn't locked while she was gone?"

"No, apparently they're very casual about that sort of thing. Some of the private offices aren't even secured after they close up at night, although they all seem to have been fitted with locks."

"Dandy. For a place so crowded with people, there seems to be an awful lot that goes unobserved around here."

"You sound surprised."

"Not surprised, just tired. And angry. I think we're being played with, Ben. I have this feeling that if I could just concentrate a little harder, everything would be real obvious. But I can't seem to focus."

"Maybe you need special filters for your glasses."

Henderson gave him a mock glare. "On the other hand, this is your investigation and not mine, so why should I get upset?" Henderson leaned back in the heavily padded chair, hands clasped behind his head.

"So what's next?"

"The broken drawer might not matter. It could have happened a long time ago. But it smells suspicious to me, and I have an old and usually very wise nose. How are the interviews going?"

"All the minor players are pretty much taken care of. You want to get started with the stars in the cast?"

"I suppose there's no good reason to put it off any longer." He rose to his feet and took one last lingering glance around the office. The furnishings were expensive and well maintained, but it all still seemed cool, austere. "Lead on."

Back in her own office, Vicki was suffering from a severe case of frazzled nerves. Ben had reached the scene before her father and had taken her initial statement himself while arrangements were being made to secure the area. She had answered his questions truthfully, completely, and succinctly, surprising herself by how calmly she was dealing with things. Alone, she tried to relax and was dismayed to find that she was light-headed and slightly sick to her stomach.

To get her mind off the situation, she poured herself a cup of coffee, using hot water and instant from a bottle she kept concealed in her desk, sweetened it from her store of sealed packets of sugar. Most people in the office were very careful about what they consumed on company premises, and even the cafeteria had reported a significant drop in customers. The coffee was hot and rich and helped considerably.

Vicki suddenly remembered the files she'd copied and turned to her computer. They were on her private network share, which meant that only she and the two network administrators could access them, but she thought it might be better to move them to her hard drive instead. She was just about to do that very thing when Linda Marzocchi walked into the office without knocking.

"Vicki, you're not trying to work, are you?"

A sense of *deja vu* swept over her. Sighing, she stared down at the keyboard, hoping she would seem depressed or preoccupied rather than just rude or nervous. "Just fiddling around, trying to keep busy, keeping my mind off . . . you know."

"Yeah. Hey, I hear you were the one who found the body." Linda parked herself in one of the chairs and Vicki turned around resignedly.

"That's right. He was up in the balcony. I just stumbled onto him, almost literally."

"I don't mean to sound ghoulish, but how did it happen? How was he killed, I mean."

"I'm sorry, Linda, but I really can't talk about that. The police, you know. They told me not to tell anyone the details and frankly," she paused dramatically, "I don't even want to think about it right now."

Linda was momentarily nonplused, then hastened to make little of the matter. "Of course, sorry, I shouldn't have asked. I've watched enough television to know better. I imagine it must have been quite a shock." She laughed, but it sounded nervous, crackled around the edges.

Vicki was anxious to get rid of Linda, but didn't want to alienate the other woman. "Don't worry. I'm not really thinking too clearly myself. I was just sitting here quietly, trying to adjust to the situation. It was a pretty big shock, seeing him there. It's not something I'm going to forget soon."

"Yeah, I know what you mean. Or I think I know anyway." She laughed again. "I'm not sure I know what I mean, is the problem. This whole thing is getting really scary. I mean, who's going to be next?"

It took a while longer before Vicki was able to convince her friend that she really needed to be alone for awhile and despite her attempt to be tactful about it, she sensed that Linda was somewhat offended. Vicki felt sorry about that, but she was growing increasingly anxious to find out just what it was that Paula Danforth was so determined to keep secret.

So naturally Mark Ross walked in just as she was about to try again.

"Whew!" He leaned back against the inside of the closed door. "What a circus this has turned out to be. The police are everywhere this time. We must have half the force in the building." He moved around the corner of her desk, and Vicki resignedly turned to face him.

"What's up?"

"Are you all right, kid?" His expression turned serious. "In all the confusion, it never occurred to me to ask before. You must have gone through a really rough period, finding him that way."

"I'm fine, just a little shaky. It hasn't really sunk in completely. It's hard to think of Ed Catterall as dead. He was always so much alive."

He nodded. "It's going to be a major loss for us all. The Board is going to have to put someone in here real fast to take over Ed's spot, and whoever it is will play everything very conservative until he knows his way around." Angrily, he slapped the palm of one hand against his hip. "And just when things were starting to jell around here. Ed's ways weren't always gentle, but he sure got things accomplished. He's going to be hard to replace and we don't have time for a leisurely transition."

"You don't think they'll give the job to you?"

"What? Me? No way. I wouldn't take it even if they offered it. That's beyond my capabilities. A few years from now, maybe. No, if anyone here is going to get the nod, it'll be Joslin, but he's made a few enemies on the Board, enough to kill his chances I think. They'll go outside, or appoint one of themselves. They'll probably do that as an interim measure in any case. I just hope whoever they end up with isn't going to wipe out all the advances we've made. At best, things are going to slow to a crawl."

"I don't think I'd worry about that too much. The Board seems quite shrewd, and they certainly supported Ed's initiatives. They recognize how much he turned things around, that his reforms are paying off. Even the people on the production line feel more confident about their future with us."

"At least we should all be secure in our jobs for the time being. Three key people gone in less than two weeks. And that doesn't count Luis Mello, who'll be leaving in another week. It wouldn't surprise me if there were sudden merit increases for a number of people who might otherwise decide this is the right time to make a career move."

"Or who are too scared to stay. They have to be worrying about who's going to be next. I know I am."

Ross seemed momentarily disoriented. "Yeah, I guess you're right. It's hard to accept that there's a conscious purpose behind all of this. It feels more like a series of random disasters than a cohesive plan."

Vicki agreed with him. "It just doesn't seem possible that the three murders are connected. Someone's off their nut, striking out at random, or they have a grudge against Standard and are just picking off targets of opportunity."

"The police sure don't seem to be getting anywhere." He sounded resentful, and Vicki resented his resentment.

"There's not a whole lot they can do." Vicki rose to her father's defense. "The killer has either been very clever or very lucky. You can't deduce from clues unless you have the clues first."

Ross looked unconvinced. "I hope you're right, but I can't say that makes me feel any better. I'm not sure what time Catterall was killed, but he'd already left his office when I called him at 9:15. Given the time you found him, there was plenty of opportunity for almost anyone to have slipped away and clobbered him."

"Eventually every criminal makes a mistake. Maybe this time he's forgotten something that will break things open."

"I hope you're right." He dropped his arms to his sides. "Hey, that's not the reason I stopped by. None of us are going to be allowed to leave the building for a while, so I called the deli down the street and they're sending up a bunch of sandwiches. We'll have them in the Customer Service office in about . . ." he glanced at her clock, "ten or fifteen minutes. The company is picking up the tab, so if you're hungry, feel free to stop by. The early birds get the choice worms."

"Okay, thanks. I'm not really hungry, but maybe after a bit. That's a good idea."

"Think nothing of it. Not even murder can convince my stomach that there is a good reason to skip a meal." He tapped his mid-section, which showed only a very slight bulge over the beltline.

Vicki waited patiently while Ross made small talk for another few seconds, then finally left. As soon as the door closed, she rose, crossed to it, and turned the lock. If someone came by, perhaps they'd assume she was too distraught to have company. Right now she wanted to examine those files.

She moved the files to her hard drive and began scanning the list of filenames. Some of them were self-explanatory: "Schedule" was most likely the projected assignment of typists to various departments, "Staffnotes" was Jenny's summary of the weekly staff meetings, and so on. Many others were cryptic, intentionally or not, and none were suggestive enough to attract her immediate interest. But there had to be something here that was important to Paula Danforth, so important that she would risk stealing it from Jenny's office.

Shifting to a more comfortable position, Vicki prepared to start loading and reading each file in turn.

THIRTEEN

Paula Danforth was the first name on Henderson's list. Although Danforth had been a strong suspect previously, Vicki had given her an ironclad alibi this time. He couldn't think of any way in which Danforth could have murdered Ed Catterall, although that didn't mean she hadn't killed Antonelli or Grissom or both of the previous victims. She was visibly nervous but understandably so, and Henderson unscientifically decided she wasn't cool-headed enough to have been involved unless she was a consummate actor. She quickly confirmed Vicki's story almost word for word. He asked her to summarize her activities for the morning in some detail, but her brief account was otherwise unremarkable.

Mitchell appeared next. He had been romantically involved with the Grissom woman, although it was possible that they'd had a recent falling out. They had checked with Grissom's family and friends and no one reported any tension between the two, but that didn't mean it hadn't been there. Mitchell was an unlikely suspect, but he couldn't be ruled out.

When Mitchell arrived, he seemed distant, uninvolved, certainly not nervous or upset. There was an absent look in his eyes, and he had to be asked twice before he sat down.

"Mr. Mitchell, could you please summarize your morning's activities for me?"

Mitchell nodded, but several seconds passed before he actually spoke. "I arrived here shortly after 8:00; I was late this morning because I stopped for coffee and donuts and the line was a lot longer than usual. No one makes coffee here anymore, you know." He sketched a brief smile, but it was forced. "I stayed in my office for twenty or thirty minutes, then walked over to see Jason—Jason Capwell, the Chief Accountant. He was tied up with some sort of personnel problem and asked me to come back after an hour, which I did. That would have been 9:00."

"What did you do during that hour?"

"I stopped in personnel for a minute, but no one was around. Miss Sanders was in her office, but I didn't speak to her. I had another donut and read my e-mail, answered a few, browsed the Internet for a few minutes. Then I went back to see Jason."

"And how long were you with him?"

Mitchell looked momentarily uncertain. "We were discussing the possibility of tying the purchasing and accounts payable system into a single unit. I won't bore you with details, but we eventually decided that we needed to have some idea of how the files were handled in data processing. The mainframe isn't as flexible as a spreadsheet and we didn't know if there was room to add fields that would allow us to apportion expenses to specific departments, for example."

There was a pause, and Mitchell looked up to see if Henderson was following him. There was a hint of contempt in Mitchell's eyes and Henderson's hackles rose. Mitchell disliked him, he realized, and looked down on him, probably tagging him as a redneck cop with little education. That was all right. He preferred to be underestimated. It gave him a slight advantage. "Go on, Mr. Mitchell."

"We spent about forty minutes in Jason's office, then went down to see Ms. Marzocchi in data processing. She pulled the documentation and we started working through it. Jason was called away after a few minutes—I really can't be certain how long he was gone—but I remained there until 10:15."

"And then where did you go?"

"I had started to go out into the factory but the receptionist paged me and said that the sales rep from Talleyrand Packaging Systems was in the lobby to see me. He was very early for his appointment, but that was all to the good because if he'd arrived as scheduled, he'd have invited me to lunch and I can't stand the man. I picked him up in the lobby and took him to my office."

"And how long did he stay?"

"We were still together when the alarm was raised. I was just in the process of explaining that I couldn't take an early lunch."

"Did you see Mr. Catterall at any time this morning?"

"No, I don't think so."

"Thank you, Mr. Mitchell. We'll call you again if we have any further questions."

Mitchell looked surprised, but rose obligingly. He stopped before he reached the door, glanced back. Ben Dardenian opened the door and entered the room behind him, saying nothing.

"Detective Henderson." Mitchell's voice sounded uncharacteristically thick, as though he was struggling to remain calm. "I was not a particular fan of Mr. Catterall, although my reasons are personal and instinctive rather than because of anything the man ever said or did. But I was very fond of Miss Grissom, and if there is anything I can do to help find the person who murdered them, I am at your service."

Henderson kept his face expressionless. "What makes

you think they were both killed by the same person?"

A series of conflicting expressions chased each other across Mitchell's face. There was confusion, surprise, anger, and perhaps even sardonic humor before he recovered. "That possibility had never even occurred to me. I suppose you're right. It's frightening to know that someone you see every day is a killer, but it's depressing to think that there might be more than one."

"Yeah, well, it's a frightening and depressing world we live in, Mr. Mitchell."

Mitchell's face softened and when he spoke again, his voice was warmer. "I don't envy you your job."

Mitchell turned and was gone.

Dardenian made a disgusted sound as he approached.

"What's the matter, Ben? Not more problems?"

"No, nothing like that. I just don't like that man particularly."

"Why not?" Henderson knew what caused his own antipathy, but he was curious about his partner's aversion. Ben rarely let his feelings show. "He seems cooperative enough, and I very much doubt we'll be able to break his alibi."

"Oh, I don't think he's the murderer. But he's too slick, too manipulative. When people are so aggressively open about things, I start to wonder if my pocket is being picked. We know that he was romantically involved with his boss, for one thing."

"That's not a crime. It's not even particularly uncommon, Ben."

Dardenian ignored the interruption. "He was romantically involved with his boss without the knowledge of their employer. That's dishonest on the face of it. Now he admits that he never particularly liked Catterall, despite the fact that Catterall was responsible for his getting a job here."

"You're reaching for that one. Catterall hired Grissom who hired Mitchell."

"This is an old Yankee business, Walt. Companies like this think affirmative action means having a token minority representative at meetings to keep the EEO off their backs. But for whatever reasons he had, Catterall conformed to the spirit, not just the letter of the law. He put minorities and women into positions of power and rewarded them for their performance, not their connections. He might not have been the nicest guy on the block but he was fair and Mitchell prospered because of him."

"Vicki respected Catterall, but I don't think she liked him. I can't say that I cared for the man myself."

"Who said you were a good judge of character?" Dardenian asked with a smile. "I'm just naturally suspicious when a potential murder suspect goes out of the way to tell the investigating officer that he disliked the victim. Most people in Mitchell's position would have kept quiet about it."

"Maybe Mitchell just doesn't give a damn what we think, because he knows he didn't commit the murder."

"I don't think he did, so maybe you're right. But I still don't like him and I don't think I'd trust anything he said without getting it confirmed. Remember that story he and the Grissom woman gave us about their visit to receiving? I found that hard to believe then, impossible now."

Henderson was thoughtful. "You're right. I'd been assuming that they went down there for some privacy. But what if they did separate? What if one of them killed Antonelli? What if both of them did it? Two people would have had a better chance of disabling him. Mitchell holds him down while Grissom operates the controls. Then Mitchell knocks his lover off after his alibi is established."

"Then who killed Catterall, and why? We've already established that it couldn't possibly be Mitchell. That puts us back in a two-demon scenario."

Henderson swore, not under his breath. "All right, all right. Stick around for this next interview, will you? I want a second opinion."

A uniformed officer escorted Ross into the room. He greeted the two detectives warmly and waited to be invited before taking a seat. Henderson regarded him with more curiosity than usual. Vicki had mentioned Ross a surprising number of times recently, and he thought he knew his daughter well enough to perceive the early stages of something more than friendship. Henderson had ambivalent feelings about that possibility. One part of his mind still hoped that she and Danny would reconcile, even though he knew there was little chance. He had even heard that Danny was involved with someone new. Vicki had refused alimony and was doing well enough for herself, but Walt was old fashioned enough to believe that she wouldn't be really secure until she was married again. Walt also wanted grandchildren badly, and in his more introspective moments admitted to himself that this was the root of his objection to her career.

Ross appeared calm and in full control of himself. "If this keeps up, you fellows will need to have a permanent office here."

Henderson frowned. "This is hardly a joking matter, Mr. Ross."

The younger man looked contrite. "Sorry. Nervous habit. I always make jokes when I'm under a lot of stress. Gets me into trouble sometimes."

"Mr. Ross," Henderson looked down, pretending to consult his notes. "I understand that you now hold Frank Antonelli's position."

"More or less. Some of the lines of authority have been changing, and now, naturally, everything is even more uncertain because we don't know who will be taking over in Ed's place. It's likely to be pretty chaotic around here for a time."

"I don't suppose you'd be in line for the job?"

"No, not a chance," he shook his head violently. "I don't have enough experience and I don't have any friends on the Board. I doubt that anyone presently with the company will even be considered. They'll have to go outside, and in the interim I imagine the Board will call the shots themselves."

"So you don't consider yourself a candidate?"

Ross laughed. "That would certainly give me a motive, wouldn't it? Sorry, but there's just no way. I don't suppose you'd believe me if I told you I would refuse the position even if offered, but it's true. I know my limitations. I'm a systems analyst first and an administrator second, Detective Henderson. I'm pretty good at what I do, but it takes a while to absorb new skills. Even the manufacturing job is proving to be a strain. I suddenly find myself retroactively more sympathetic to Frank's problems. If I was pushed into Catterall's job right now, I'd either get myself fired for incompetence or I'd self-destruct and jump off a bridge somewhere."

Henderson kept his expression neutral as he changed the subject. "What time did you arrive at work this morning, Mr. Ross?"

"Just before 7:00, same as always. Now that I've taken over manufacturing, it's particularly important to establish my presence here. It's hard to demand punctuality from your subordinates if you're casual about your own attendance. I had a series of individual meetings with department supervisors all morning; I'm still learning a lot about the separate departments. I can get you a copy of the schedule if you want."

"We'll look at it later. For the time being, let's just deal with the period from 9:00 on."

Ross nodded. "So the murder was committed after 9:00?"

"I never said that."

"No, you didn't. Let's see, at 9:00 I met with Luis Mello. He gave us notice, you know, so I've been spending a disproportionate amount of time in the press area. We haven't decided what to do about replacing him yet. There really isn't anyone within the department with the kind of leadership abilities that are needed. One of the men is marginally qualified, but he asked not to be considered."

Henderson cleared his throat impatiently.

"Sorry, didn't mean to ramble. Things have been piling up in my mind lately. After that, I met with Tony Capra in the plating office at about 9:30. Luis walked out with me and then went to his own department. Tony is a hard worker, but he has a recurring problem with paperwork and counts. We were supposed to have a quick discussion, no more than fifteen minutes, but it ran well over that while he gave me some really inventive reasons why nothing was his fault and we were asking too much of him. I was a couple of minutes later for my next meeting, with Manny Soares in autopolish. Some of the factory workers may have noticed me, but I'm afraid I don't really have an alibi for the next five or ten minutes. Fortunately, Manny was a little late himself, so I didn't keep him waiting."

"Is it common for your supervisors to be late for meetings?"

"Sometimes it's unavoidable. If there's a serious problem on the floor, they deal with it first. They usually page and explain if it's going to be long. Even Antonelli cut them slack there."

"How long did you spend with Soares?"

"About twenty minutes. It would have been longer, but we overlapped with the meeting I had scheduled with Art Richardson and I told him I'd try to get back to him later."

"Richardson runs the warehouse, doesn't he? So you went down there."

"No, as a matter of fact I had asked him to come up to autopolish. There are too many interruptions down in receiving; it's impossible to carry on a logical conversation. Art doesn't like to delegate anything to his crew when he's around, so they have to chase him down to ask questions constantly. It's one of his traits I'd like to break, but it's so ingrained by now that it's probably a lost cause. Anyway, he showed up on time and I cut the meeting with Manny short."

"And how long were you and Richardson together?"

"Quite a while. We were interrupted when Vicki paged me and said she'd found the body in the balcony. I called the police from the office out on the production floor."

"That would have been over an hour later."

Ross nodded his head. "Normally I try to hold them to thirty minutes or less, but this was an unusual case." He massaged his chin with one hand, and continued in a level, emotionless tone. "Some of the changes I've announced are not too popular. One of the reasons this company has lagged behind the rest of the industry is because we hold onto outdated systems with surprising tenacity. Information management is the wave of the future, and the timeliness and accuracy of all aspects of information reporting are going to be crucial to the financial success of any business from now on. We have a pretty good infrastructure, but if the numbers aren't good going in, then the data coming out is useless. We've had problems with reporting accuracy in every department, some worse than others, some totally unacceptable. A few of the line supervisors resist change, particularly when it's imposed by someone they consider a newcomer. One area has been of particular concern to me. I have reason to believe that our receiving records have been inflated at times, that we've been recording and paying for more material than actually arrives on site."

Henderson didn't blink. "You think Richardson has a sweetheart deal with some of your suppliers. They short count you and he gets part of the take."

Ross looked uncomfortable for the first time. "I can't prove anything so I have to tread softly, as I'm sure you understand. But I had made it quite clear that there was going to be some kind of random spot checking. Richardson was indignant at what he characterized as a lack of confidence in his abilities, but I wasn't about to be bluffed. He advised me this morning that he was going to accept a job offer at another company and I was caught somewhat unprepared. Under ordinary circumstances, I'd have accepted his resignation immediately, but I was concerned that more change would just stir things up further. Outsiders are already reluctant to apply for jobs here, and none of the other people in receiving are supervisory material. I was hoping to convince him to hold off for a while."

"Did you succeed?"

"I'm not sure. I think he was wavering, but then everything hit the fan and I haven't spoken to him since."

"Were you aware of anything peculiar in the relationship between Richardson and Antonelli, anything that might have led you to believe there was a special understanding between them?"

Ross looked quite honestly puzzled. "I'm not even sure I understand the question, let alone how to answer. I don't think they liked each other, if that's what you mean. At least they almost never talked. But most of the time when Frank was talking, it was to chew someone out, and Richardson ran his department efficiently enough to avoid Frank's attention."

"Did you see or talk to Catterall at any time during the day?"

Ross hesitated for a few seconds. "Briefly, early this morning, somewhere around 8:00. He paged me to ask about lead times for water pitchers. Joslin in sales had suggested some kind of promotion and he was concerned that we wouldn't have enough warning to respond with the quantities required. And I called his office at 9:15 to ask him about a problem with the overhead distribution, but his secretary answered and said he wasn't there."

"You didn't page him?"

"No. It wasn't that urgent."

"And that was your only contact with Catterall today?"

"That was it. I was supposed to get back to him after lunch about the water pitchers. We have a pretty primitive method of measuring workload here. It's one of the problems we're going to have to address in detail very soon. How can we know how much additional business we can accept when we don't know what our total capacity is?" Ross suddenly recollected himself. "Sorry, didn't mean to get technical."

"And there's nothing else you can think of that might have a bearing on his murder?"

Ross shook his head. "Sorry, I really wish I could. Catterall made some enemies here, but none of them were serious enough to explain a murder. We all tend to get so focused on our own jobs that we have trouble appreciating the problems that others have to deal with."

Henderson immediately sensed that Ross had something else to say, but was reluctant to volunteer it without some prodding. So he obliged. "I had the impression that Catterall was quite popular for a CEO."

"He was respected by most people, but I don't think anyone actively liked him. Ed was always too impersonal to develop friendships. Oh, he knew the names and ages of everyone's children and asked about them all the time, but it was like a catechism he'd memorized. And there's no question that he turned things around in terms of profit. But Ed was a decision maker, and a lot of his decisions—even the ones that were proven right—offended and irritated people."

Henderson felt his patience slip. "Mr. Ross, if you're trying to tell me something specific, please be frank about it and stop wasting my time."

Ross raised his eyes and locked them with Henderson's. "All right, I'll tell you, but I honestly don't think this will be of any help. Catterall believed that it was more important to always make a decision promptly than to always make the right decision. Sometimes he was proven wrong. Joslin in sales, for example, lost a significant battle with Carlisle, the advertising manager, because Catterall chose to implement the new, economy-priced line that has been using up such a disproportionate amount of our manufacturing capacity. Carlisle has powerful friends on the Board who would like to see him become the next Vice President of Sales and Joslin has been trying to shore up his own position. Catterall's decision came at a very awkward time and Joslin lost a lot of ground, which naturally only reinforced Carlisle's position."

"Are you saying Joslin had reason to want Catterall gone?"

"No, because Catterall later admitted to Joslin, publicly in fact, that if he had it to do over again, he would have reduced the scale of the new line dramatically. Carlisle might have been worried that the next decision would go against him simply because Catterall felt the need to even things up, and that was a potential weapon for Joslin."

"Doesn't Carlisle work for Joslin? That's what the organizational chart indicates."

"Organization charts show the formal lines of power. The informal power structure is what really runs the company. Joslin and Carlisle head two opposing power centers within the sales and general administrative infrastructure, and each has allies on the Board."

"Did Catterall have other enemies within the company?"

Ross replied with a pained expression. "That's too strong a word. Jason Capwell, the Controller, was quite upset about Catterall's asset management program. Carl Romero tried to be a Catterall clone, spouting the official line all the time, but Ed had a low opinion of Romero and used to make jokes at his expense, and not always behind his back. For that matter, I didn't like the way he put me on the spot, forcing me into Antonelli's job without massaging the supervisors first. They had their backs up from the very first day.

"Mello says he's leaving because there is more opportunity for advancement elsewhere, and the murder certainly didn't help, but I think he was also concerned that someone with almost no production background was going to be his new boss. I can sympathize with that. I asked Ed to help smooth things over but he was either incapable of understanding the problem or he felt that the tension would bring out our competitive sides, force us to compete against each other to excel. That was his management style." Ross fell silent.

Henderson waited while the silence lengthened. He suspected that there was more that Ross could have said, but that he was reluctant to go any further. It was probably better to let things go for the moment and get back to Ross later.

"I think that's all we need from you right now, Mr. Ross. I would appreciate it if you would remain on the premises until the interviews are completed and we've specifically released you."

Ross nodded. "I seem to be in charge at the moment. Until someone from the Board arrives, I'm effectively in command." He laughed nervously. "Which means I'm going to have to answer a lot of questions that I'm not prepared for when they do arrive. Awkward facts don't carry much weight with the Board when they have a potentially bad effect on the bottom line."

"I'm afraid some disruption is inevitable."

"I realize that. But even if you catch the killer and we're able to revive the morale here and avoid losing any more frightened people, there's also the unpleasant fact that three murders are going to cause a lot of publicity that we really don't need."

"I thought any publicity was good publicity."

He shook his head. "Not always. The market for silverplate is very conservative. We've already had a few customers cancel orders without explanation. I know it doesn't make any sense, but this is the kind of scandal that could convince some of the major buyers to drop our line altogether."

"I'm sure the families of the three victims will be heartbroken to hear that you've lost market share because of their deaths."

Ross stiffened. "Detective Henderson, I am well aware of the tragedy involved. I was rather fond of Jenny Grissom, and Ed Catterall did a great deal to advance my career. My personal feelings are one thing; my responsibility to this company is another. You have no right to judge me because I choose to continue to perform those duties for which I am being paid."

Henderson considered an angry rejoinder, but finally nodded. "Maybe you're right, Mr. Ross. Maybe the nature of my job makes me insensitive to the obligations of others. But I take my job every bit as seriously as you do, and I intend to get it done regardless of the cost. I think that's all we need from you right now. We'll let you know if we require any further information."

He looked down at his notebook until the other man had left the room.

FOURTEEN

Luis Mello twisted uncomfortably in his seat, obviously anxious to be somewhere else. Anywhere else.

"I understand you're going to be leaving Standard Silver, Mr. Mello."

"That's right. I had another job offer and, under the circumstances, I decided it was time to make a move."

"What circumstances in particular?"

Mello looked puzzled. "The murders, of course. What else would I be talking about? Would you stay here while people are dying all around you?"

Henderson ignored the question. "What time did you arrive this morning?"

Mello's first two hours were of little consequence and Henderson waited impatiently until he reached the critical time. "I spent a few minutes talking to Mr. Ross when he came through my area. After that I was helping Alex Rose set up the first draw tool for the top ring of the 102 Epergne on press number 14. I left him just before 9:30 to talk to Manny Soares. We spent about half an hour together."

"Where was that?"

"In my office, the press room office."

"What did you talk about?"

Mello looked uncomfortable. "It wasn't anything in particular. Just shop stuff, you know, schedules and stuff."

Henderson sensed there was more. "We'll be talking to Mr. Soares, you know. It won't look good if he tells us a different story."

Mello looked as though he was going to hang tough, but then his shoulders relaxed. "Look, I'm leaving so it doesn't matter to me, but Manny's got no place to go and he's a friend. I don't want to get him into trouble."

"Unless it has something to do with the murders, what you say here will remain confidential."

Mello shifted nervously. "Manny's not too happy with some of the changes Ross is making out on the floor. He was a little bit outspoken about it and I know he was pissing Ross off. Ross is okay, but he's finally getting to run his own show and he wants everyone to play on the same team. I thought it might be a good idea to tell Manny he was only hurting himself, that he should give Ross the benefit of the doubt until his new systems had a chance to prove themselves. Ross has been cutting him some slack, but I know it won't last. And Manny has been having some personal problems as well."

"What kind of personal problems?"

Mello looked uncomfortable. "He gets into moods, you know, depressed. He won't see anyone about it."

"What do you think of Ross as a boss?"

Mello's mouth twisted in distaste. "Like I said, Ross isn't a bad guy, but I don't think he's going to last. I wasn't a big fan of Frank Antonelli, but at least the man understood that production is more than just work orders and schedules and piece counts. You have to get out on the floor to see what it's really all about, and walking through the plant once or twice a day isn't going to get the job done. All the reports and projections and charts and forecasts in the world won't get one more piece produced. Ross is a paper pusher. He tries hard enough and some of his ideas are good, but he isn't going to be able to make a difference where it counts. The people on the floor won't follow him unless he leads."

"Is that why you're leaving?"

"It's part of it."

"So you stayed with Soares until . . . when? . . . 10:00?"

"Yeah. Manny had to go to a meeting with Ross."

"What did you do after that?"

"Matty came in just as Manny was leaving to tell me the small lift truck had stopped working. Matty's one of the forklift operators, Matty Mello. No relation. Receiving delivers the raw coil stock to the press room, and we use our own forklift to move it to the right piece of equipment. Our truck is smaller and it fits down some of the aisles where the big one won't go, but it won't handle as heavy a load. We've been having a lot of trouble with it lately, and this time the maintenance people just couldn't get it restarted. I was still there when we heard about Mr. Catterall being found dead."

"And you never left the area at all?"

"Not once." He smiled. "There were three or four people with me, I'm happy to say."

"Could you give us their names? Just so we can check it out."

Mello named one man from the press room, the maintenance worker who had labored over the forklift for over an hour, a material handler who'd been pressed into duty as his assistant, and a fourth man from receiving. "There were a couple of more who stood around and watched for a while."

"And when exactly did you hear about Catterall's death?"

"Just before lunch. Ross called each of the supervisors individually to tell us there'd been a death. At least he had the courtesy not to pretend it was an accident."

"Catterall made a point of walking through the factory every day, didn't he?"

"Pretty much. He knew most of the workers by name, their first name at least. He was pretty popular with the hourly people. Something like that makes a big difference here, the personal touch."

"So I would imagine." Henderson was curious about the tension between Mello and Ross, but let it drop for now. He thanked Mello and told him he could leave.

When Manny Soares entered the room a minute later, Henderson was startled by the man's appearance. He appeared to have aged dramatically in a matter of days. He sat down sullenly, his head bowed forward, deep wrinkles under his eyes, his hands held together tensely in his lap.

Soares confirmed Mello's account of their meeting at 9:30, but was even less specific about what they had discussed. "You know, we talked about production. Jobs that had to get done. Making sure we met priorities, how the new boss was making out, that sort of thing."

"Luis Mello told us that the two of you weren't entirely happy with the changes Ross has been making."

Soares' eyes shifted about the room, searching for something innocuous on which to focus. "You know how it is, new bosses always want to change things, to show they're in charge. It wasn't nothing out of the usual."

Henderson tapped his pencil against his chin. "Ross says you showed up late for your meeting."

Resentment showed plainly this time. "It was only a minute or two. And he just made it on time himself, at that."

"How long did you stay?"

"Maybe fifteen minutes. I left when Richardson showed up. I had things to do."

"And where did you go when you left Ross?"

"Up to personnel for a grievance hearing. Velasquez was waiting for me outside the office. Little worm thought he was going to get me this time, but even Romero wouldn't let him off the hook."

"Who is this Velasquez?"

"Shop Steward for the union. He grieved against me for using operators on set-ups, to keep the big rotary polishers going. The bastard said it was a violation of the contract because it wasn't in their job descriptions."

"He accompanied you to personnel?"

"Sure, followed along with me, telling me how I was going to lose this one. It sure wasn't his day. The field rep wouldn't even look at him after he shot his mouth off some and made things even worse."

"Field rep?" Henderson was puzzled, thrown off his gait.

"Field rep. Union guy from the international, a real asshole. He comes in whenever we have a grievance hearing. But this time he didn't say nothing, just talked to Velasquez in private and called everything off after Romero read him the riot act."

"And Velasquez accompanied you all the way to personnel?"

"He sure did, running his mouth right along."

"And after you arrived, you never left the personnel office until the call from Ross?"

"That's right. Velasquez left after the rep told him they had no case, but Romero wanted me to stay behind and sign the paperwork. Ross called Romero and he told me about what happened."

Henderson sat back abruptly. "All right, Mr. Soares, that's all we need for now."

He waited until the supervisor had left the room. "Ben, check out this Velasquez character. I don't think Soares was lying, but let's check everything. Someone will have to talk to Romero to find out if Soares left the office, even briefly, but I don't expect to find anything there either."

Dardenian nodded. "No problem." He glanced down at his watch. "Want to break for lunch?"

"No. Have someone send out for sandwiches. You know what I like. I want to get this done. It looks like everyone is going to have an alibi this time, and I want to get past all the bad news as soon as possible and move on. Danforth was with Vicki, Ross was with Mello or Soares or maybe Richardson, depending on when Catterall was actually killed. Mitchell, Mello, and Soares all have interlocking alibis and if Richardson confirms the story Ross told us, he's probably out of the running as well. That only leaves D'Angelo and Capra from the original list of suspects, and I have a feeling they're not going to pan out either. Someone's playing with us, and I don't like it. I seriously don't like it."

As Henderson had expected, Richardson confirmed that he had arrived at the office in autopolish shortly before 10:30, and that Ross had spent the next hour trying to talk him out of leaving Standard. "The place just ain't the same any more, you know," he said defensively. "Frank was a tough boss, but he made people move, got them all heading in the same direction. This Ross guy is soft, spends all of his time reading reports, trying to be a nice guy, walks around in nice clothes without any grease on 'em. I just don't think he's gonna make it, and a lot of people might lose out before the top brass wises up and puts in somebody with real manufacturing experience."

"Mr. Richardson, you arrived at the office at, let us say, 10:20. What were you doing during the hour before that?"

"Unloading trucks. Or one truck anyway. The salt and

pepper glasses from Crystallite came by commercial carrier again, and they didn't bother to skid the damned things. Nine hundred tiny little cases of glass piled up in a forty footer." Richardson looked genuinely offended. "We got maybe four or five percent breakage; it's concealed damage, so we won't know until we check every carton. And the boxes were scattered all over the inside of the truck, so we had to pack them up on skids ourselves before we could even start to move them. Should have taken ten minutes and ended up taking nearly an hour."

"Isn't it unusual for you to be involved with the actual unloading of the truck? I thought you were the supervisor."

"A man who can't do the work his people do isn't much of a boss, now is he? I get out there and pitch in when it's needed, and sometimes even when it isn't. Gets you the respect of the people that way. And this was such a mess, I wanted to handle it myself. Matty, my right hand man, he's a hard worker, but not too smart, see? He'd have loused up the count or something and they'd all be doing more bitching than working."

"You never left the truck then?"

"Nope. Stayed with it right through the end. We were just finishing up when I had to leave to see Ross."

Henderson searched his notes. "You keep a log of arrival and departure times for all trucks, don't you?"

"I don't. My clerk does. He's got it all written down."

"And you can provide us the names of the people who worked with you unloading this glass?"

"Sure, it was Howard and Mel and Matty. They were all there. The truck driver too. Gus something, I think his name is. He comes in here a lot. He's with Faulkner Trucking."

Henderson paused, pondering whether or not to play the

card he'd been holding in reserve. Nothing else had worked, he decided, so why not?

"Mr. Richardson, why were you blackmailing Frank Antonelli?"

The change in the other man was visible and significant. His face froze and his complexion paled visibly under the coat of grease and soot. His shoulders slumped noticeably and the muscles tensed in his thighs, back, and hands. Deep furrows suddenly lined his face, much deeper than they had been previously. Small, intensely bright eyes darted around the room, as though seeking an escape route.

"What do you mean?" His voice was shaking.

Henderson sat back and folded his arms. "Don't waste my time, Richardson. We know part of the story already. Antonelli had been paying you off for at least three years. Didn't it ever occur to you that by accepting his personal checks, you were leaving a trail obvious to anyone who was looking for it?"

Richardson's mouth opened and closed, fish-like, but no words came forth. He glanced toward Dardenian, saw no rescue there, and turned toward the blank wall, not meeting the detective's eyes. "I don't know what you're talking about," he said quietly. "I used to help Frank with his cars, restoring them. He paid me for that sometimes. That's all there was to it."

Henderson leaned forward suddenly. "Don't play games with me, Richardson. The only reason we haven't pulled you in and charged you already is because we're after bigger fish, and because the victim is dead and can't be hurt further. So if you don't want to find yourself under arrest, maybe you'd better tell us the truth!"

Richardson turned back, one eye jumping nervously. For a long moment, Henderson thought the other man was about to burst into tears. "It wasn't blackmail. Not really. I never asked for the money." Richardson seemed to collapse back into the chair, suddenly much smaller and more vulnerable than he had been only a moment before. "Frank was getting on my back a lot at the time; I had some new people working for me and they screwed a few things up. And I borrowed a few things once and Frank found out about it. I returned them real quick so there wasn't any way he could make anything out of it, but he let me know real quiet-like that he wasn't too happy with me. I needed some insurance and when Romero hired the Garcia kid, everything sort of fell into my lap."

"Slow down and start again from the beginning."

Richardson looked up at him. "I think I need a lawyer before I go any further."

Henderson nodded. "That's certainly your right. But if you bring a lawyer into this, the blackmail issue is going to become even more important than it is now because a lawyer will insist that we charge you if we want to ask more questions. If you decide to cooperate with us instead, you may help find the person responsible for three deaths. That's our only concern at the moment, not the money you extorted from a dead man. We're only concerned insofar as it affects the murders. Like I said, now that Antonelli's dead, no one's being hurt any more."

Richardson appeared doubtful. "My deal with Frank won't come into it then?"

"Not unless it's germane to the case."

Richardson glanced at Dardenian again, licked his lips, finally nodded, more to himself than to anyone else. "This kid Garcia knew me from a private club up in Boston. It's a kind of sex club, not exactly illegit, but . . . well, shady."

"So you hired him?"

"No, no way. I don't hire people I know from the outside. Romero hired him. I didn't even know about it until Romero brought him down as a temporary hire while Gomes was out on disability."

"So Garcia worked for you?"

"For a couple of weeks. Then Gomes came back earlier than we expected and we didn't have anyplace else to put him, so he got laid off. But by then he'd seen another familiar face in the building and he told me about it. It was Frank Antonelli."

Henderson nodded. "Go on." For the first time, he thought they might have a useful lead. He still couldn't predict the destination, but at least they were in motion. "So Garcia told you that your boss was gay but not out, so you decided to blackmail him."

"No, that wasn't it!" Richardson raised both hands in protest. "Not exactly anyway. I just sort of hinted to Frank that Garcia thought he looked familiar, had him confused with someone he used to know in Boston. That place in Boston, it goes both ways, so I don't know if he was gay or straight. Anyway, Frank just nodded, never let on that he was upset at all, but then once a month he'd drop an envelope off for me with a check in it."

"And I suppose you never mentioned the matter again."

"No, never. Garcia was gone, like I said. I kept the first few checks for a long time, months, never cashed them. Then I needed some money in a hurry, had to replace my car, and that seemed the easiest way. I just kept on after that, and the checks kept coming."

"And that's all there was to it? You never discussed the matter again?" Henderson made no effort to disguise his disbelief. "You expect me to believe that Antonelli paid you all that money even though you never said anything about exposing him?"

"Never! I swear that's all there was to it! I didn't threaten him, not then, not ever! I didn't even think of it as blackmail, exactly. I mean, I never asked for anything, did I? When I told him, I hoped that he'd ease up on me a little, that's all."

Richardson seemed to have regained some of his composure, relieved to have finally revealed his secret. Henderson was disappointed, but not surprised, realizing that the story he had just heard was probably pretty close to the truth. He felt certain that Richardson had made it obvious that he was dangling a sword over Antonelli's head, and had probably hinted that he knew more than he was saying. They might well never know exactly what Antonelli was afraid of, and it probably didn't matter.

Henderson was also reasonably confident that Richardson had not murdered Frank Antonelli; he would not have slaughtered the goose that laid the golden eggs. And even more certainly, he could not have killed Ed Catterall, assuming his alibi held up.

Tony Capra seemed much more self-confident than he had during his previous interview. Antonelli's death must have made things considerably easier for him. Ross might be equally critical of the man's performance, but his personal style would have been less abusive, and he probably had too many problems to deal with to devote much time to the errant plating counts. Capra seemed almost cheerful as he sat down, nodded briefly to Dardenian, crossed his arms, and leaned back in the chair. Henderson noted that his forearms were ringed by ugly masses of scar tissue.

Capra must have followed Henderson's eyes because he looked down suddenly, then pulled his arms back. "Sorry," he said. "That's why I usually wear a long-sleeved shirt even when it's hot. I had a bad accident with some acid a few years back, messed my arms up real bad. The skin gets irritated easily and I have to watch for infections. I can't even wear a watch."

Capra confirmed the details of the meeting with Mark Ross. "Ross was after me to work out some better way of figuring what pieces were plated. The guys I have working for me, well, they try hard but they're not really clerical types. Sometimes they count bad, sometimes they write down the wrong item number. Two-quart and three-quart covers look a lot alike if you don't see them together, but they use a different amount of silver and it screws up the production counts when they get confused. You see, the work tickets get separated from the jobs at plating, so it's a lot harder to match things up here than it is in any other department."

"We don't need all the details right now."

"No, of course not." Capra gave a nervous little laugh, quickly cut it off. "Anyway, Ross wanted me to set something up with Donna, that's Donna D'Angelo, to keep the runs together when they came off the plating line. That way we could record the counts in bulk rather than one plating rack at a time. We wouldn't have to spend so much time matching items to issues either, see?"

"How long did this meeting last?"

Capra scratched his head. "Fifteen minutes, I think. Ross had to rush off for another meeting at quarter past, but I think we might have started early. I'm not sure."

"And what did you do after this meeting?"

"Went right in to see her. Donna, that is. She was working with this trainee right near the end of the plating line, and she yelled over to me when I stepped out of the office. Wanted to bitch," he caught himself, "she wanted me to check the plating thickness on the brandy snifters."

"How long did you spend with her?"

"We were still working on it when Ross called us. We checked the plate on the snifter first; it was right on spec. Then we went to look over the layout of the floor where they do the unracking. I suggested that we try unracking right onto the big dollies. Those are the wheeled trucks we use to move the work around where there aren't any conveyors. Anyway we were looking at those at the entrance to the finishing room when we got the call."

"And the two of you were together all of that time?"

"Sure. It sounded like a real good idea to me. The front office has been on my back for months about the silver usage and the counts, even though I keep telling them the problem is in their figures, not on the production floor. This way, someone else is double-checking before the reports go in instead of after, so the numbers would be fixed before they even saw them. A lot of the pressure would be off of my back."

"So having Ross as your new boss is working out for you?"

"Well, up to now anyway, it looks good." He started to smile but it didn't last. "Hey, I mean, you know, he's got some good ideas. But I didn't have anything against Frank either. He was a tough boss, but he wasn't unfair or anything. Just a little difficult to deal with sometimes. He had a bad temper. But I wasn't mad at him or anything like that."

The man seemed so hopelessly desperate to wriggle off an imaginary hook that Henderson almost said something to reassure him. Almost. "We'll be talking to you again, Mr. Capra, in due course. But that's all we need for the time being." Let the man squirm for a while, he told himself. Capra struck him as the type of man who would never have the guts to use dangerous knowledge directly, but he might well have kept his eye to a few keyholes hoping to gain some advantage. Particularly if his own performance had been subject to a great deal of criticism.

The more he learned about the people running Standard Silver, the more amazed he was that his daughter insisted she actually enjoyed working here. Sometimes the company of criminals seemed to Henderson every bit as appealing as the company of supposedly honest men and women.

Henderson stretched his legs while waiting for Donna D'Angelo, who arrived with a cigarette sticking out of one corner of her mouth. She sat down without being invited and barely glanced in his direction.

"What can I do for you this time, Mr. Henderson?"

Henderson was mildly irritated and mildly amused. He returned to his seat and played with his notebook for a few seconds just to ensure that she recognized who was in charge of the interview. For some reason, she seemed positively belligerent this time, in contrast to her previous cooperation. "When was the last time you saw Edward Catterall?"

"Yesterday," she sighed, "about 1:00 or just after. He was standing in the hallway talking to the guard when I came back from lunch. I never saw him again."

"Then you didn't see him today at all?"

"That's what I said. He took a walk through the factory and offices almost every day, but I didn't notice him this morning. He liked to talk to some of the people on the line. He used to call it 'participative management.' " She grimaced. "It was all a show, but a lot of people appreciate good showmanship, and I suppose it didn't do any harm."

"You work for Mark Ross now."

"That's right." Her tone was noncommittal.

"Did you see him today?"

"Only from a distance. He was in the office with someone, Luis Mello I think, first thing this morning, and then later with Tony in plating. Tony came out right afterwards to see me with some suggestions Ross had made." She nodded, but it wasn't meant for him; she was reviewing some internal checklist or script she'd prepared. "It wasn't necessarily a bad idea either, surprising since he hasn't spent much time on the floor. It's not quite as easy as it sounded when we first started talking about it, but I think its doable. Tony and I went over some of the possibilities. Do you want the details?"

Henderson shook his head. "Mr. Capra has already filled us in."

"Okay, anyway I figured I could save some material handling time at the same time by having the unrackers sort directly onto our big dollies. We must have been together for two hours at least, maybe even longer."

"What time was this?"

"We stopped when Ross paged me and told me Catterall had been found dead. That was pretty close to lunchtime. My stomach was growling a mile a minute. And I know it was exactly 10:00 when we went to look for the dollies because the timekeeper was calling coffee break in packing when we walked through the archway. So I guess it was almost exactly two hours."

"And you and Capra were within sight of one another for that entire time?"

"We could have reached out and held hands if we'd wanted. It's loud out there, even in the packing area. You go more than a yard away from someone, you have to shout to be heard."

"Was there anything out of the ordinary today, no matter how inconsequential?"

She shook her head. "I can't think of a thing."

"You can go then, Miss D'Angelo."

She rose and walked to the door, then hesitated. "Detective," she said quietly. "Ed Catterall wasn't a particularly warm man, maybe not even a nice man, but he did a lot of good for people because he let them have a chance when he thought they deserved it. Are you going to find the son of a bitch who killed him or not?"

"We will, Miss D'Angelo. Sooner or later, we will."

He remained seated, watching the door close, wondering if he had just told a lie. Because if everyone's story checked out with the witnesses they'd named, none of the people who were in a position to kill Frank Antonelli had any chance at all of killing Edward Catterall.

And that didn't make any sense at all.

FIFTEEN

Someone knocked on her door. Vicki cautiously minimized the window she was reading before turning away from the computer and rising to her feet. She'd been reading Jenny's memos, the current one a proposal to combine some reports that significantly overlapped. Vicki was impressed by the dead woman's efforts; the memos she had read were rich with possibilities. Despite her comparatively short time with Standard, she had developed a quite sophisticated understanding of its manufacturing systems and accounting principles, and her familiarity with data processing systems was even deeper than Vicki had suspected. Unfortunately, she had yet to find anything that might justify Paula Danforth's extraordinary effort to steal copies of the files.

The knock was repeated. "I'm coming!" She glanced at her watch, saw that half of the afternoon had passed. Her stomach growled warningly and she realized that she hadn't eaten anything since her toast and coffee that morning.

"Hi." Ross stood in the hall with his hands clasped behind his back. "I was starting to worry about you; you never came by for sandwiches. When people don't show up at the times they are expected, I tend to get worried."

"Yeah, well . . ." She made a confused, dismissive gesture, stepped back so that he could enter. "I just got involved in something and lost track of time."

As he entered, he handed her something wrapped in plain white paper. "I saved you a ham and cheese. The lettuce isn't very fresh, I'm afraid."

She smiled and accepted it gratefully. "Thanks. Now that I think about it, I'm half starved. Even wilted lettuce will do." She peeked into the sandwich.

"Almost everything was gone by the time I realized you hadn't put in an appearance. The tuna was actually pretty good."

She sat down and took a bite; the bread was slightly stale. "It's fine. All it has to do is hold me until supper. Thanks for thinking of me."

"Vicki . . ." Ross turned away, started walking around the office with his hands jammed into his pants pockets, not looking in her direction. "Ed's death is going to cause a lot of upheaval here. I know this may sound a little premature, but it might be to our mutual advantage to work out some strategies in advance, so that whoever ends up taking over knows that we're on top of things. There's no reason why we can't cooperate; the tension between you and Frank was a waste of time. If we want to hold onto the improvements we've made, I think we're going to have to move quickly. I just heard that Powell is flying in to represent the Board, and while I don't think Joslin will get the job, he has a lot of influence, and he'll be pushing his own agenda regardless of who takes over. You know he has unrealistically high expectations for quality and no appreciation at all for how much it will cost. I think you and I can find the right balance, but not if he's pushing and prodding at us separately."

She nodded, her mouth full of sandwich. "You're probably right," she said after a moment. "He sends angry memos whenever a customer complains about quality, justified or not, and even though he's the champion of the economy line, he expects our standards to be just as high there as on the top end stuff. He doesn't even want to listen when I tell him we can't possibly inspect every piece a full hundred percent. We could get Paula involved as well."

"Right," he turned in her direction. "But Paula's not going to be much of a factor, really. She doesn't have the strength to create policy, although she's good at implementing it. She'll follow our lead so long as she keeps her own department and can call herself a manager."

Vicki felt her hackles rise slightly at this characterization of the other woman, but when she thought about it for a few seconds, she realized it was an accurate assessment. Paula would be perfectly content to be told what the new policies would be; she lacked the self-confidence to initiate major changes in procedure on her own. She enjoyed her title and did a good job, but she was blessed with a good staff and that made things operate much more smoothly than it might otherwise. Certainly she would never have the self-confidence necessary to oppose Joslin openly, not on any subject.

"I agree with you, I suppose, but we're not going to be able to generate much enthusiasm so long as these murders are hanging over us. Even if the killer doesn't strike again, people are going to be on edge for a long time. And I wouldn't be surprised if we saw more resignations."

Ross nodded. "One of the secretaries told Romero that this is her last day. He tried to talk her out of it but she was terrified."

"I'm not surprised. You noticed that I locked my door?"

"You're not alone in that." He approached her desk, stood in front of it without sitting. "We can't just suspend everything until things are cleared up, if they ever are. I'm not confident that the police will ever get to the bottom of this."

Vicki bristled again. Ross did not, after all, know about her relationship to Henderson, and even her father admitted that they weren't making any progress. "Maybe you're right. But I'm just too jumpy to talk about it right now."

"Fair enough." He glanced at his watch. "What about supper tonight? We could leave your car here and go over to Pirandello's and talk about it there. I'll treat."

A silent alarm went off in the back of Vicki's head, but she wasn't sure whether or not to pay attention to it. Ross probably had something in mind above and beyond planning corporate strategy. She had dated a couple of times since the divorce, but never seriously, and she had a low opinion of office romances. Mark had a tendency to flirt, but as far as she knew, he was not involved with anyone from Standard. She preferred to keep her personal and professional lives separate and she still wasn't completely past the lingering unpleasantness of her failed marriage. On the other hand, she genuinely liked Ross, and admired his drive to succeed.

After all, she told herself, it's a business supper for a legitimate business purpose. There was no reason why they could not be sociable. But if anyone saw them there together, rumors would spread like wildfire.

"I don't know, Mark. This hasn't been a great day. I really feel wrung out. A hot shower and early bed seem like a much better idea. Some other time?"

"It's up to you. I just thought you might want company when you left. After finding the body and everything that followed, it's not surprising that your nerves are on edge. I'm not trying to be overbearing, but I wanted to offer any support I could. But it really is important that we get something formulated soon. A couple of days might make a big difference around here; things are going to move quickly."

She smiled and relaxed. "I appreciate your concern. Let me think about it for a while and I'll get back to you."

"Sure thing." Ross looked as though he was about to say more, but he was forestalled by another knock on the door.

"Come in." Vicki heard the exasperation in her voice. Wasn't she ever going to have a chance to finish reading the purloined files?

It was one of the uniformed officers. "Miss Sanders? Detective Henderson would like to see you for a moment. He's in Conference Room A. Right down the hall."

"All right, I know where it is. I'll be along in just a moment. You'll excuse me, Mark?"

"Of course. I'll check back with you later. Give it some thought."

She nodded, powered down her computer, and stood up, nodding to the officer. "Lead on."

Henderson was alone in the conference room when she arrived. A fan of manila folders lay spread across the table, and a ruled pad was set to one side, covered with her father's distinctive indecipherable scrawl.

"How's it going, Dad?"

Instead of answering, Henderson picked up one of the folders and handed it to her. The label had her name on it. She accepted it with a puzzled look, opened it, and began reading the contents. Her expression changed by degrees as she read on, betraying her increasing anger by subtle alterations of the set of her chin, the angle of her jaw. When she was done, she looked up at him and her expression was fierce.

"We found this in Catterall's office," he said quietly. "There's a separate folder for everyone in middle management and up, even the floor supervisors."

Vicki closed the folder and dropped it on the desk. "That nosy bastard!" It was barely more than a whisper.

"This is the same nosy bastard you described to me as a topnotch manager a while back."

Vicki glanced down at the discarded folder and looked over at him. She sighed and her face relaxed slightly, but there was still visible anger. "He was very good at his job: effective, decisive, and with a broad general understanding of his people and the processes involved. I'm not surprised that he did background checks, but I'm amazed at the degree of detail. They even talked to my goddamned neighbors!"

"My guess is that Catterall was looking for leverage, something in the background of his managers that he could use to manipulate them if the occasion arose. Even if he never made use of the material here," he tapped the pile of folders, "he knew that he could if he wanted to. That gave him power, secret power."

She glanced down at the spread of folders. "Are the others as complete as mine?"

"Most of them are much more detailed. There are copies of police records from twenty years ago, for example. There are photographs of Richardson with a young man who is heavily into body piercing, a complete transcription of the Danforth divorce proceedings, and notes on things so innocuous I don't understand what reason Catterall could have for compiling them. What difference did it make to him that Ross was quite a jock in high school, quarterbacked the football team and played basketball, for example? Why keep a copy of the appraisal on Paul Joslin's wife's jewelry? What use is Luis Mello's military service record when it reflects only exemplary conduct? What difference does it make what Manny Soares' relatives in Portugal do for a living? How is it relevant that your head of maintenance had his income tax return audited four years ago and paid a small fine?"

"Maybe he was just nosy. He did have a tendency to involve himself in every facet of the company's operation. He always made certain that he knew everyone by name, sometimes even the names of people's wives and kids. It had its plus side; the people who didn't know him well liked him a lot."

Henderson began to gather the folders into a pile. "Listen, Vicki," he continued without meeting her eyes. "Sit down, will you? Can't you find an excuse to take some vacation time?"

She made an impatient noise and continued to stand. "We've been through this already, Dad. I have a job to do, and it's going to be even busier now." She bit her lip. "You still don't have any clear idea who is responsible, do you?"

"We don't even have a murky idea! This time around there are too many alibis. There are a few people who just might have had time to run upstairs and hit Catterall over the head, but it doesn't seem to be possible for any of them to have killed Antonelli. My guess is that some of the times we were told were off a little, through error or lies or both. That might have given someone just enough time to run upstairs and murder Catterall, although it would be taking quite a chance."

"There are a half dozen ways to enter the stockroom."

"I know. And we think that five minutes would have been long enough to get there, get the job done, and get away. But unless someone changes their story, we haven't much chance of breaking any of the alibis. Your Mr. Ross, for example, admits running from one meeting to another. That made me slightly suspicious, particularly when everyone was being so vague about their timing. He was one of the few who actually spent some time unobserved. But I don't believe we're dealing with multiple killers and unless you're going to change your story about the day Antonelli was killed, we're still without a credible suspect."

She shook her head. "He was never out of my sight. Sorry. I'd like to help."

Henderson stood up and began pacing. "If we have to assume that there are two different murderers, then there are dozens of people who could have killed Catterall. There's certainly no lack of motive." He gestured toward the folders. "The motive might well be in one of those. Something might have showed up that was dangerous to our killer, and Catterall could have revealed that he knew about it, innocently or not. But if that was the case, the information is probably lost now. The desk drawer was forced and I would be very surprised if whatever incriminating information existed has not been removed and destroyed. The Grissom murder doesn't help us at all either; almost anyone could have poisoned her sugar bowl. Captain Nicholas thinks we have a psycho killing at random, but my instincts tell me something else. I think we're being played with. The killer is on a power trip; Catterall would have liked him."

Vicki frowned. "But if you're sure that no one could have committed all three murders, doesn't that mean either two separate killers or a conspiracy?"

"I know." Henderson shook his head wearily. "Which means that either my instincts are wrong or that there is something screwed up in our reconstruction of what's been happening. If the latter is the case, then the killer hasn't just concealed what he's done; he's managed to create false evidence. Somewhere along the line we have been gulled into believing something that isn't true."

"So where do you go from here?"

Henderson ran both hands through his rapidly graying hair. "I don't know. Review all the testimony again, I suppose, and hope that we spot something that doesn't ring true. We've been through all of those," he indicated the secret personnel files, "but there isn't anything startling other than the fact of their very existence. Like I said, the killer had ample time to purge his file."

"Or hers."

"Or hers," he agreed.

"So whoever murdered Catterall came down here afterward and ransacked the office? Doesn't that help?"

"It might, if we knew when the break-in took place. It might have been today, but it might also have been yesterday, last month, last year. We don't know if Catterall was aware of the pilferage."

"Did you check with his secretary? I can see Ed keeping things quiet, but if he found something missing, wouldn't he have checked with her to see if she knew something?"

"She seemed to think otherwise, told us Catterall kept a lot to himself and didn't even want her in his office when he wasn't around. And she wasn't at her own desk very long this morning either. The desk could have been pilfered at any time and she might not have noticed. The locks on the office doors are all pretty simple, not really meant to keep any determined intruder out. You can open them with a credit card."

"Yes, I know," she said softly, her voice trailing off. "Look, Dad, I understand that you're worried about me and I appreciate it, honestly. But when all of this is cleared up, I still have to earn a living here. I don't have enough experience yet to make the jump to another employer, at least not in as good a job. If there's anything I can do to help, let me know, but I am not going to sneak off and hide until the danger is over."

He turned toward her, but recognized the tone in her

voice. "I suppose I shouldn't blame you. I know I wouldn't be willing to cut and run if I were in your place. On the other hand, you can't really blame me for making one more effort. So do what you have to do, but be careful, will you, Vicki? I don't want you to underestimate the danger. Whoever is responsible is smart, deadly, and ruthless. If more killings will further this person's agenda, or feed his passion for power, he'll act without compunction. Trust no one."

"I'll be careful," she agreed. "Very careful."

Back in her office, Vicki rebooted her computer and resumed her own private investigation, wondering if she should have mentioned the CD to her father. It hadn't occurred to her while she was with him and she considered going back immediately. On the other hand, the contents seemed innocuous, and even if Paula had acted suspiciously by stealing the CD, it might have nothing at all to do with the murders. Maybe the two women traded pornography, or talked about others at the company. If it was something entirely innocuous, she would have wasted her father's time as well as her own.

She was soon immersed in reading a series of memos, including proposals for pay increases, a suggestion for revising the entire clerical structure in sales, answers to complaints about the service provided by the clerical pool—most of which seemed to originate in sales as well, along with routine requests for information, responses to other requests, and other trivial matters. Predictably, it was in one of the very last files that she discovered what it was that Paula Danforth had been so interested to retrieve, and although she checked the last few anyway, there was nothing else of any particular interest.

Satisfied that she had finally learned something, Vicki

took the precaution of password-protecting the file in question and erasing the others. Paula Danforth had been actively looking for another job, and had asked Jenny Grissom for help composing a resume and cover letter. Paula had been openly concerned that her job was going to be eliminated, and no one would have blamed her for looking elsewhere, but she was also a worrier who would not have wanted people to know that she was being "disloyal." Vicki couldn't see any possible way this could be related to the murders, and she was depressed by the thought that she'd wasted her time for such a trivial revelation.

She glanced at her wristwatch and was surprised to see that it was a few minutes after five. Most of the office would have cleared out by now, assuming that the police were willing to let them go. She collected her things, turned out the lights, and started down the corridor, walking past a uniformed officer who nodded without changing expression. He was a new face, someone she hadn't seen before.

Ignoring him, she walked down toward the front entrance. Ben Dardenian was talking to two uniformed officers and all three fell silent when she approached.

"Can we go home or do we have to wait here?"

Ben kept a serious face. "You'll have to give the officer on duty your name when you leave. But otherwise you're free to go at any time."

"Thank you." She turned to the uniformed officer. "I'm Victoria Sanders and I'm done for the day."

He made a note on the clipboard he was holding and nodded to her. She gave Ben an amused glance, which he studiously ignored, and started to leave.

"Hey, Vicki! Wait up!" She turned to see Mark Ross approaching. "I'm on my way out. I'll walk you to your car."

He paused to give his name to the officer. Dardenian had already disappeared.

Ross joined Vicki in the lobby. "My offer is still open, you know. Supper at Pirandello's, or somewhere else if you'd like."

Her first inclination was to beg off, but she hesitated. Did she really want to go home to her empty apartment right now? Mark was pleasant enough company and he treated her as an equal, not just a precocious child. Even Catterall had been somewhat condescending at times. It felt good to have someone actually interested in her opinions and willing to give them his undivided attention.

"Sure, why not? I'm famished and all I have at home is cold leftovers."

"We could leave your car here and pick it up on the way back."

She considered the logistics of it quickly and shook her head. "We both have to take the highway. It makes more sense if we meet at the restaurant. That way you won't have to drive me all the way back here, and then turn around and go home."

"All right. I'll meet you there."

She was a little nervous when they were seated together, but Mark was contagiously relaxed and she was soon feeling much better than she had during the afternoon. The food was good and she ate more than usual, but declined a second glass of wine. Mark summarized for her some of the rumors that had been making the rounds that day, even going so far as to imitate Jason Capwell's pedantic style, and Vicki shook her head in wonder at their marvelous illogic.

They talked business a little, but not nearly enough to justify getting together, and then turned to personal matters. Mark, it turned out, was a voracious reader, particularly of classic murder mystery writers like P. D. James, John Dickson Carr, Earl Derr Biggers, and John Rhode.

"Never expected to find myself in one of them though."

Vicki had heard enough crime stories from her father to last her a lifetime. Her reading taste tended to be more mainstream—John Irving, Donald Barthelme, William Goldman, and John Barth—although she'd read the Harry Potter books and Tolkien and enjoyed an occasional light fantasy.

The subject shifted from books to movies and through some verbal sleight of hand that Vicki never quite figured out, she found herself agreeing to go to a late-night movie. There was a new suspense thriller playing that interested them both, and the theater was only a few minutes from the restaurant. They left her car in the lot at Pirandello's and Mark drove. They sat together companionably but neither spoke a word from the opening splash screen to the closing credit.

When they emerged from the theatre two hours later, it had cooled off noticeably. Ross seemed a bit preoccupied and Vicki wondered if he wanted to pursue things any further. She was of two minds on the subject herself. Did she want Ross to make a pass, no matter how gentle? She wasn't sure how she'd react. She was mildly attracted to the man, and that was rare enough in itself to be worth noting.

"Are you cold? It's pretty chilly out here."

She laughed a little nervously. "It's beginning to feel like September already."

"How about a nightcap back at Pirandello's when we get back?"

"I don't know, Mark. Ask me again when we get there. I'm already getting sleepy, and another drink might push me over the edge. I still have to drive home, you know."

For a second, she thought he was going to suggest that she not drive home at all, but he didn't. "Good point. Shall we go?"

When they reached the car, they still had to wait for the rush of traffic to clear away. Ross lit himself a cigarette, offered her one reflexively, even though he knew she didn't smoke.

"What'd you think of the film?" she asked.

"Not bad. It was quite a risk to make such a high profile movie with a cast of relative unknowns. The script was really good; I thought the dialogue was sensational."

She nodded, but didn't speak until Ross had successfully pulled out into a gap in the traffic. "I thought they did a great job of balancing the humor with the suspense."

Ross nodded. "Hitchcock knew how to do it right. Remember *North by Northwest*? This felt a little like Hitchcock, in fact. The plot twists and the surprise ending in particular."

"Yeah, he was a master of misdirection. The ending wasn't much of a surprise though. It was obvious from the beginning that Troughton was murdered, that it was just made to look like a suicide."

"Hitchcock would have made it look fresh. He would have found a way to surprise us anyway."

"Yeah, maybe he'd have had someone fix up a suicide to look like murder."

There was a short silence as Ross made a left turn and the lights of the restaurant became visible. He asked her about her plans for the following morning, but she barely heard him. She had the oddest feeling that some part of her mind had just realized something important. Fortunately, Ross seemed equally preoccupied and he just nodded in response to her vague reply.

Vicki wondered if something in the movie had triggered this reaction, some parallel between the events on the screen and those in the real world. The wine, the lateness of the hour, and her general exhaustion after an emotionally draining day all conspired to slow her thinking and dull her senses.

But she knew something was there, almost within her grasp. It might not be the solution, but it was something that she needed to remember, something she'd seen or heard that didn't fit.

But what was it?

Sixteen

As they drove, Vicki sank back into the seat, trying to pursue the phantom thought and identify it. Ross seemed similarly self-involved. He glanced in her direction occasionally, but he didn't say anything.

Something was wrong with their perception of what had taken place. If it was impossible for the same person to have committed all three murders, then they had to accept that not all of the murders were committed by the same person. But Vicki just couldn't believe that there were two separate murderers involved. If no one person had murdered all three victims, and if her instincts were right and there was only one killer, then the inescapable conclusion was that there had not been three murders after all. One of them was something else. What if suicide had been made to look like murder? Frank Antonelli must have known that he had a potentially terminal illness. He was paying blackmail to conceal a past indiscretion. And he had devoted his life to a job which had become increasingly difficult, had perhaps even suspected that it was only a matter of time until Catterall forced him out of his job. He had no family, no close friends, and a very unpromising future. What if Frank Antonelli had decided not to go quietly into the darkness? What if he had decided instead to kill himself in a way that would embarrass Catterall and the company that no longer valued him?

But why would he try to make it look like murder? And how? Vicki knew that the safeguards could be bypassed.

The controls could have been set so that one button would make the press function, but the settings would have remained unchanged afterward. It would be even easier just to tape one of them down so that the contact was made, then depress the other. Anything like that would have left behind physical evidence. The only explanation that made sense was that someone had come by after the fact, removed the evidence in order to cover up the fact that Antonelli had taken his own life. But why would anyone do that?

"Mark," she said at last. "That morning when Frank died, you went looking for him but couldn't find him."

"That's right. I didn't go out into the Press Department; if I had, I probably would have been the one who found the body."

"I think someone else did find him. Before Luis did, I mean."

"I don't understand."

"Just hear me out. Frank was seriously ill, you know. One of the policemen mentioned it." This wasn't even a lie; her father was, after all, a police officer.

Mark shook his head. "I would never have guessed," he said quietly. "But Frank never was one to talk about himself."

"Listen. I think Frank killed himself that night, rigged the press somehow so that he could run it alone."

"The police checked the press, Vicki. There's no way he could have done it."

"No, there just wasn't any evidence when the police arrived to indicate how he had done it. Someone else found him, either late the night before or early in the morning. Whoever it was realized that Frank had killed himself, or maybe they even thought it was an accident. It didn't matter. Our mystery person removed everything that would tell us what really happened so that we would all think Frank had been murdered."

"I suppose that's possible, but why in the world would anyone bother to do all that? Frank was dead either way."

It was all starting to become clear to her. "Because whoever it was wanted to commit a genuine murder, and a bogus one would confuse matters even further. Maybe Jenny's murder was another diversion; the poisoned sugar bowl could have killed any of us. I think Ed Catterall was probably the target right from the start."

The road was poorly lighted and wound through overarching stands of tightly packed trees.

"Where in the world are we, Mark?"

"Scenic route through Ashton Woods. I thought it might be romantic, although this conversation is anything but."

"Sorry, I didn't mean to spoil the evening, but everything seems to be falling into place all at once."

She lapsed back into silence, reviewing conversations in her mind. There was something else nagging at her, something important; she could always tell when she was on the brink of solving a problem. It was like hearing the soundtrack slowly start to wind up to the point where the killer appeared at the window.

"I still don't see why your mysterious villain would draw police attention to the company even before he had committed a crime. All that would do is increase the chance of being caught in a mistake."

"Not if he had an alibi for the time of Frank's death and . . ."

The words were barely out of her mouth when she realized that only two people had established an alibi for the time Frank Antonelli died. Vicki Sanders and Mark Ross.

And as if a floodgate had finally been opened, she remembered something else that had happened that day, something that should have occurred to her long before. With an involuntary gasp, she turned to face Mark Ross.

"I was afraid you were going to figure it out," he said softly, reaching down to take something from beneath the seat. "This is a gun in my hand, Vicki. I'm really sorry about this; I was really looking forward to working with you. You're a smart girl, but this time you were just a little bit too smart."

"I should have realized it a long time ago," she said quietly, frightened but fascinated as well, still working things out. "That morning, on the way in, you told me you knew Frank was already there because his car was in the lot. But you couldn't have known that because Frank had parked down behind the receiving area. It would have been hidden from the street."

"You're right, and that's why I've been paying so much attention to you since that morning. I knew that it was a slip at the time, but the words were out of my mouth before I had time to think, and since you didn't pick up on it, I hoped that I had gotten away with it. It was my one error of planning in this entire affair. The first rule of a successful lie is to tell as much of the truth as possible. But you have to be careful which truths you tell."

"Why did you do it, Mark? Was it Ed Catterall you were after all along?"

"Of course. If you hadn't had this wonderful burst of intuition, the killing would have been over now. It was necessary, you know. Catterall really wasn't a knight in shining armor. He was a real bastard. Among other things . . ."

She gambled that he would be reluctant to shoot her in his own car, particularly without having told her the entire story. Mark always liked to describe his victories, and this particular one must have been clamoring for release for days. With her left foot, she reached across and stamped hard on the gas pedal. The car jerked forward, then came to a jerky halt as he instinctively moved his foot to the brake. The engine stuttered, then stalled, and she struck at him with a clenched fist. Ross raised his arm, deflected her blow easily, but she had released her seat belt and now she lunged at him, trying to grab hold of the hand that held the weapon. Her martial arts skills were rusty, but her father had made sure she knew how to defend herself. The side of her hand struck his wrist solidly enough to numb his fingers for a few seconds. The weapon fell to the floor between the pedals as the car shuddered to a stop, its engine silent.

Ross swung a backhanded blow at her face, but the angle was awkward and all he managed was to brush her shoulder. She thought about diving forward to recover the handgun, but even if Ross wasn't the athletic type, he was still bigger and stronger than she was, and particularly within the confined space of the car, there was little doubt he could overpower her. Instead, she let him lean forward to grope for it while she opened the door and slipped out.

It was incredibly dark, the sky completely overcast, there were no streetlights, and dense forest marched right up to the edge of the road on both sides. This worked both for and against her as she plunged in among the trees. Branches slapped against her face, one striking painfully across her right cheek, bringing tears from that eye. She refrained from calling out, knowing her only chance was to hide. Fortunately she was wearing practical shoes, not heels, because the terrain was rugged and uneven.

After forcing her way a good distance from the road, she stopped, crouched, and tried to look back the way she had come. Ross had restarted the engine and maneuvered the car so that his headlights shone directly into the wooded area where she had fled, although her flight had taken her at enough of an angle that she was presently outside the arc of illumination. The engine continued to run, but she was sure that she had heard one of the doors slam. He would try to find her; of that she was certain. He had no chance if she survived the evening. No one knew they'd gone out together. Her car would eventually turn up at Pirandello's, and there was a chance that the waiter might remember that she'd been with a man, might even identify him if given the opportunity. It wouldn't be much of a consolation to her if Ross was finally tripped up, but only because of her murder. If he caught her, he might well take the keys and move the car to some other location, further confusing the situation. Thinking that, she reached into her pocket and drew out her keys, then dropped them on the ground. At least she could deny him that option.

She was torn between two possible courses of action, flight or concealment. Running blindly through the woods would be foolish; she'd make too much noise. He had certainly recovered his weapon, so a physical confrontation was out of the question. Ashton Woods was a very small state park, but it was large enough that the sound of a handgun would be swallowed up and lost. If he dragged her body into some dark corner and covered it, days or even weeks might pass before someone stumbled across it. Headlong flight was impossible, but inaction was just as risky. She wasn't far enough from the car to feel safe. She would have to move at least a short distance.

Even as she realized this, she saw the cone of a flashlight beam moving in her general direction.

Vicki began to back away slowly, one step at a time, still

crouching, trying to keep as much foliage as possible between herself and Ross.

Moving backward at a very slight angle, she began to edge away from the flashlight. Ross was moving quickly but methodically and began to draw closer. He didn't need to worry about making noise, which gave him far more freedom of movement than Vicki. The flashlight beam danced in the night air, diffused by light mist that rose from a nearby bog. It was hard to judge distances in the murkiness, but she thought he was moving in a pattern that would eventually lead him away from her.

Then came the crack of a gunshot.

He hadn't seen her; the gun hadn't even been fired in her general direction. It had been a random shot designed to upset her, drive her to run. She didn't panic, but she was startled by the sound, lost her balance, and fell awkwardly, banging her hip against a truncated stump. She managed not to cry out as sharp pain lanced through her thigh, but the damage was already done. She heard the crashing and crackling of someone running through the woods, moving closer with every step, and heard Ross curse loudly. Hopefully he'd taken a branch across the face, preferably at eye level. He wouldn't know her exact position yet, but he had to have gotten a general idea.

There wasn't enough time to try to find a hiding place. Scrambling to her feet, she ran a zigzag course through the forest, aided occasionally by the sweep of the flashlight. Ross didn't call out, and he may not have seen her through the dense foliage, but he could not help hearing her. She hit a dark spot and ran at full speed into a tree. Her left shoulder went numb and she gasped with the pain, then stumbled onward. Vines caught at her ankles as she moved away, and she had to slow down to keep from tripping. She could still hear Ross moving behind her, but he didn't seem to be as close. She made a sharp turn to the right, hoping that he would continue on his present course and eventually start to diverge from hers.

At the last possible moment, a gap in the clouds let enough light through to show her that she was headed directly toward a towering boulder, at least three stories high. She came to a stop when she reached it, touching it with her hands to orient herself, and the clouds closed up again and cut off her light. The cool stone surface was damp, either condensation from the air or the slow trickle from a pool of water located higher. With one hand pressed against the stony surface as a guide, Vicki felt her way around its curve, using her other hand to ward off branches. Every few seconds she paused, hoping to find a cavity large enough to conceal her, but the only imperfections she found were narrow cracks.

"Vicki!" The voice came from somewhere behind her, not as close as she had feared, not as far away as she had hoped. She didn't reply. Ross hadn't expected her to do so. He was simply trying to rattle her into giving away her position.

Instead she paused, listening for his footsteps, trying to estimate his position, but any sound he might have been making was masked by the whispering of a surprisingly brisk wind that sprang up suddenly, sighing its way through the branches. The headlights still flickered in the distance, almost completely obscured now, and shadows jumped where they touched. Vicki couldn't see the flashlight anywhere, but that didn't reassure her. Ross could be just a few meters away around the curve of the boulder.

A car engine grumbled in the distance, perhaps on another leg of the twisting park road. She froze, wondering if she should try to reach the highway and flag someone down. Unfortunately, she had become so disoriented that she was no longer sure in which direction the highway lay.

She estimated that she had come halfway around the circle of stone by now. To continue in the same fashion might well bring her toward Ross instead of away from him. She turned slowly and took one tentative step away, and her foot came down on a piece of very dry wood which cracked loudly. Stumbling forward, she almost lost her footing altogether.

Crouching with her back to the rock, Vicki reached out and felt along the ground ahead of her. There was a thick layer of dead branches and pine needles here, some crumbling into powder at her touch. There was no way that she could move forward without advertising her presence loudly. She edged slowly back until she was pressed up against the boulder once again.

The flashlight appeared to her right, moving steadily in her general direction. Whether by chance or because of the sound of the snapping branch, Ross was moving around the opposite side of the boulder, sweeping the light back and forth in small arcs as he advanced. Vicki crouched where she was, her heart pounding, unwilling to risk headlong flight when he was this close.

"Vicki, you're just making things more difficult." He didn't shout this time, actually spoke in a normal conversational tone. But his voice held a hint of tension, anger, or perhaps fear. She hoped it was the latter. "I'm sorry that things turned out this way. You and I would have made a really good team, I think. It's just one more thing to hold against that bastard Catterall."

Vicki forced herself to breathe slowly and easily, dropped to her knees and lowered her head. The flashlight came closer, then stopped and began moving in a slow sweep that looked as though it was coming right toward her.

"The son of a bitch was blackmailing me, you know. Not for money, of course. He knew how little I was getting, knew how much more I was worth. He wanted to impress the Board with his talent for keeping costs under control. That's the real reason he was the champion of all of you struggling yuppies; he gave you fancy titles and responsibilities and paid you twenty percent or more below the going rate for the position. He wasn't an altruist. He was an opportunist."

The light swept across the rock face just above her head as Ross moved past, but it didn't hesitate and she was sure she hadn't been spotted. That was the good news. The bad news was that his voice was growing steadily louder; he was getting very close.

She heard his footsteps and held her breath. Then the footsteps stopped and the flashlight abruptly flicked off. The darkness was nearly absolute and she felt as though she'd gone blind. The wind was chill and goose pimples broke out all over her body. She clenched her jaws to prevent her teeth from chattering

The silence continued. Either Ross was remaining motionless in an attempt to detect her movement, or he was moving so stealthily that she could not separate the sounds he was making from the general background noise caused by swaying branches and rustling wind. Panic screamed at her to stand up and run and keep running until she reached lights and safety, but reason told her that she'd never make it that far. She calmed herself by thinking of her father's reaction if she became hysterical. He would be greatly disappointed.

A branch snapped loudly during a moment in which the

wind was silent rather than while it was still blowing. It had to be Ross, moving without benefit of his flashlight now. She had another moment of terror when another gap opened overhead and the pale disc of the moon glowed in the sky, but it only lasted a few seconds before being swallowed up by another mass of cloud.

Her right leg was beginning to cramp. She couldn't risk not being able to run if necessary, so she very slowly stood up instead, cautiously, listening for any sound that might tell her where Ross was. She didn't think she'd be easy to spot if she remained motionless; thank heaven she'd worn sensible shoes and dark clothing today.

What happened next might have been simple mischance, or perhaps she had given herself away in some other fashion. The flashlight snapped on quite suddenly, aimed only a meter or so to her left, and right at eye level. If she had remained motionless, Ross might not have noticed her, but it didn't matter. This time she moved instinctively, turning away and lurching forward with her arms raised to protect her eyes. She intended to stay close to the boulder, race around its circumference, taking advantage of whatever cover it provided, and then perhaps run directly to the car. Ross had left the keys in it because the engine was still running, and if she could get there far enough ahead of him, she might be able to pull back onto the road and escape before he caught up.

She probably wouldn't have made it in any case, but the question became moot because she ran directly into the thick bole of a pine tree.

Fortunately, she was crouched forward and took the blow on her left shoulder rather than her face. There was a jarring pain and she was knocked backward and sideways, spinning around before finally losing her balance completely and falling backward over some other obstruction, a bush or small tree. By the time she had gotten herself untangled and was struggling to her feet, Ross had crossed the distance separating them. He pushed the flashlight forward, holding it less than a foot from her face.

"That's about enough, Vicki, don't you think?"

Her shoulder hurt and she was breathing heavily, but her fear was tempered by anger. What right, after all, did Mark Ross have to come into her life and mess it up this way? She stood up, very slowly, with her arms tight against her body.

"So what's it going to be now, Mark? A fourth killing? How many more will you have to commit to hide what you've done? You'll have to run the presses yourself, box up the items, and ship them out at this rate."

"You forget, I didn't murder Frank. He killed himself in the most bloody repulsive fashion I can imagine. Leave it to Frank to cause trouble even on his way off the stage. I have to admit it gave me some satisfaction, depriving him of his dramatic exit." He laughed unpleasantly. "Frank was quite the actor, you know. He wrote a suicide note, explaining how Catterall was destroying his life's work and would inevitably ruin the company. It was actually quite pathetic." Ross laughed nervously, and the flashlight beam wavered erratically. Vicki watched carefully, looking for a chance to knock it out of his hand and escape into the darkness, hopefully without getting shot in the back.

"So you made his suicide look like a murder."

"Of course. I was quite proud of myself for thinking so quickly. It only took a couple of minutes. Frank used the gauging block, taped it inside one of the press guards so that the button couldn't release, then pressed the other himself." Ross sighed. "That took balls, I have to admit. I can think of lots of pleasanter ways to go. Anyway, I unwrapped the tape, put everything back where it belonged, stuck the note in my pocket, even reset Frank's watch a few minutes earlier, so that it would show the exact time when you and I were out in the factory together. I knew my alibi would stick anyway, but if that gave me a little more leeway, it was all to the good."

Cautiously, Vicki took a half step backward and to one side. "And Jenny? What did you have against her?"

"Why, nothing at all. You won't believe me, but I'm actually quite sorry about that. Jenny was a good worker, and she wasn't half attractive either. But I needed a second murder, something to establish that there was a serial killer at work, and her office was accessible and empty. Catterall never actually believed our story, you know. He told me he thought the two of us were sleeping together and had collaborated on our stories to provide each other an alibi. Naturally he thought you were the dupe, since I was the one with the history of violence."

Vicki didn't have to pretend to be puzzled and she wanted to keep him talking. "What history of violence?"

"Ed Catterall was a nosy bastard, Vicki. He hired private detectives to check on our backgrounds. I thought I'd covered my tracks pretty well, but someone did a really good job, turned up something that I thought was forever hidden. I'd almost forgotten about it myself."

"Is that why you killed him?"

"That's why I had to kill him. I broke into his desk a few days ago, made it obvious that someone had gone through the personnel folders, but I didn't take anything. He called me when he discovered the break-in and I played innocent, even accused him of being sloppy with material that could send me to jail."

"Why didn't you destroy the evidence?"

"He would just have requested a new copy from whatever agency he had hired. No, I just wanted to establish some uncertainty in his mind, a suspicion that someone else knew what he was doing."

Vicki took another half step, but the flashlight moved as Ross stepped forward, closer to her. She couldn't see the handgun; the light was dazzling at this close range, and the surrounding darkness impenetrable.

"Saturday morning I stopped by the factory, and used the maintenance key to get into Catterall's office. This time I did take the relevant information from my file. Then I called him early this morning and told him that I had received an anonymous phone call threatening blackmail. I also told him that the caller was obviously the same person who had broken into his desk, and that I knew how to find out who it was. We agreed to meet secretly in the balcony so we could decide what to do, and then I scheduled a meeting with Tony Capra and got him so upset that it was easy to mislead him about the time. I imagine you can work out the rest for yourself."

Vicki knew if she was going to do anything, it would have to be soon. "There's one thing I don't understand."

Ross sounded amused. "We sound like we're doing the dialogue from a mediocre thriller, but it's not going to matter. What did I leave out?"

Vicki pivoted on her left leg and kicked out with the other. She was aiming beyond the hand that held the flashlight, but she misjudged the distance. Or perhaps Ross moved at just the wrong time. Instead of kicking the gun out of his hand, she hit the flashlight. It went spinning out into the darkness.

Treacherous footing hampered her again, and her pivot foot twisted painfully, causing her to fall heavily to one side, but this time it was a godsend. There was a sharp "Crack!" as she fell; Ross had fired into the darkness. She rolled frantically to one side, but Ross had retreated, afraid that she would try to wrestle the handgun away from him. He backed directly into a patch of thorny brush that clutched at his arm and by the time he had ripped his arm free, Vicki was running desperately down a shallow slope.

The gun fired again, sounding tinny in the open space, although the ricochet as a round struck the rock face close by was depressingly loud. Vicki ran toward the darker shadows, picking up some scratches in the process but thankfully not hitting anything solid enough to hurt, and heard Ross swearing somewhere behind her.

When the ground began to rise again, she risked a glance back and saw the flashlight bobbing back and forth. Ross had retrieved it before giving chase, which had given her at least a slight head start, although she would have been happier if the flashlight had been broken. She had gained enough ground to consider running for the still idling car, but she was nervous about the headlights. If she was silhouetted against them, Ross might be able to pick her off even from a distance.

What other choice have you got? she asked herself silently, and began to run.

She might have made it too, if she hadn't forgotten about the gully. The same narrow defile into which she had fallen earlier tripped her up again. But this time when she fell, a sharp root pressed up against her diaphragm and her breath exploded outward. Stunned, she rolled off the root with a barely suppressed groan, shifted her body awkwardly toward the dirt wall, and desperately tried to draw in air without noisily betraying her location.

She heard Ross running nearby, rapid, heavy footsteps, ending abruptly as he came to a stop. Light blinked above her head and passed on. The paralysis in her chest and side began to ease and she thought that just possibly she might be able to move again. The wind was picking up once more, brisk, playful, tossing branches about as if it were autumn. Leaves brushed against one another softly, whispering in the darkness. The background noise might cover any small sounds she made, but they afforded Ross the same protection. She couldn't tell where he was, in what direction he had gone, or whether he was still moving or motionless, waiting for her to break cover.

Then a glob of moist soil fell onto her left cheek.

Vicki felt an incredible urge to sneeze and had to exert all of her self-control to suppress it. She didn't dare raise a hand to her face.

Another bit of dirt, heavier this time, brushed the side of her neck and came to rest on her shoulder. Something crackled just above her head.

Ross was standing directly above her on the lip of the gully, the flashlight off, his body just faintly visible against the slightly lighter background provided by a patch of sky. Vicki's heart almost stopped, which might have saved Ross the necessity of committing another murder. She could just barely detect a faint motion, probably his head moving slowly back and forth, like a radar set scanning for a signal. If he glanced down, he might see her even without the light. She had no way of knowing how well she blended in with the background and she couldn't take the chance.

Drawing a long, slow breath, she tensed her muscles, then reached up quickly, snagged one ankle, and pulled down with all the strength she possessed. Ross let out a cry of dismay as he lost his footing and fell heavily on his back, then began sliding down into the gully, thrashing wildly. The flashlight went flying and came to rest pointing off into the distance. Vicki lunged forward and caught hold of his right wrist with both hands, trying to force him to drop the handgun. Ross swung at her with his left fist, but she ducked her head and caught the blow on her shoulder. Desperate, she threw all of her weight onto his arm, slamming it down against the ground. He lost the weapon, but his other hand was in her hair, yanking her back, and then both of them were tumbling and sliding, one after the other, until they reached the bottom of the gully.

She knew she couldn't match his strength and weight, so she clawed at his face, then rolled away when he raised his hands to protect his eyes. He lunged toward her but missed, and Vicki started scrambling up the opposite slope on hands and knees. Ross was no longer interested in talking, but she could hear his heavy breathing as he followed in the same fashion. He caught hold of her right calf once, his fingers tearing her stocking, but she kicked free before he could tighten his grip. Mercifully, the slope was more gradual on this side and she reached the top and got unsteadily to her feet. The headlights were off to her left; she'd actually lost a little ground, but she turned and began running toward the car. It was easier as the light grew brighter and illuminated obstacles in her path.

Ross was right behind her. She could hear him coming.

Although Vicki would reach the car first, she realized it would do her no good. Ross was too close; there would not be enough time to open the door, climb inside, and drive off. Even without a weapon, he was quite capable of murder, and she was no more interested in being strangled or beaten to death than she was in being shot.

So instead of running straight to the car, she came to a sudden stop when she reached the road, spun around to face her pursuer.

Ross stopped as well, a couple of meters away, then slowly, cautiously moved forward.

"Nice try," he said hoarsely, his breathing heavy, labored. "If I was a little younger, you wouldn't have made it this far. You're a tenacious woman, Vicki. I really meant it when I said I was sorry that you were caught up in all this."

Vicki contorted her face, trying to look terrified. It wasn't hard; she felt close to fainting for the first time in her life. If she was going to have any chance at all, it would have to be by trickery. She couldn't hope to match him physically.

"I'm afraid this would have been easier if you hadn't made me lose the gun," he said quietly, menacingly, "but I think it's time to put an end to this."

As he stepped forward, raising both arms, she spun and kicked again, this time aiming directly between his legs. She hadn't had a ballet lesson in a long time and she wasn't sure that she could still do what was necessary, but she was sure as hell going to give it a try.

Ross had anticipated the kick and was prepared for it. He twisted his body so that one hip would deflect the kick, but it never landed. Vicki turned the kick into a pirouette, spun around in a complete circle. Then she took two quick steps forward, planted one foot, and pivoted again, lashing out with a high kick aimed directly at Ross' face.

Ross ducked away, but her foot scraped across his left cheek and ear. With a cry of pain and fury, he retreated a step, head lowered, arms raised protectively. This was the best chance she would likely get, so Vicki adjusted her stance and kicked out again, this time hitting him right between the thighs. Ross doubled over, gasping, his knees slowly folding as he sank to the ground with his arms folded across his groin.

Vicki almost turned away from him. She was confident she could now reach the car and drive off before he recovered. Ross could run and hide, but the police would find him sooner or later. That wasn't good enough for her. "This one's for Jenny, you bastard." She took two quick steps forward and lashed out her right leg. The side of her foot slammed into the underside of his chin. Ross flew backward as though he'd been shot, landing on his back. Vicki thought she might have killed him, but when she checked, he was still breathing.

There was no rope in the trunk of the car, but there was a roll of copper wire in the tool kit and that worked well enough.

Seventeen

"Ross was an egotist," Henderson observed as he handed one beer to his partner and another to his daughter. The remains of a house special pizza sat on the coffee table. "He thought that he was so much smarter than anyone at Standard or in the police force that he could get away with anything. And let's face it, he almost got away with it."

"I suppose we should have suspected something when Soares said he showed up out of breath for their 10:00 meeting. That was out of character for him; he always tried to project a calm, cool image."

"It wasn't much of a risk. The layout of the factory meant that he could make his way through plating to the shipping balcony and back without being observed unless he had extraordinarily bad luck. Under normal circumstances, no one works on the far side of the plating line, and that long partitioned walkway from the office through the shipping area masks everything from view. There was a very remote chance that someone from the inspection area might have been looking in the wrong direction, but the odds were in his favor."

Vicki took a long drink, wincing slightly as she raised her head. Her collision with the tree the night before had left her with a painful bruise from shoulder to armpit. "He'd already hidden the wrench somewhere up there, I imagine?"

"So he says. He was apparently thinking about a fourth murder to confuse things further. The chief candidate seems to have been Tony Capra. Ross is pretty openly contemptuous of him, seemed to feel the company would be better off with a new plating supervisor." Henderson made a disgusted sound and drank from his own beer as he sat heavily into his chair. "That line he gave you about Antonelli wanting to fire Capra was apparently fiction as well. A safe one; the only person who could have contradicted him was dead."

"Did you retrieve the material he stole from Catterall's office?"

"Not directly. He burned the original copy. Blake, Anderson, and Shorter were willing to provide another copy once we convinced them that Standard Silver was their client, not Edward Catterall. They agreed to send a copy to the Board of Directors and they forwarded it to us."

Dardenian nodded. "It confirms the details of his confession. Mark Ross is actually Martin Adamski, wanted for questioning in a murder case in Sandusky, Ohio, about eight years ago. He skipped out before he was seriously suspected and assumed the identity of Mark Ross of Toledo a couple of years later. The real Ross went to Notre Dame on a football scholarship, but died of spinal meningitis during his freshman year. We're not sure how Adamski tumbled onto his identity."

Vicki smacked her head with her free palm. "Idiot that I am, I remember you saying that Catterall's files described him as a jock. He knew less about sports than I did. I should have noticed that, just like I should have realized he was lying about having seen Frank's car that morning."

"Don't blame yourself, Vicki," Dardenian said mildly. "There was absolutely no way he could have murdered Antonelli, remember? There was no reason for you to question the inconsistency." He glanced at the wall clock and got to his feet. "Hey, I've got to get going. If I don't see my wife soon, she won't recognize me."

Henderson showed his partner out, then walked slowly back into the living room. "How are things sorting themselves out at Standard?"

Vicki settled back into her seat. "As well as can be expected. Things are still pretty confused. Wilson is taking over as interim President and they're looking for someone from the outside to assume the position on a permanent basis. All of the pending promotions and major changes are on hold, but Wilson personally called me in today and told me not to worry, that I would still be a full manager within months if I was willing to stay on. I don't think Paula is going to get the production control job though; he said something about some positions requiring tougher personalities than the people Catterall had in mind. Bill Elliot's back, and there's been talk about having him take over responsibility for receiving as well as shipping, now that Art Richardson is leaving."

"He didn't decide to stay then? I thought with Ross out of the picture, he might reconsider."

"No, I guess the offer he had was good enough that he's leaving anyway."

"And you're planning to stay?"

"Sure, at least until something better comes along. Standard isn't the most thriving company in the world, but at least I'm getting the kind of experience that looks good on a resume."

They were both quiet for a while and Vicki was wondering if it was time for her to go home when her father cleared his throat awkwardly. "Vicki, I owe you an apology."

"Probably," she admitted. "What for?"

"It's hard for a man, for me anyway, to face the fact that

his only daughter is a grown, competent woman. You know, your mother was smart as a whip, smarter than I ever was, and strong-willed besides. But whenever there was a big risk to be taken, she always deferred to me. Probably part of it was that she felt I wanted it that way, and being the age that I am, she was probably right."

Vicki had a good idea what he was building up to. "Don't worry about it, Dad. I think I understand."

"No, I need to finish. I need to say this." He raised his head and met her eyes squarely. "You're my only daughter, my only child. It's hard for me to admit even now that you're an adult, that you can make your own decisions. I guess I thought of Danny as kind of a substitute for me, someone to watch over you when I couldn't. When you divorced him, it was almost as if you were disowning me."

She leaned forward and put her hand on his knee. "Dad, you know that's not true."

"Sure I know. I know that you never felt that way about it. But I did. And what I really want to tell you now is that I'm proud of you for wanting to stand on your own, even when it feels wrong to me. My heart might still tell me that you're my little girl and that you need protecting, but my head knows that you're an intelligent, strong-willed, adult woman." He laughed shortly. "And not as helpless as I thought either."

"You never know when dancing lessons are going to come in handy," she said wryly. She finished her beer and rose. "Thanks, Dad. I love you too, you know." Reaching over, she ruffled his head. "I have to go. Work tomorrow, lots of it, and I have to start early. No, don't get up." She picked up her bag and crossed to the front door.

"Vicki," he said, still seated. "There's one other thing."

She glanced back. "What's that?"

He shifted uncomfortably in his seat. "You were right in leaving Danny, and I was wrong. He was never good enough for you."

She turned completely around, tilting her head to one side as she stared at him. "Okay, I'm glad to hear you say that, but what inspired this sudden reappraisal?"

He lifted a folded newspaper from the floor and waved it at her. "Remember I told you we were short-handed because we had so many officers on loan to some federal task force?"

"Yeah, I remember."

"Well, they just indicted your ex-husband for money laundering."

She laughed first, but only by a split second, and then they were both laughing, loudly and continuously, and it felt really good.

About the Author

DON D'AMMASSA is the author of three previous novels, *Blood Beast*, *Servants of Chaos*, and *Scarab*, as well as over a hundred short stories that have appeared in *Analog*, *Isaac Asimov's Science Fiction*, and other magazines and anthologies. He has been a book reviewer for *Science Fiction Chronicle* for twenty-five years, and is currently writing full time.